M000252231

Danger by Design

copyright©2017 by Helen Macie Osterman.
All rights reserved.
No part of this book may be used or reproduced in any manner without permission from the publisher.

Cover design by Robyn Hyzy

ISBN-978-0-9986852-3-6

Second edition
Pebble Creek Press
Homer Glen, IL

Danger by Design

A Net Petrone Mystery

Helen Macie Osterman

Dedication
To all those scammed by the unscrupulous in our midst

Acknowledgments

Net Petrone is a new character, much different from Emma Winberry. I want to thank my writers' group for their valuable critique, and Lynn Schoorl and John Morton, my first readers.

Chapter 1

George Watkins returned to his hotel room at the Waldorf in New York City, tired but gratified that his speech had gone so well. The CEO of the investment firm he worked for was considering giving George the promotion he coveted, and tonight might just solidify that decision.

His bed had been turned down and a chocolate mint left on the pillow. He smiled, ate the mint, and then threw himself on the bed with a sigh of relief that the evening was over.

After a few more obligatory meetings and some necessary networking, he could go home, probably the day after tomorrow. He thought about having a drink but decided that he had imbibed enough liquor that evening.

The red light blinking on the phone caught his attention. Probably his wife. After twenty years of marriage, they still missed each other when they were apart. He smiled as he pressed nine and a recorded voice said he had a message. After a brief pause, he was surprised to hear his mother's voice, shaky and barely audible.

"George, I want you to come over as soon as you get back in town." She whispered so softly that he barely heard the words. The message continued. "I've made a terrible mistake. I have rewritten my will and had it witnessed by two of the neighbor ladies. I'm going to put it in a secure place. When you get here, we'll go to the lawyer and have it properly executed."

George could tell by the tone of her voice that something was wrong. She was recently behaving in an erratic manner. She would stop in the middle of a conversation, stare at nothing, then say something like, "You wouldn't understand. It's beyond all of us." He and his brother had seriously considered a psychiatric evaluation to determine her competency. The next words made the hairs on the back of his neck stand up.

"They're watching me. I believe I'm in danger. Come as soon as you can."

The message ended abruptly. George stared at the phone. Should he call her back? Maybe he would call his brother and ask him to check in on their mother, but it was just past midnight in Chicago and he didn't want to disturb the family, especially with a disabled child to care for. It was probably just another one of his mother's fantasies. They were becoming more paranoid recently.

He sat on the bed for a long time, overcome by exhaustion, and decided that tomorrow would be soon enough.

Chapter 2

Three months later

"Why did I let them talk me into this?" Net Petrone gingerly braced her right knee with both hands and, inch by inch, moved it over to the side of the bed.

"Ugh," she groaned as she reached for her walker and pulled all of her five foot two inches to a standing position. "I can do this," she repeated over and over as she made her way to the bathroom. She avoided looking in the mirror, wasn't ready to confront her sleep-deprived face and unruly hair.

After tending to the call of nature, she sat on the chair strategically placed next to the sink, and splashed water on her face. For a long time she stayed there wondering how she had reached this stage in her life.

It seemed like yesterday that her son, Vince, was a little boy getting into all the diabolical mischief that seemed to be born into boys. Now his son, Dominic, was doing all the same things. She avoided thinking about her daughter, Donna. Not now. She couldn't handle that.

Oh why did women become widows just when they needed help? It wasn't fair.

"Stop feeling sorry for yourself, Antoinette Petrone," she scolded. She removed the dressing on her knee, did a thorough examination, as the visiting nurse instructed, and decided that all was well. A line of silver-colored staples ran down her kneecap. They were so even that she wondered if the doctor had used a ruler. She had trouble visualizing the metal joint that now replaced the one she was born with.

"Net, are you up?" a voice called from the front door.

"Just barely, Ruth. Come in."

Ruth Borden, from the townhouse next door, peeked into the bathroom. "Need help getting dressed?" Her soft white hair was pulled back and tied with a red ribbon. She had one of those classic faces that improve with age: large clear eyes, high cheek bones and a bow mouth.

"I need help with these damned anti-embolic stockings. Whoever came up with that idea never had to wear them."

Ruth smiled as she heard her friend grumbling. "You know how important they are," she said as she deftly rolled the elastic stocking up Net's leg to the thigh. "Besides, didn't you say that after today you wouldn't need them anymore?" She put on the other one and gave them one last tug.

"I hope so," Net said. She turned to her friend. "What would I have done without your help? You've been here the entire three weeks since I got home. That's a real friend." Her voice dropped to a whisper as her throat tightened. The past few days, Ruth gave Net some independence, but she was only a phone call away.

"You would have done the same for me," Ruth said. "Suppose I start breakfast?"

"Good." Net sat for a moment listening to her friend bustling around in the kitchen. It was a cheery sound, homey and welcoming. In the three months since she moved into this retirement community, Net and Ruth had become close friends. They were both widowed too soon and had been drawn to each other almost immediately. Each kept a key to the other's house. Ruth decided from the start that Nettie was too old fashioned a name and had begun calling her Net. A new name with a new lifestyle. Nettie liked it and insisted that everyone call her Net.

Ruth had been chauffeuring her around since her surgery three weeks earlier. Today the doctor would remove the staples and she would regain some of her freedom.

* * *

After the trip to the medical center, the staple removal, and the advancement to a cane, Net felt liberated. She decided to treat her friend to lunch.

"How does it feel now that you've graduated, so to speak?" Ruth asked

"Much better, and I don't need that walker anymore. This trusty cane will do me for a while."

Ruth stopped the car in front of a neighborhood restaurant in the center of a strip mall. She let her friend out and proceeded to park. Net took a deep breath of the early spring air. It felt good. Tomorrow the therapist would discharge her from home visits and Net would be able to attend therapy in an outpatient facility for three more weeks. She was definitely on the mend.

They walked into the restaurant that sported large planters decorating the foyer and hanging plants at each window. Net sighed; sometimes she missed her yard with the large garden, talking with the neighbors over the back fence, but all that was behind her now. It was time to move on.

Gingerly she slid into a booth opposite Ruth and they both looked at the specials of the day.

"I'll have a grilled cheese and a cup of soup," Ruth said putting down the menu.

Net shrugged. "I don't feel too hungry, but I'm supposed to keep up my energy. So I'll have the same."

"Coffee?" the waitress asked as she came by with a pot in each hand, one of regular and one of decaf.

"Yes, please," Ruth said. "Regular."

"Same for me." The women turned their cups upright and breathed in the hearty aroma.

Ruth rested her arms on the table and looked her friend in the eye. "So, have you decided to sign up for the genealogy class? It starts next week."

Net made a face that said she wasn't too keen on the idea. "Do I really want to know? My mother came from Genoa so maybe I'm descended from nobility." She raised her eyes and lifted her chin. "But my father came from Naples. God only knows what cutthroats and robbers he sprang from."

Ruth laughed. "You're being a melodramatic Italian, as usual. They were probably fishermen."

"So where did your parents come from?" Net asked as the waitress put their lunch in front of them.

"My mother's family came from Salzburg, in Austria, so maybe I'm a descendent of Mozart. And my father came from somewhere near London. Royalty perhaps?" She turned her head and assumed a theatrical pose.

"Sure, and I'm related to Caruso." Net picked up her sandwich and took a bite. "All right, I'll do it or you'll never give me any peace."

They finished off their lunch with apple pie a la mode.

* * *

Later that afternoon, after taking a pain pill, Net settled on the sofa, an ice pack on her knee, a cozy mystery in hand, and two pillows under her head. She looked around the comfortable living room with all her old furniture. It was light and airy but didn't feel like home, yet.

She wiggled into a comfortable position and breathed a deep sigh. The drug began to take effect and her eyes closed as the ringing of the phone jolted her. Fortunately it was within reach or she would have let the answering machine pick it up. Couldn't do that. If it was her son or Ruth they would think something was wrong.

Net grabbed the phone with one hand and steadied the ice pack with the other. It had become her indispensible companion.

"Hello."

"Hi, Net," a familiar voice said. "How's it going?"

"Fine, Sam. I had the staples removed today and am recuperating according to schedule. The only thing they don't tell you is that you probably won't be able to sleep at night."

"I'm sorry," he said. "I wish I could do something. You need anything?"

"No, no. Vince and his wife, Melissa, have taken care of everything. And my friend, Ruth, lives right next door. So all bases are covered."

"Oh."

She heard the disappointment in his voice. Net had known Sam Urbino most of her life, and she knew that he wanted to be more than friends.

"How about some Italian pastries? I can go right to the Turano bakery and pick up a box of fresh ones."

"Sam, I'm carrying ten pounds too many now and I can't do much exercise. Let's wait a few weeks 'til I can go back to the pool for my water classes. Then I'll take you up on the pastries." She wiggled into a more comfortable position.

"You got it. Anything you need, you let me know."

"I will, and thanks so much for the flowers. They're beautiful." Her eyes rested on a colorful spring bouquet sitting on the coffee table.

"It was the least I could do," he said.

"Listen, I'll call you when I'm able to get around better and you can take me out to dinner. How does that sound?"

"Great."

She heard the hopeful tone in his voice, but she didn't want to raise false hopes. To her, Sam Urbino would always be like a brother.

After she ended the call and lay back on the pillows, Net allowed her mind to go through the past years. She, Sam, and Joe Petrone had grown up in the same Italian neighborhood in Melrose Park, a suburb of Chicago. She had been a tomboy: climbed trees, played baseball in the alley, rode bicycles all over town. The three were inseparable.

Net always felt something special for Joe and when they reached puberty, she realized she was in love with him and always had been. But Joe flirted with all the girls. He was charismatic with dark curly hair and his sparkling black eyes could charm the skin off a snake.

Sam, on the other hand, short and stocky, lacked the charisma that surrounded Joe. But he was always there to help Net when she fell down, to wipe her tears and walk her home. She depended on him like an older brother, but her heart belonged to Joe.

When they grew up, Net became a grade school teacher, Sam went into accounting, and Joe became a partner in his father's construction business. During those years the three grew apart until Joe came back into her life like a steamroller. He wined and dined her in grand fashion.

Before she knew what had happened, they were engaged. Six months later they were married and she never regretted it. She loved him with all her heart and soul and he returned that love. Joe was a model husband and, to her knowledge, had always been faithful.

Net wiped away the tears that always leaked out when she thought of the past. Joe Petrone had lived life to the fullest and died with dignity of a sudden heart attack. He left Net financially independent but totally bereft.

Now, five years later, she still hadn't accepted the loss.

'

Chapter 3

The following day Net and Ruth drove to the main building of the facility where the programs were held. It was ordinarily a brisk walk, but Net wasn't ready to take on that distance yet. She was up to a block, before she succumbed to pain and exhaustion. Bart, the charming young therapist from Holland, had told her to go easy, and increase her endurance gradually. He gave her written instructions in the exercises she was to do and watched her during the therapy sessions. Net did as she was told, but was eager to resume her normal routine and lying on the sofa with an ice pack on her knee was not part of it.

"Where do we sign up?" Net asked her friend as they walked into the activity center.

"Don't sound so eager," Ruth chided. "There's Margo. She'll know."

The activity director, Margo Brewster, stood in a corner animatedly talking to a tall thin man. A pencil line mustache crawled across his upper lip like a black worm. As the women walked into the room the stranger looked at them, his eyes narrowing, his lips pulling back in a smile that appeared pasted on.

Margo turned. "Ah, ladies, welcome. Let me introduce you to Professor Andrew Marcus, genealogy expert."

Professor Marcus bowed and extended his hand as Margo continued the introductions. "This is Ruth Borden and Antoinette Petrone."

Net winced at the mention of her Christian name. It sounded so "old country."

When Professor Marcus shook Net's hand, she was surprised that his hand felt warm and strong. "I do hope you ladies are planning to sign up for my class. We sometimes uncover some very interesting ancestors." His eyes seemed to be sending her a message that Net didn't comprehend.

By now she was leaning heavily on her cane. "I must sit down, Margo."

"Oh yes, I almost forgot. You've recently had knee surgery." The woman pulled out a chair and Net quickly occupied it with a sigh of relief. "How are you feeling?" Margo gushed.

"Better every day." Net tried to smile, but it was difficult. She hated insincerity.

The professor turned to the activity director. "Miss Brewster, now that everything is arranged, I'll take my leave. I hope to see you ladies next week." He gave a slight bow, turned, and walked away.

Net frowned at Ruth and mouthed, "Don't like him."

Ruth simply ignored her. "We're here to sign up for the class," she said.

"Good. So far we have ten interested parties. Here are the forms and a couple of pens. Just leave them on my desk when you're finished. I have a meeting in a few minutes."

"Before you go," Net said, "I just remembered that there is still a box of possessions of the former owner of my townhouse. It's in the garage."

"What's in it?" Margo asked.

"I have no idea. It's on the top shelf. Someone will need a ladder to retrieve it."

"I'll call Mrs. Watkins' son and remind him. He probably forgot all about it. Bye ladies." She waltzed out of the room.

"She's too gushy for my taste," Net grumbled examining the form in front of her. "Why does he need all this information? I don't want to answer all these personal questions." At that moment she felt that she would rather be on her sofa with an ice pack and a book.

"Don't be so stubborn," Ruth said. "These are the usual questions that are asked for statistical analysis."

"So now you're a statistician."

"Just fill out the form," Ruth said through gritted teeth.

Net let out a sigh, picked up a pen and began to print: name, address, phone, e-mail, gender, age. Here she hesitated then wrote sixty-five-ish. She had been sixty- five-ish for a long time but refused to admit that the hands of time were inching toward the next decade.

* * *

By the following week Net was surprised at how much more active she was: did her exercises regularly, was doing exceptionally well in physical therapy. Bart told her she would soon be able to resume her water aerobic classes. Life was finally returning to normal.

When she and Ruth walked into the activity center for the first genealogy class, they were both surprised to see the number of people there; many were residents of the apartment building that was part of the complex. Some leaned on canes, others used walkers, some sat in wheelchairs.

Net wore a simple pantsuit with an elastic waist. She took a deep breath. That ten pounds definitely needed to come off. Ruth also wore a pantsuit, but, since she was tall and slim, whatever she wore looked smart and stylish.

"How are you feeling?" a diminutive woman asked Net. Before she could answer, the woman began a history of her own surgical procedures with all their complications.

Net simply smiled and walked away as soon as she could. "Cheerful soul," she whispered to Ruth.

Her friend grinned. "She relishes doom and gloom, that one. Let's sit over here where there's plenty of light. I need to have my glasses checked." Ruth pulled out a pair of designer glasses that appeared expensive.

They sat down and opened the notebooks they had purchased for the class and waited ... and waited. The chattering around them diminished when Margo Brewster walked into the room.

"I'm so happy to see so many of you interested in resurrecting your ancestry. Professor Marcus is running a little late this morning but he assured me he would be here. In the meantime I'll go over the activities for the next month."

Margo's voice droned on but Net wasn't listening. She noticed a woman dressed in black sitting in a corner. She sat like a statue, neither moving nor showing any facial expression whatsoever.

"Ruth, have you seen that woman before?" Net whispered.

Her friend looked across the room. "Never. She reminds me of a character from *The Addams Family*." Ruth giggled as the woman turned her gaze to them.

Net froze. The *Malocchio,* the Evil Eye. She could feel it. Immediately she extended her index finger and her pinkie while holding the others folded back and clutched the twenty-four carat gold *corno*, the horn shaped amulet she always wore for protection. She breathed a sigh of relief. This gesture was a time worn remedy for warding off the curse. Even though Net had been born and reared in the Chicago area, her Neapolitan grandmother had instilled in her the dangers of the Evil Eye, the ability of certain people to do harm took merely a look.

"Be careful of that woman," she whispered to Ruth. "She's evil."

Ruth frowned and turned down the side of her mouth, but said nothing.

At that moment Professor Marcus entered the room. "I'm sorry I'm late. A little trouble with my car. I want to extend a warm welcome to all of you," he said in a deep bass voice. "I expect most of you to have a stimulating and enlightening experience during this initial six week course." His eyes examined everyone in the room, apparently taking stock.

Net felt strange vibrations emanating from him. He's up to something, she thought.

"Let me introduce you to my associate, Cassandra Dolton." He nodded to the woman in black. She joined him at the table and studied the group.

"Cassandra will be invaluable to you in your ancestral search. Feel free to come to her with any questions you may have."

The woman nodded and sat down again.

Net frowned. What am I doing here? she wondered. Then, with a sigh, she decided to give it a try. After all, for the next few weeks she would be unable to resume her normal routine anyway.

"What I want you to do," the professor continued, "is to open your notebooks and begin to write the names of all the family members you can recall. Just put down their names and who they are in relation to you."

As he examined the group, Net noticed some blank stares from the participants.

A slight furrow crossed his brow. "Let's get started with your immediate family, parents and grandparents. Cassandra and I will come around and give you any assistance you need."

Net gave Ruth a frown and began to write. She started with her parents and her only sibling, Molly, a divorced sophisticate, living on Chicago's Gold Coast. Being ten years Net's junior, she had little time for more than an obligatory family gathering. She had visited Net after her surgery, had to give her credit for that. But Net would probably not see her again until Thanksgiving.

Molly was involved with Second City and belonged to an Improv Group—had always been a frustrated actress. Her only daughter, Lena, had left home as soon as she was old enough and lived with a roommate in some artsy section of the city. Net shook her head. This was the extent of her family other than her son and his family.

That was all she wanted to remember right now. With the excuse that her knee was sore, she and Ruth left the class early.

Chapter 4

He sat at a massive desk, his hands tented, a pensive expression on his face.

"Anyone with any promise?" he asked the woman sitting across from him.

She shrugged. "It's too soon to tell."

A frown crossed his face. "We need to speed things up. There's been a lag in donations. If we're going to reach our goal at the allotted time, you know what's needed."

She nodded. Then, without another word, rose from the chair and soundlessly left the room.

He examined the items around him: an antique vase, an original Picasso sketch, a statuette smuggled in from an archeological dig. He caressed each one as if it were a seductive woman. His slippered feet sank into the colorful Persian rug covering the floor. He liked expensive things, felt he deserved them. After all, he was helping save the planet and all its inhabitants. He envisioned clean air, the rivers devoid of waste, the rain forests replenished. This was his calling.

Didn't that mean that he deserved the best? Of course it did. And he would have his heart's desire, no matter what the price.

Chapter 5

Net heard the front doorbell but didn't respond. She sat at the kitchen table, her chin cupped in her hands, her eyes staring out the window.

"Net," Ruth called coming into the room. "Are you here?"

"I'm here."

"Why didn't you answer the doorbell?"

"Eh, I knew if it was you, you'd let yourself in. Anybody else I don't want to talk to." She motioned her head toward the counter top. "Have a cup of coffee."

Ruth poured herself some, refilled Net's cup and sat down. "Now what's wrong? I see tear stains down your face. Are you in pain?" She took her friend's hand and gave it a squeeze.

Net lowered her chin to her chest and slowly moved her head from side to side. "How do you define pain, my friend? It's not my knee that hurts." She raised her tear-filled eyes to Ruth. Before her sat a pad of paper with a list of names.

"It's this genealogy stuff. I got through parents, grandparents, siblings, all those people. But when I come to those I love and miss the most, I can't go on. It's too painful."

Ruth put her hand over Net's. "It's your daughter, isn't it?"

Net nodded.

"I never asked you about her, felt it was none of my business. That you would tell me when you were ready."

Again a nod.

"Maybe it's time," Ruth said.

"I suppose it is. All these years I've been hoping and praying and waiting. I want to talk about her now."

Ruth settled back in her chair. "I'm listening."

Net took a deep breath, and sat for a moment gathering her thoughts.

"After Joe and I married, I had trouble carrying a baby—three miscarriages, one after another. Then Vince was born. Joe was thrilled to have a son, one who looked just like him." She stopped for a moment. Then she smiled at Ruth. "But we both wanted more children. Didn't want Vince to grow up an only child. We had just about given up when, five years later, I got pregnant again. This time everything went right and Donnatella was born."

Net closed her eyes again and remembered the perfect baby: ten fingers, ten toes, two huge blue eyes that never changed color, and a fuzzy head that eventually grew a crop of golden curls.

"She resembled my grandmother: fair, blond, and blue-eyed." Net let out a laugh. "I was so protective of that baby, always afraid someone would put the Evil Eye on her." She reached for a tissue as a tear escaped.

"Donna was a perfect child, always obedient, smiling and happy, good in school ... until she became a teenager. Then everything changed. She got in with the wrong crowd. Joe was always out looking for her when she didn't come home on time.

"When she was fifteen, she ran away. I found a note in her room saying she needed to find herself." Net turned pain-filled eyes to her friend.

"Did she come back?" Ruth whispered.

Net shook her head. "We searched everywhere—contacted all her friends and classmates. Joe even offered a reward. The police listed her as a missing person; we hired private detectives. But there was no sign of her anywhere." She stopped for a moment and took a deep breath. "I bought a statue of St. Anthony, patron saint of lost articles and missing persons, and prayed to him every day. On June 30th, his feast day, I would put a bouquet of flowers in front of the statue." Sadly she shook her head. "I guess he wasn't listening." She hesitated and stared out the window.

"Joe was never the same. Everywhere we went we saw someone who looked like Donna."

"I don't know what to say," Ruth said, feeling tears stinging the back of her own eyes. "That's a terrible burden to carry all these years. I can't imagine what you've been through."

"Every time the body of a young girl matching her description was found, we went to the morgue to see if it was Donna. Joe would have to hold me up. Once I fainted in his arms." She stopped for a moment, reliving the experience. "I was always relieved when it was someone else. But that meant another mother would be devastated." Net stopped for a moment and closed her eyes then let out a sound between a laugh and a sob. "You know what's funny? I still think she'll come back someday. She'd be thirty-five years old now, but I know I'd recognize her if I saw her." Net never visualized her daughter as being dead. That would be bad luck. She always saw her happy somewhere, maybe with a family. It was the only way she could cope.

* * *

The following day Net received a phone call from Margo Brewster telling her that George Watkins, son of the former owner of the townhouse, would be stopping by that afternoon.

"Will that be convenient?" Margo asked.

"I'll be here," Net replied. "What time can I expect him?"

"He said between four and five."

"All right." She disconnected the call and resumed her exercise routine. It was getting easier but still left her with some residual soreness.

When she finished, Net sat at the bay window in the living room gazing out at the flowering dogwoods that dotted the property. They put on a spectacular display.

She stared again at the flowering trees and remembered the day Vince had driven her there to check out the retirement center.

She had found every reason under the sun to stall him, but he would not hear of it.

"Ma, all I want you to do is look at the place. Is that asking too much?"

"All right, I'll look, but that's all." She sat back in the car with her arms folded across her ample bosom, a determined frown on her still attractive face.

17

As he drove south on Harlem Avenue, she examined the unfamiliar terrain. "Where are we going, Indiana?" she asked a sarcastic tone to her voice.

"I told you it's in Palos Park, lots of forest preserves and fresh air. It's a new place, only five years old, and it's only about a twenty minute drive to our new house."

"Humph." She knew she was being stubborn, couldn't remain in the old house especially since Vince and Melissa were buying a house in Orland Park.

When they arrived at the Palos Retirement Center, Net admired the strategically placed flowerbeds marking the entrance to the gated community. Even though it was still winter, she could imagine how they might look in the spring. She saw a number of buildings in the distance as Vince drove down the two-lane road.

"Here's the main building," he said parking in the visitor's lot.

As he helped his mother out of the car, she winced as she bore weight on her right knee. It had bothered her for some time, but she tried to ignore it. She knew she couldn't do that for much longer.

Vince led her into a foyer decorated with large potted plants. Tasteful watercolor paintings graced the walls. A well dressed middle-aged woman greeted them and led the way to the administrator's office.

"This looks expensive," Net whispered to her son.

"Pa left you plenty of money. I already checked. You can afford it, believe me." He scrutinized her with his father's black eyes as if waiting for her to object.

"Humph, so you know all my affairs."

Vince let out a frustrated sigh. "I'm your lawyer for chrissakes." He held out his arms in a theatrical gesture. "Sometimes you make me crazy, Ma."

Mrs. Thompson, the administrator, shook hands and took them on a tour of the main building. She led them through activity rooms, a library, a gym, and the main dining room. Residents had the option of paying for prepared meals if they so chose.

She pointed out another three-story building housing apartments and an assisted living facility.

"We're interested in the townhouses," Vince said.

"Of course, but I thought you should see all the amenities we have to offer." She led them past a chapel with modern stained glass windows breaking the light into its spectral colors.

"Is this place run by a religious organization?" Net asked.

"No," Mrs. Thompson answered. "The chapel is non-denominational. There are services on Saturday and Sunday for anyone who wishes to attend."

Net grunted. She had been raised a Catholic, but after Donna disappeared and her prayers went unanswered, she stopped going to church. What good did it do? But many of the old habits persisted. She found herself making the sign of the cross whenever anything frightened her.

Mrs. Thompson escorted them outside and Net climbed into Vince's car. They followed her to a townhouse that was presently vacant. On the way they passed a pond where a crust of ice decorated the periphery.

"See. Ma, there's a nice walking path around that pond and I'll bet there are ducks and geese in the summer."

Net didn't answer but she did like the feel of the place. The grounds were well tended with flowerbeds dotting the area ready to send out spring bulbs.

They pulled up behind Mrs. Thompson's car and walked into a townhouse with light airy rooms: a large cheery living room with a bay window, two full baths, one with a walk-in shower, a large bedroom and a smaller one that could be used as a sewing room or an office. The kitchen at the rear of the house sported new-looking appliances and plenty of wall cabinets. A sliding glass door led to a small patio.

"This is great, Ma," Vince whispered. "Everything you need."

Net had to agree. It was much nicer than she had anticipated.

"There are buzzers on the walls in the bathrooms, the kitchen, and the master bedroom should you need help," Mrs. Thompson said.

Net made a face. She wasn't an invalid for heaven's sake.

The woman looked at them expectantly.

"Thanks a lot," Vince said extending his hand. "We'll get back to you real soon."

Net said nothing. Simply gave her a half-hearted smile.

Now, here she was, three months later, living in the very townhouse and enjoying it, although she would never admit that to her son.

Chapter 6

Promptly at four P.M. the doorbell rang. Net looked out the peephole and saw Margo Brewster accompanied by a middle-aged balding man wearing a blue sport coat over gray slacks. She opened the door and greeted them.

"Mrs. Petrone," Margo said in her too sweet voice, "I thought you would feel more comfortable if I introduced you to Mr. Watkins." An artificial smile plastered her face.

"Thank you," Net said. She turned to the man and noticed the dark circles under his eyes and the deep furrow between his brows. "How do you do, Mr. Watkins. I'll open the garage door and you can retrieve the box."

"Then I'll leave you two," Margo said with a two-finger wave.

"You do that," Net said between gritted teeth. She noticed the half-smile on George Watkins' face and the slight roll of his eyes. She liked him immediately.

"Mrs. Petrone, I apologize for this intrusion. Mother's affairs have left my brother and me in quite a legal mess."

She pushed the button and the garage door slid up with a few squeaks and groans. "No problem. There it is, up there." She pointed to a large cardboard box in the corner of the top shelf. I wonder what kind of legal mess, she pondered. But it's none of my business. "There's a small ladder you can use." She indicated the old two-step ladder she had brought from the other house.

He climbed up, pulled down the box and was about to walk out to his car, then turned to her.

"Is something wrong?" Net asked.

"May I speak with you for a moment?"

"Sure. Come inside. I have a fresh pitcher of lemonade." Net preceded him into the kitchen and took two glasses from the cupboard.

George Watkins put the box on the floor and began pulling at the packing tape. "Do you mind if I open this now?"

"Go ahead." Net shrugged. As long as he didn't leave her a mess. Her curiosity was aroused as he pulled out one useless looking item after another: an old music box, a souvenir from Florida, a metal goblet, a vase with a broken handle.

"This is all junk," he said shaking his head, a desperate tone in his voice. Meticulously he examined every piece of wrapping paper. "Nothing."

"Please sit down. I get the feeling you're searching for something in particular," she said as she put the glasses on the table.

"Yes, but I haven't found it." He rubbed his forehead. "Oh God, I don't know what to do." He picked up the glass and took a swallow, then another.

"You want to tell me about it? Don't know if I can help, but I'm a good listener." Net grabbed the cookie jar from the counter and set it on the table. "Biscotti—have one."

"Thanks." He munched the almond-flavored biscuit with approval. "Very good."

"My sister made them. Now, tell me what the problem is."

George Watkins finished his drink and sat back in his chair. "Have you ever heard of the Society for the Fifth Beneficence?"

"The what?" Net stared at him in confusion.

"I figured you hadn't. You haven't been here long enough."

"Exactly what is it?" Net's curiosity was piqued. "Is it a cult of some sort?"

"You're exactly right. My mother, some of the other ladies in this complex and others all over the area were suckered in with all kinds of outlandish promises. But I'm getting ahead of myself." He picked up his empty glass then put it down again.

Net poured more lemonade and waited. She had nothing better to do and this sounded intriguing.

"Mother only had two children, my brother and me," he continued. "But my nephew has a severe physical disability, cerebral palsy. He needs constant care. It really puts a financial and physical strain on the family. Mother always helped out while she was living, God bless her. In her will she made provisions for my nephew and left the rest of her assets to my brother and me."

A suspicion began to take root in Net's mind. She had read too many books about ruthless people.

George sipped his lemonade and took another biscotti. "These are really good."

"My sister's secret recipe. She gives it to no one. Superstitious old Italian." She gave a slight grunt.

"To make a long story short," he continued, "Mom got involved with this Society and told me she had changed her will, leaving everything to them for the greater good of mankind." He dropped his chin into the palm of his hand as if the burden was too great to bear.

"May I ask how much money was involved?" Net said.

"Close to a million dollars."

"Oh *Madonna mia*, that's a lot of money. And nothing for your disabled nephew?"

"Nothing. By then Mother had completely changed. They brainwashed her. I tried to talk to her but she said I couldn't understand her 'higher calling'."

"Was she mentally competent?" Net asked.

"According to the doctor she was. Believe me, we tried to reason with her but she was firm in her decision. She gave the attorney a copy of the new will and he assured us it was legal and negated the former will." He rubbed his eyes with the palms of his hands then looked at Net.

"After that her behavior became erratic. My brother and I considered having another psychiatric evaluation. She had become extremely paranoid, claimed to hear noises all the time when no one was there." He let out a deep sigh.

"One day while I was on a business trip to New York, she called and left a message on the phone. Her voice sounded strained and she was whispering. She said she had made a terrible mistake and had made out a new will that was witnessed by two of the neighbor ladies. She said it was in a safe place and as soon as I returned we would go to the lawyer." He rubbed his hands over his eyes and gave a slight shake of his head.

Net wanted to prod him to go on, but she knew he needed time to collect his thoughts.

He looked into her eyes with an expression of pain. "Then she said she was being watched and felt that she might be in danger. Because she had been acting so paranoid lately, I felt she was exaggerating. She was doing a lot of that recently. After all, she lived here in this secure gated community. That assumption was a mistake. I decided to wait 'till morning. I'll regret that for the rest of my life." He let out another sigh. Tears filled his eyes as he pulled a handkerchief from his pocket. "I never saw her alive again. She had a fatal heart attack that very night."

"The *Malocchio*," Net blurted out making the sign of the cross multiple times. She noticed the inquisitive look George Watkins gave her.

She shrugged. "An old Italian superstition. If someone puts the Evil Eye on a person, bad things can happen. But, as I said, it's only superstition." She, herself, wasn't convinced of that, but she didn't share her beliefs with the man.

"Was there anything suspicious about her death?" Net asked.

"No. According to the doctor it was another heart attack. She had a number of them in the past and we knew her days were numbered."

"I'm sorry," she said. "I wish I could help you."

"My brother and I are contesting the will but it will be a long legal battle and we may not win. We're trying to prove that she wasn't competent and was coerced into signing it. I don't need the money but my nephew does. He'll need care for the rest of his life." He stopped for a moment, and then continued.

"My sister-in-law, Myra, has been caring for her son since be became ill. While Mom was alive, she paid for a woman to come in and help as needed. My nephew, Luke, is a bright seventeen-year-old. He can walk a short way with forearm crutches, but he tends to fall a lot. He communicates by means of a computer. His speech is so garbled that most people can't understand him. But he needs help in dressing, bathing, and eating." He stopped again and ran his hands down his face.

"Was it a birth injury?" Net asked.

"No. He had a severe case of meningitis when he was three with complicating brain damage." He shook his head and looked around as if he just became aware of his surroundings. "I've taken up enough of your time. But if, by any chance, you come across an envelope or some papers of any kind, please call me." He placed a business card on the table.

"I certainly will."

Mr. Watkins hesitated for a moment. "The lawyer said that if we can find the two people who witnessed Mother's signature, we might be able to question them."

That sounded plausible.

"I wrote down the names on a piece of paper. Perhaps they're residents here."

"I've only been in this place a few months," Net said. "But my friend, Ruth, has lived here since it opened. I'll ask her." She took the piece of paper without reading the names, and slid it into her pocket.

He got up and looked at the items from the box. "Thank you, again, for your kind hospitality and your sympathetic ear. Do you want any of these?" he asked beginning to replace them.

Net thought for a moment. "My niece, Lena, is studying art. Always bugging me for something to use for a still life. Leave that music box, the goblet and the broken vase. If she doesn't want them, I'll dispose of them."

He finished packing the box, thanked her again, and left.

Net sat for a long time thinking of the injustice of the entire situation. What would her favorite amateur sleuth, Emma Winberry, do? She had just finished reading her most recent mystery. The protagonist had gotten herself into serious trouble, but everything worked out in the end. But that was fiction. This was real life.

* * *

Net pondered what George Watkins had told her about his mother. Her heart went out to the disabled nephew and her resentment grew at the people who had obviously scammed Mrs. Watkins into changing her will. I'll ask Ruth if she ever heard of this society, she thought. Then she wondered where the will might be hidden, if, indeed there even was one. She looked around. All the cupboards had been cleaned out when she moved in as well as the bathroom cabinets. An old buffet had been left in the dining room with some tablecloths and linens in the bottom drawer. George Watkins didn't mentioned it when he was there and Net had forgotten all about it.

"I think I'll pull everything out of that bottom drawer and see if the will might be in there," she said aloud. She switched on the radio to a light classical station, sat on a chair, and, with a grunt, pulled out the heavy drawer.

A linen tablecloth lay on top. It bore a few red wine stains but was otherwise usable. She set it aside on the dining room table. Underneath were napkins to match, holiday table runners, and a heavy hand crocheted bedspread on the very bottom. Net pulled it out, spread it on her lap and marveled at the hours of work that went into such a piece.

She remembered her grandmother listening to the Italian soap operas on the radio and crocheting medallion after medallion before attaching them together. Everyone in the family had dresser scarves, table runners, and bedspreads made from the same pattern. When she was a child, Net believed Gram could make those things with her eyes closed.

A knock at the door followed by Ruth's cheery voice brought her back to the present.

"Come in, Ruth, I'm in the dining room."

"What on earth ..." Her friend scrutinized the items lying around.

"I'm searching through this drawer. Come here and help me. You can kneel down and I can't. See if there are any papers or envelopes tucked away in there."

Ruth gave her an inquisitive look, and then did as she asked. "I don't see anything here. What am I supposed to be looking for?" She sat back on her heel then looked again. "Wait a minute. " She stuck her head in a far corner of the drawer. "There's something here."

"Is it an envelope?" Net's excited voice asked.

"No. It's some sort of pin." Ruth pulled herself back and sat on the floor. "Will you look at this." She held a long sharp pin with a crystal knob on one end.

"What is it?" Net asked, her brow furrowed.

"I think it's an old fashioned hat pin—like women in the last century wore to hold those huge hats in place. They all had long hair, you know, and the pin went right through the mass of curls."

"God, it looks lethal," Net said gingerly taking the pin from her friend's hand. "How long is this thing?"

Ruth eyeballed it. "I'll bet it's eight or nine inches long."

"I wonder if it's valuable," Net said.

Ruth shrugged. "Maybe to a collector."

"I'll phone Mr. Watkins and ask him about it. But he was hoping to find something else." She placed the pin in the center of the dining room table.

"Let's put this stuff back." Net handed Ruth the items and she arranged them neatly in the drawer.

"All right," Ruth said. "That's done. Now will you tell me what this is all about?"

With a grunt, Net pulled herself up from the chair and preceded her friend into the kitchen. They nibbled on chocolate chip cookies while Net told Ruth the tragic story.

"My God," Ruth said, "a real mystery. And right here."

Net pulled the piece of paper with the names of the witnesses out of her pocket. "Do you recognize these names?" When she read them, her eyes widened. "Look at this. One of them is Cassandra Dolton, the woman from the genealogy class."

"No," Ruth said grabbing the paper and staring. "You're right."

"Do you recognize the other name?" Net asked.

"Uh uh," Ruth said shaking her head and biting down on her lower lip. "The plot thickens."

Net nodded. "Have you ever heard of that society?"

Ruth thought for a moment. "I seem to remember something about some of the residents joining an organization a couple of years ago. Don't know if it's the same one."

"Do you remember who they were?" Net persisted.

"Let me think." Ruth furrowed her brow. "Mrs. Peters, I believe. She's in assisted living now. Has mobility problems."

"Can we go and talk to her?" Net was warming to the prospect of investigating something that sounded very suspicious.

"I guess so. It certainly won't hurt," Ruth answered.

"Let's go right now," Net said.

"You're really into this, aren't you?"

Net shrugged. "Those amateur sleuths I read about are always solving mysteries."

"Don't most of them get into deep trouble doing it?" Ruth raised her eyebrows.

Net put her hands on her hips. "We're only going to ask a few questions. Besides, we don't have anything else to do right now."

"Did you do all of your genealogy homework?" Ruth asked.
Net frowned. "As much as I intend to."

Chapter 7

They found Mrs. Peters sitting in a wheelchair in a large atrium of the assisted living section. She was humming to herself and examining her fingers. Net and Ruth looked at each other wondering how 'with it' she was.

"Hello, Mrs. Peters, do you remember me? Ruth Borden?"

"Huh?" The woman gazed at her with a blank stare.

"Ruth Borden. We used to live near each other in the townhouses." Ruth sat next to the woman, smiled and took her hand.

Mrs. Peters screwed up her wrinkled face, stared, and shook her head. "Don't remember."

Ruth turned to her friend. "I don't think we're going to get through to her," she whispered.

"Can't hear ya," Mrs. Peters shouted. "Hearing aids are dead."

"Mrs. Peters," Ruth tried again, "did you ever join a society when you lived in the townhouse?"

"A what?" She cupped her hand behind her ear.

"A society." Ruth practically yelled.

"Don't know what you're talking about," came the reply.

Just then a diminutive woman struggling with a walker came up to them. "She doesn't remember much since her stroke," she said. "I'm Martha Grimes. I remember that society."

"You do?" Net tried to contain her excitement.

"It had a strange name. Society for the Fifth something or other."

"Beneficence," Net said.

"That's it. Didn't make much sense to me but it sounded important."

"Did you join?" Net asked.

"No." The woman shook her head emphatically. "I'm a devout Catholic and don't join secret societies." She scanned the room suspiciously as if expecting someone to be listening.

"So it was secret?" Net persisted.

"Oh yes. The ones who joined couldn't talk about it to anyone. Strict rules."

Net gave Ruth a knowing glance.

"Did you know Ella Watkins?" she asked.

"I did," Martha Grimes answered. "She was real nice. Poor Ella, I went to her memorial service in the chapel just a few months ago."

Net extended her hand. "I bought her townhouse, Net Petrone, and this is Ruth Borden."

"Lovely to meet you." The woman took Net's hand and smiled.

"Did Ella Watkins join that society?" Net asked although she already knew the answer.

Martha gave a sigh and a slight shake of her head. "I'm afraid so. She had always been so friendly. Then, all of a sudden, she kept to herself. Took a lot of walks alone, as if she was thinking about something." She raised her glistening eyes to the two women. "Then she was gone."

Net hesitated for a moment then asked, "Do you, by any chance, know of a hand written will that Mrs. Watkins claimed she wrote just before her death?"

Martha Grimes slowly shook her head. "No, I'm sorry, I don't. But then, as I said, she was staying pretty much to herself."

Suddenly Mrs. Peters chimed in. "I know," she shouted. "I signed it. I did."

The three women gave her a dubious look.

"I did," she insisted. "I signed the will." Then she began babbling something incomprehensible.

"I wouldn't put too much credence in that statement," Martha Grimes said. Then she chuckled. "Ask her if she signed The Declaration of Independence."

Net asked.

"Eh? Can't hear you," Mrs. Peters said.

"I asked if you signed The Declaration of Independence," Net shouted.

"I signed it, yes I did. I signed everything," Mrs. Peters answered. Then she began to sing as she took an imaginary pen in her hand and made circles in the air.

"I see what you mean," Net said. She decided not to tell George Watkins about Mrs. Peters. There was no sense in giving him false hopes.

"Well, thank you so much, Mrs. Grimes. It was nice talking to you," Ruth said as they got up to leave.

"Come back again," she said. "I don't get much company."

"We will."

They walked out of the building to Ruth's car. "What do you make of that?" Net asked.

"I have no idea, but I think we should stay out of it. I, for one, have no intention of getting involved with a secret society and I don't think you should, either." She started the engine and drove faster than her usual speed.

When Net returned to her townhouse, she reexamined the hatpin they had found. She didn't see any need to bother George Watkins with it at this time. Out of curiosity she took out a ruler and measured it–nine inches. From the decorative head to the sharp point.

"My God," she muttered. "That could be used as a weapon." She held it up to her neck. With enough force, it could go right through.

"Fool," she scolded herself. "It would snap off. You read too many mysteries." Still, it might come in handy. She didn't think George Watkins would mind if she kept it for a while.

Taking out the black leather purse she always carried, she slid the hatpin down the side and nestled it in a seam. Only the head was visible. It simply appeared to be a decoration. No one would ever know what it really was. She wasn't sure why she did that, but felt it might come in handy. One never knew.

* * *

The following day Net reluctantly joined Ruth for the genealogy class. A few of the people who had been present the previous week were missing.

"There'll probably be fewer here each week," Net whispered to Ruth.

"That always happens," her friend responded.

Professor Marcus walked in the door followed by Cassandra Dolton. He scanned the group, smiled, and said, "It looks like we lost a few folks." He gave a poor imitation of a laugh. "Let's get right down to business. Today I'll show you how to get the information you will need to research your ancestors."

Net squirmed in her seat. She really didn't want to be here, was doing it only to pacify Ruth.

"Cassandra will pass out some sheets with names of web sites and organizations that will help you. You may be surprised to learn that the Church of Jesus Christ of Latter-day Saints is one of the premier genealogy organizations in the world."

He stopped for effect, but Net wasn't impressed. She heard a few remarks from some of the others. "For those of you who don't have computers or are unfamiliar with the Internet, Miss Brewster tells me there are computers in another room and she will be glad to have someone help you with your research."

He went on to tell them how to fill out various research forms as Cassandra passed them around. But Net wasn't listening. She was studying his associate. She felt an evil vibration emanating from the woman. Every time she came near, Net covertly extended her index finger and pinkie with one hand and grasped her gold *corno* with the other. At one point Cassandra met her eyes as if to say, 'I know what you're doing and it won't help.' Net shivered. She noticed that the woman raised one eyebrow only. Net never trusted anyone who could do that. It wasn't natural. She decided then and there that she would drop this course.

* * *

"I'm sorry, Ruth, those people give me the willies. I'm not going back and neither should you. That Cassandra Dolton must be involved in that society since she witnessed Mrs. Watkins's will."

"Even if she is, what does that have to do with the genealogy class?" Ruth asked.

"Maybe that's the way they get women involved with the society, did you think of that? She's evil, a *strega*, a witch. She might put the *Malocchio* on you. Be careful, Ruth."

Ruth looked disappointed. "It's too bad you feel that way. I'm really getting into this. I'll just stay until I have all the information I need to continue on my own, okay?"

"If that's what you want to do. You go ahead and research your ancestors. I choose to leave the past alone," Net said firmly "Case closed."

Ruth sighed. "Okay, if you feel that strongly."

"I do. Now I'm going to lie down with a book and an ice pack. Talk to you later."

Chapter 8

Sam had been calling almost every day. Finally Net told him she was ready to go out to dinner. They hadn't seen each other since she was in the hospital and she had been so filled with pain killers that she remembered little of his visits.

When the doorbell rang, she glanced in the mirror one last time and decided she looked passable. She wore new navy silk pants, with a silver thread running down the sides. A silver tunic and red scarf set off the ensemble nicely. Her curly hair cupped her face and she had put on a little eye shadow above her chocolate brown eyes. She liked the effect.

Net opened the door to a grinning Sam, flowers in one hand and a box of chocolates in the other. He stood there for a moment, eyes shining a little too brightly. He was the only man she knew who cried as freely as a woman. Then, of course, he was Italian.

"Hi Sam." She took the flowers and buried her nose in the fragrant carnations. He put the candy down on the end table as Net retrieved a vase and filled it with water. She put the flowers in it and smiled at him.

"How about a nice hug?" Arms wide, he embraced her carefully as if she were a Dresden doll in danger of breaking.

She hugged him back. "It's good to see you, Sam."

"Let me look at you." He held her at arms' length and studied her from head to toe. "You lost weight, but you're as pretty as ever."

"You're an incurable romantic." She ran her hands through his gray curly hair, still thick, and laughed. "I was never pretty, just a plain Jane."

"Not to me. You're the prettiest woman in the world."

She knew she had to put a stop to this kind of talk as soon as possible. After a brief tour of the tour house, he nodded his approval.

"I'm hungry," Net said. "Shall we go?"

"Okay." He held the door open and followed her out holding her arm firmly. He helped her climb into his roomy Cadillac and drove slowly out of the complex.

"It's nice here," he said as they passed beds of spring flowers planted to bloom in succession. A row of Bradford pear trees lined the drive, their branches heavy with tiny white flowers.

"Yeah, they hire people to plant just the right flowers. Believe me, they don't spare any expense in this place." She let out a "humph."

"You like it, don't you?" he asked, an anxious tone in his voice.

"Oh sure, how could I not like it. I've got everything I need: a nice place to live, all sorts of activities. They're always arranging trips somewhere."

"I hear a 'but' in your voice," he said.

"It's not the old neighborhood. I miss hearing the kids playing outside, old Mrs. Morelli scolding them to stay out of her garden, the trucks going down the street ..." She stopped. Knew if she didn't she'd start to cry.

"Those were all the things you used to complain about."

"I know, but now I miss them. Everybody is old here." She sighed. "Oh Sam, we're never satisfied, are we?"

"You know, Net, you gotta be happy inside yourself. Then, no matter where you live, it'll be home."

"Well, aren't you the philosopher." He had surprised her with that statement.

"I been reading, even going to church."

Net was speechless. Sam had never been a church-goer except for weddings and funerals.

"What changed you?" she asked.

He shrugged. "Getting old, I guess. I'm even thinking of selling the old homestead and moving into one of them condominiums."

Sam still lived in the house his parents had owned in Melrose Park. Through the years he had upgraded the place until now it must be worth quite a tidy sum.

"Boy, are you full of surprises today," she said.

He turned south on Harlem Avenue and drove to a new restaurant that had recently opened. "I heard they got good food here," he said pulling up to the door.

"I can walk, Sam. You don't have to let me out at the door."

"But I want to." He helped her out of the car, sat her on a bench outside the door, then parked .

They walked into a modern structure decorated with pictures of street scenes of European cities. Soft classical music played in the background.

"This is nice," Net said.

"Sure is."

"Table for two, sir?" the hostess asked picking up two menus and leading them to a booth next to a large window. "Will this be satisfactory?"

Sam looked at Net. "Fine," she said. Carefully she slid into the booth and he sat facing her.

Studying the menu, her eyes widened at the prices. "Did you know this place was so expensive?" she asked.

"It's only money. Nothing's too good for my favorite gal. This is a celebration, remember?"

She cocked her head and raised her eyebrows.

"Your recovery," he said with a grin.

"That sounds good." After browsing the entrees she ordered the roast beef with baked potato and fresh asparagus. Sam ordered a steak with the same sides.

"How would you like that done, sir?" the waiter asked.

"Rare, please, and bring us each a glass of wine."

Net screwed up her face. Sam rarely drank alcohol.

He smiled. "We're celebrating, remember?"

The waiter brought him a wine list and stood by while he examined it.

"Merlot okay?"

"Fine," she answered.

Everything was perfectly prepared and served. After they had finished, Sam sat back with a contented sigh. "That was good. Did you enjoy your dinner?" He was always so anxious to please.

"Oh yes. The roast beef was so tender you could cut it with a fork. And the trimmings were delicious."

Sam's smile of satisfaction almost brought tears to her eyes.

"Are you ready for dessert?" the waiter asked.

Net grimaced. "I'm pretty full. What do you have that's light?"

He rattled off a list of exotic confections. "We also have a small ice cream sundae."

"I'll have that, vanilla with chocolate sauce," Net said.

"Same for me," Sam agreed.

"Coffee?" he asked.

They both nodded.

"This was a real treat," Net said. "I almost feel like myself again. You have no idea how frustrating it is not to be able to do the things you want. I went back to the pool this week. That water felt heavenly. But I still have to take things slowly."

"Are you in any pain anymore?" he asked, a concerned expression on his face.

"Eh, just a little aching when I'm on my feet too much. Otherwise, I'm right as rain." She laughed. "I wonder where that expression came from."

"Beats me. We say so many things just because our parents did. Most of them don't mean anything."

"You're right," she said as the waiter set their coffee and desserts on the table.

"Dig in," Sam said spooning the ice cream into his mouth.

"Remember when we were kids," Net said after sampling the flavors. "You were always the first one outside when the Good Humor truck came around."

"Yeah, the good old days. We didn't worry about anything, just had fun." He glanced past her as if reliving that time.

"You know, Sam, I've been thinking about Donna so much lately. It's almost as if she's reaching out to me but, for some reason, can't make the connection. Does that sound foolish?"

He reached over and took her hand. "You're never gonna forget her, you know that." His deep brown eyes shared her pain.

She didn't pull her hand away. Right now she needed the support of someone she cared about. "I know she's alive. A mother can feel that." Her eyes met his and a tear sneaked out. "Someday ...."

He reached up and tenderly wiped the tear with his finger.

She let out a breath and waved her hand. "It's probably that genealogy class I've been taking. We had to list all the immediate family members then go back as far as we could remember."

"Why are you taking that?" he asked. The waiter put down the bill; Sam examined it and left money in the folder.

She shrugged. "Ruth wanted to and I thought it might be a good idea. But I think I'm gonna drop it. I don't particularly like the instructor." She didn't mention Cassandra and the bad vibes she got from the woman. Sam would be upset and worry unnecessarily.

"Don't do anything because somebody else wants you to. Please yourself." With a determined nod of his head he helped her out of the booth.

She smiled. "Thanks, Sam, for both the dinner and the advice."

"Anytime. You just come to me. I'll always be there for you."

She squeezed his arm as they walked out of the restaurant into a perfect spring evening.

Chapter 9

A few days later Net received a plain cream-colored envelope. It was hand addressed in calligraphy style. She searched the front and back for a return address, but found none. Something about it made her nervous. She made the sign of the cross then went into the kitchen, took a knife and slit the top of the envelope. Inside was one sheet of the same paper. In script style print it read:

> *You are invited to a lecture about the future of this planet.*
> *Environmental issues are a concern to all of us.*
> *Learn what you, as an individual, can do to help.*
> *Place: Church of the Redemption*
> *(followed by an address on Wolf Road)*
> *Time: Thursday, May 15th, 7 PM.*
> *We look forward to seeing you.*
> *Brother Rupert.*

At the bottom in small print read: *printed on recycled paper.* What in the world is this all about? Why no name of the organization? Net was tempted to throw it in the recycling, but her curiosity was piqued. Just then she heard a knock at the door. She opened it to a bewildered Ruth holding a similar envelope.

"You got one, too?" Net said.

"Yes. Who is this Brother Rupert and what is this all about?" Ruth asked.

Net shrugged. "Sit down and we'll talk about it. I wonder if everybody in the complex got one?"

They sat at the kitchen table and Net poured two glasses of fresh lemonade and put a plate of chocolate chip cookies on the table.

Ruth compared the envelopes. They were identical, each addressed by name. "They're not sent to occupant so somebody has a list of names. They sell those, you know."

Net nodded as she chewed on a cookie. "It's probably a scam. You get there and they have their hands out for a donation."

"Maybe it's just a lecture. There's no mention of a fee." Ruth said. "Some churches have them sponsored by a woman's guild or something."

Net frowned. "They don't usually send out invitations. The only time I've received anything like this is to a wedding."

"You're right. What do you think we should do?" Ruth asked.

Net scratched her head and pushed her curly hair away from her face. "First, let's find out who else got one."

"Good thinking," Ruth agreed. "I'll ask some of the people at the genealogy class this afternoon. Are you sure you're not coming?"

"Absolutely. I don't trust that Dolton woman and neither should you. You go without me and I'll take a walk around, see if I can find anyone else who got an invitation."

"Okay." Ruth sighed. "I have a few phone calls to make. See you later."

* * *

Net decided to call the church and see what they could tell her. She looked up the number and punched it into the phone.

"Church of the Redemption, may I help you?" a pleasant sounding woman's voice answered.

"Hello, I would like some information," Net answered.

"Certainly. Our services are held every Sunday at nine and eleven. We have a prayer group that meets on Wednesday evenings at seven."

"Thank you, but that's not what I wanted to know. I received an invitation about a lecture on May fifteenth. It was rather vague. I wanted more details."

"Oh, I can't help you there," the woman said. "When we're not using the church hall we sometimes rent it out for lectures and meetings by various organizations."

"What organization is sponsoring this lecture?" Net persisted.

"Just a moment and I'll check that."

Net waited tapping her foot on the floor. A few minutes later the woman returned.

"Sorry to keep you waiting. The pastor is not the most organized person. All I can find is that it is an environmental group and the talk will be about issues confronting society today and what we can do to help. It sounds quite informative."

"What's the name of the organization?" Net asked.

Hesitation on the other end. "I don't seem to have that information." Her tone sounded perplexed.

"Thank you very much," Net said. "Goodbye."

She sat for a moment, thinking. What organization doesn't identify itself? Maybe it's new and they don't have a name yet. There's certainly nothing secret about the problems with the environment. I'm sure they want money.

She got up and looked outside. The sun was shining with the promise of a lovely day. Net slipped on a light jacket, put the invitation in her pocket and started out the door. Then she remembered her cane. She wasn't sure how far she was going to walk and didn't want to come home limping in pain.

Locking up came automatically to her. She took a deep breath of fresh air, and started down the walk. For the next half-hour she rang a dozen doorbells and spoke to the residents. Only one had received an invitation. Net recognized her as a member of the genealogy class. Was that where they had gotten the list of names? She was eager to talk to Ruth later, but now she was tired and her knee ached. "Boy will I ever get my energy back?" she muttered as she opened her front door, plopped down on the sofa, and put her feet up.

* * *

"Huh?" Net shook her head. Was that someone at the door? She must have fallen asleep. "Coming," she called, easing herself off the couch. She opened the door to an excited Ruth. "Hi."

"Did I wake you?' her friend asked.

"I didn't mean to fall asleep. Was tired after my long walk."

"Guess what?" Ruth said. "Six people in the genealogy class got one of these invitations. Did you find anyone else?"

Net nodded. "Only one lady who was in the class. So they sold our names. That makes me angry. I think we should tell Margo Brewster."

"So do I," Ruth agreed. "We gave them that information in good faith and they go and sell it to some environmental organization. Who knows who else they sold it to."

"Let's go right now," Net said.

They walked out the door, got into Ruth's car and drove to the main building, but Margo Brewster wasn't in her office. The door was locked with a sticky note saying she wouldn't be back until the following day.

The women walked into one of the activity rooms where a few ladies were milling around talking excitedly. "Listen," Ruth whispered.

"I heard that this Brother Rupert goes around the world lecturing about global warming and the melting of the ice caps," one woman was saying.

"And," another added, "he's predicting all kinds of catastrophes if we don't do something about it."

"Excuse me," Net interrupted "Where did you hear about this man?"

"In my bridge group," she answered. "Lot's of the ladies go to his lectures. They say he's a very dynamic speaker."

Net and Ruth exchanged glances.

"We got an invitation to hear him speak at a neighboring church on May fifteenth," Net said.

"Oh, don't miss it. I'm going, too. Some people are actually comparing him to Ghandi," she said in a reverential tone.

Humph, Net thought, maybe he'll appear with a shaved head, wearing sandals and a sheet wrapped around him like a toga. She wasn't impressed by these accolades.

"Thank you," Ruth said as they walked away. "Now I *am* curious."

"So am I," Net said. "I suppose there's no harm in listening to what the man has to say. We don't have to give him any money."

"Okay. I'll go if you do," Ruth said.

"Agreed."

As they were leaving the building Net felt someone staring at her. The hairs on the back of her neck stood up. She immediately extended her second and fifth fingers, clutched her *corno for protection*, and slowly turned around. There was no one there. Was it her imagination? Probably, but she shivered as she followed Ruth out the door.

Chapter 10

The following day Net hurried to answer the phone. She had been on the patio arranging a few potted plants. "Hello," she said.

"Mrs. Petrone?" a male voice asked.

"Yes."

"This is Professor Marcus from the genealogy class."

Damn, what does he want? He's probably the one who sold our names.

When she didn't respond, he continued. "May I ask why you decided to drop the class?"

Was that disappointment she heard in his voice? Maybe he got paid by the number of participants. "I just decided it wasn't something that interested me. I only tried it because a friend of mine was going."

"I'm sorry to hear that. We'll be getting into some interesting research in the next few weeks, even may be able to uncover relatives you've lost touch with."

Net gripped the phone and reached for a chair. "What do you mean by that?" she asked in a demanding tone.

"I know about your daughter," he said softly. "We may be able to help you find her."

She gasped. "How come you know all about me?" She became irate, felt as though her privacy had been invaded.

"We research our clients. It isn't difficult these days to do an Internet search. I'm sorry if I've upset you, but I really may be able to help you."

She took a deep breath and struggled for control. "Listen Professor Marcus or whatever your real name is, my husband and I hired private detectives to search for our daughter. If they couldn't find her, I don't know what you think *you* can do. Now, *please*, stay out of my life!" She pushed the disconnect button and struggled to control her trembling hands.

"I've got to think," she said aloud. Grabbing her car keys and a sweater, she ran into the garage, pushed the door opener, and got in her car. She backed out a little faster than she should have but gained control as she drove down the street.

With no destination in mind, she drove south on Harlem Avenue, past a number of strip malls, restaurants and past the expanse of Cook County Forest Preserves. Without thinking, she turned onto one of the gravel roads that led to a parking lot, turned off the ignition and sat for a while trying to clear the jumble of thoughts in her mind. A few tears made their way down her cheeks. Absently she wiped them away with her hands.

A number of trails led into the woods, each with a sign denoting the length of the walk. It appeared safe enough. Net got out of the car, took her cane from the back seat, locked the car and slowly made her way down the nearest path.

Birds sang, squirrels ran through the brush, an occasional inquisitive chipmunk poked its head at her, then scampered way. She breathed in the woodsy smell. It immediately lifted her spirits.

After a ten-minute walk, she came to a bubbling stream. A fallen log beside it offered a nice place to sit and think. Net sat down, stared at the water, and noticed a turtle sunning itself on a rock. I wish I were that turtle, she thought. Then all I would have to do is find something to eat and sleep away my life.

"Oh Joe," she said, "I miss you so much." She often talked to her deceased husband, felt his nearness, the warmth of his love. "Is Donna really alive somewhere? Why doesn't she come home? Could it be possible that Professor Marcus might be able to find her when everyone else failed?" She closed her eyes as a feeling of calm and peace came over her. She felt Joe was trying to comfort her.

Net lost track of time, didn't know how long she sat there until she heard the distant rumble of thunder. She looked up through the trees and noticed the sky filling with ominous clouds. A chill wind whipped the branches of the trees.

"*Madonna mia*," she said in alarm as she got up from the fallen log. "I better hurry."

She began making her way back but it seemed much farther. Am I going the right way? She wondered. In a fit of panic she quickened her step as lightning streaked across the sky and thunder crashed. Her knee began to ach as she limped along, then, with a sigh of relief, she spotted the parking lot and almost ran to her car. By then she was limping badly but paid no attention. She unlocked the door and got in just as huge raindrops pelted the windshield.

She started the ignition and drove slowly back to Harlem Avenue. She was barely able to see through the wiper blades slashing across the window. Twice she pulled over to the side along with a number of other drivers until the rain let up.

The storm passed as she turned into her complex and the sun shone through the departing clouds. Net pulled the car into the garage, went into the house, and looked out the kitchen window at a magnificent rainbow arching across the sky. Something about it filled her with hope. The colors blended into each other so perfectly. The sight brought tears to her eyes. She stood there until the colors began to fade. Only then did she notice the blinking light on the answering machine.

* * *

When she depressed the button, her son's frantic voice came through. "Ma, Melissa's in the hospital. She fell and went into labor. We're at Palos Hospital. Please come when you get this message."

Net stood frozen trying to process Vince's words. How did she fall? Where? When was the baby due? For a moment she couldn't think. Slowly she walked to the calendar and looked at the date with a red X. Melissa's due date—five weeks away.

"*Madonna mia*," she groaned. "It's not time yet." She had to get to the hospital but didn't know where it was. "Ruth, she'll know."

Net punched in her friend's number and counted the rings. She answered on three. "Ruth, where's Palos Hospital?'

"What? Are you all right?"

"My daughter-in-law went into early labor. She's at Palos Hospital and I don't even know how to get there." She rubbed her knee as her words came out in a staccato rhythm.

"I'll drive you. Be over in five minutes."

Thank God for friends like Ruth. She was dependable. Net rushed into the bathroom, dashed water on her face, and brushed her hair. Ringlets hung down on her forehead even though she pushed them back. Got to get a haircut, she thought. She grabbed her jacket, retrieved an ice pack from the freezer, and rushed out of the house just as Ruth's car pulled into the driveway.

When she was settled and had fastened her seat belt, Ruth asked, "Where were you in that storm? I tried to call you several times, but you weren't home."

Only then did Net remember the call from Professor Marcus. It didn't seem important now. She would tell Ruth about it later. "I went for a drive and got caught in the rain."

"Your timing was lousy."

"Tell me about it." Net sighed and closed her eyes, overcome with weariness. She placed the ice pack on her knee and felt immediate relief.

"How early is your daughter-in-law?"

"Five weeks. I don't know the details because Vince left a message on the machine. Said she fell."

"Oh, Lord!" Ruth exclaimed.

"Yeah, I don't know any more than that. Oh *Dio mio,* a mother worries."

"Especially you. At least she's far enough along that the baby should be okay. One of mine was four weeks early, a little pipsqueak. Now he's six foot three and built like a bull." Ruth was always the optimist while Net always thought the worst.

When they arrived at the hospital, the visitors' lot was almost full. A van pulled out just as Ruth turned into that row. She parked and let out a breath. "I swear, hospitals are doing a bang up business."

"That's not funny," Net said.

"Sorry."

The first thing Net noticed was a row of wheelchairs lining a wall. Another set of doors led them into a lobby. The subdued lighting lent a peaceful atmosphere.

"This is nice," Ruth said. "Look at all those comfortable chairs and sofas."

But Net barely heard her. She hurried to the information desk. "Melissa Petrone," she said anxiously. "She's in labor and delivery."

The woman behind the desk smiled. "How do you spell that, please?"

Impatiently Net spelled the name.

"She's on the second floor. Here are visitors' passes for each of you. The elevators are that way."

"Thanks." Net realized she had forgotten her cane and was favoring her right leg. She hoped Ruth wouldn't notice the limp. When Ruth grabbed her arm, she nodded a thank you.

Like the lobby, the elevators were jammed. They had to wait for a second one as the doors of the first one closed, the people in the front pushing back.

The second floor was quieter, not much hustle and bustle. They walked into the waiting room where Net spotted Vince perched on the edge of a sofa, his head in his hands.

"Son," she muttered, sitting next to him and grasping his hand.

"Ma, I'm glad you're here." His eyes were rimmed with red.

"You remember my friend, Ruth? She was kind enough to drive me."

"Thanks." He extended his hand to Ruth and motioned to her to have a seat.

"Now, tell me what happened," Net said almost afraid to hear the details.

He took a breath. "You know how big she got in the last few weeks." He shook his head. "She was carrying some laundry into the bedroom and tripped over one of Dominic's trucks. She fell forward, let go of the clothes and was able to break her fall with her hands. But she sprained her left wrist. Then her water broke."

It could have been worse, Net thought, but she better not say it. She rubbed her son's back with one hand and held onto him with the other.

"How do you feel?" he asked.

"Me? I'm fine. Back to my normal routine. Don't worry about me. Where's Dominic?"

"With Melissa's sister."

"Good. What does the doctor say?"

"He said the baby's heart rate is good and she should weigh between four and five pounds."

She—a girl. They hadn't wanted to know the sex of the baby earlier. Net's eyes filled with tears. "She's gonna be fine. I know it. Girls are strong. But why aren't you with Melissa?"

"The doctor is doing some testing and asked me to wait here."

Net continued to hold her son's hand until a nurse came out and called him. "Mr. Petrone, would you like to be with your wife now? She's in active labor and it shouldn't be long."

He jumped up from the sofa, glanced back at his mother and Ruth, and hurried after the nurse.

Ruth sat next to Net. "There must be a cafeteria somewhere. Why don't we find it instead of sitting here, waiting."

"Good idea."

They went to the nurses' station and asked directions to the cafeteria. The secretary told them where to go; they thanked her and walked to the elevator. They had to ask one more person before they found it.

"I swear these hospitals are a maze of turns and twists," she said as the adrenaline rush of the past few hours began to subside. Now she needed a boost of caffeine.

They each chose a roll and coffee and sat at a table near the window. A few clouds scudded across the sky as the sun made its journey to the west. Net tried to ignore the throbbing in her knee. Now why had she forgotten that cane?

When they were on their second cup of coffee, Net decided to tell Ruth about the phone call from Professor Marcus.

"He actually called you?" Ruth said, a furrow deepening between her eyes.

"Can you believe that? He knew all about me, and about Donna."

"How in the world did he know that?"

"He said he might be able to help me find her. Now why would he say such a cruel thing?"

"I don't know." A bewildered expression crossed Ruth's face. "So what did you say?"

"I told him to stay out of my life and not to call me again. Then I hung up." She pursed her lips and crushed the bit of roll she held in her hand. "The nerve ..."

Net wiped the crumbs off her fingers as they sat for a while saying nothing. "I'd better go back upstairs. You don't have to stay, Ruth. Vince can drive me home."

"Nonsense. Of course I'll stay."

Net knew her friend wanted to be there in case any complications arose and she was grateful to her.

When they returned to labor and delivery Net asked how Melissa Petrone was progressing.

"She just went into the delivery room. It won't be long." The woman's voice was soothing and reassuring. She had obviously been doing this for a long time.

After a short wait, a beaming Vince appeared, disheveled but smiling. "Ma, a beautiful little girl. She's tiny but yelling away."

Net hugged her son and brushed away a tear. "Can I see her?"

"In a little bit. They're taking her to a special nursery called the NICU. She'll be in an incubator for a while."

Net grasped her *corno* and muttered a prayer of thanksgiving. "How big is she?"

"Four and a half pounds. Not too bad." He let out a sigh. "Boy, I'm beat. It's hard work having babies."

Net and Ruth both laughed.

"How's Melissa?" Net asked.

"Tired, but fine. No problems."

"Good."

They sat quietly until a nurse came in and said they could see the baby. She included Ruth presuming she was a member of the family. They put gowns and masks on and walked into a room with special cribs and incubators lining the walls. Machines beeped as everyone busily attended the premies.

"Here she is," the nurse said. A sign with a pink band identified baby girl Petrone. She kicked her arms and legs and let out a lusty cry.

"Good pair of lungs," Vince said, beaming.

"She's strong and her lungs are well developed. She won't be in here long," the nurse said.

Net looked down at the tiny head wearing a pink cap and the pinched face. God bless you, baby girl. She was so overcome with emotion she couldn't talk for fear of making a fool of herself.

They spent a few minutes with the Melissa. Then, satisfied that all was well, they left the new parents alone. Only then did Net realize she hadn't asked what they planned to name the baby.

Chapter 11

Ruth pulled the car into the parking lot of the Church of the Redemption. "Look at how crowded it is already," she said searching for a spot.

"He must really be popular," Net said amazed at the number of people streaming into the building.

Ruth finally pulled into a spot between two SUVs. "I wish people wouldn't park these monsters so close to the yellow line. Will you be able to get out?"

"Sure." But when Net opened the door, she had to squeeze her body out of the narrow space. "Ugh." I'll put the *Malocchio* on these people, she thought.

As they walked into the church, the difference between the two women was striking. Net was attractive, but short and slightly overweight. Her face was pleasant, but wouldn't turn any heads. Ruth, on the other hand, was tall and regal-looking. She had cut her long gray hair and had it styled to complement her thin face. She wore a navy blue suit that appeared tailor-made, though Net knew she had bought it at the mall. Net felt no jealousy toward her friend. She accepted their differences and enjoyed her company.

They were directed to the parish hall, a large auditorium-style room where a man stood at the door handing out programs. Over half of the seats were already occupied and an excited buzz filled the room. They sat on two seats in the rear and glanced at each other, trying to listen to some of the comments, but so many people talked at the same time that it was all a jumble.

Net examined the program, printed on recycled paper. At least this shows that this group may really be concerned about the environment, she thought. First on the agenda was an introduction by a Mrs. Applewood, then a video of the damage being done to the environment by greenhouse gases followed by the feature speaker, Brother Rupert.

What more can he say after a video? Net wondered. We'll soon find out.

A tastefully dressed woman, her hair expertly coifed, stepped up to the podium, made sure the microphone was working, and called everyone's attention. She identified herself as Ardis Applewood. "Those of you who have never been to one of these meetings are in for a real treat," she said scanning the crowd. "I see some familiar faces and welcome you back. If, after you've heard the presentation, you would like to join our little family, there will be applications in the back. Just fill one out and someone will call you. Now, without further comment, we'll see the video. I must warn you that some views are disturbing, but please, take everything seriously. The future of our world is at stake."

Everyone applauded as she walked off. The lights dimmed, a large screen lowered at the back of the stage, and the video began. It lasted about twenty minutes and was no different than those that everyone had seen on television specials about the devastation to the planet.

When the lights came on, Net and Ruth looked at each other and shrugged. "Nothing new there," Ruth whispered.

Mrs. Applewood returned to the podium and said, "Now, the moment you have all been waiting for. Let me present Brother Rupert."

Deafening applause filled the room as a tall man walked slowly toward the podium. He was impeccably groomed wearing an expensive dark gray suit, light gray shirt, complemented by a red striped tie. Gold cuff links peaked out from the sleeves of his jacket at just the appropriate length.

"Looks like he had that suit made in Saville Row in London," Ruth whispered.

"What do you know about Saville Row?" Net asked suppressing a grin. A woman behind her shushed .

"Went on a tour," Ruth whispered in Net's ear.

Brother Rupert stood for a moment smiling and gazing at his admirers. He was clean-shaven with a thin grim-looking face and piercing black eyes. Then he bowed theatrically and held out his hands in supplication.

"What a phony," Net whispered. Her friend nodded.

When he finally began to speak his voice was smooth as honey. "Fellow travelers on this road we call life, thank you for your enthusiastic greeting."

More applause.

Net looked at her friend and wondered how long this performance would go on.

"Tonight," he paused. "Tonight I have a special message for all of you. We are gaining ground in our fight to save the planet." He hesitated for effect. "The devastation you saw in the video is slowly being reversed by the efforts of believers like yourselves. At this moment some of our younger members are working tirelessly in every corner of the world to reverse the damage mankind has wrought."

Net frowned. That was certainly an overstatement. There were environmental groups active and making a difference but not to the extent he was claiming. I wonder what his agenda is, she thought.

"Most of you are familiar with our little family, but for you newcomers, there is literature in the rear of the church describing our organization and, as Mrs. Applewood told you, if you are interested in joining, fill out the application and someone will call."

He went on for another half-hour talking about ways to stop pollution and emphasizing the use of renewable energy sources. When he finished with a flourish and a bow, the audience gave him a standing ovation.

Ruth frowned at Net as they struggled with the crowd to the exit. Out of curiosity, they each picked up the information.

"Wasn't he fantastic?" a woman behind them said to her partner.

"I get goose bumps every time I hear him speak," another woman said.

Net and Ruth made no comment as they headed for the door. When they were comfortable seated in the car, Ruth asked, "He is a good speaker, but did you get anything new out of his lecture?"

"Only what we've heard before on TV. He's charismatic all right, but it was more like mass hypnosis, if you ask me."

"I agree," Ruth said as she joined the queue to exit the parking lot.

"I'll read this when I get home," Net said, "but I'm willing to bet there's a nice fat fee associated with joining this organization."

* * *

When Net returned to her townhouse she was eager to have a look at the application for membership. She turned on the light on the end table and tried to settle on the sofa. Something was definitely wrong with the carpeting. It hadn't been installed properly. Shoddy workmanship. Someday I'll have it ripped out and hardwood floors installed. She moved the sofa until it was level then settled herself and opened the four-page folder.

Her breath caught in her throat. At the top in bold letters was written:

Application for Membership in the Society for the Fifth Beneficence

A chill ran up her spine—the same people who scammed poor Mrs. Watkins out of her money. Her first instinct was to tear it up and throw it in the recycling. Then she thought of the disabled grandson, his inheritance stolen from him.

Her Italian temper took hold. "Those crooks," she said between clenched teeth. "They must be stopped."

At that moment the phone rang. She grabbed it and was tempted not to answer. Don't be foolish she thought as she saw Ruth's number on the caller ID.

"Hello."

"Net, did you look at that application?" Ruth's agitated voice came over the instrument.

"I sure did and was thinking of tossing it."

"Me, too. I don't want to get involved with those people."

"But, if we don't, we'll never be able to help Mr. Watkins." Net paced and made faces, wondering what to do.

"My friend, we're not private investigators. We're two aging women trying to enjoy the rest of our lives. Do you really want to get mixed up in this intrigue?"

"Well, when you put it that way. Why don't we sleep on it. I don't want to read through the whole thing tonight. In the morning will be soon enough."

"Okay, I'll be over in the morning and we can examine the entire thing with a fresh mind. Goodnight."

But it wasn't a good night at all. In her dreams Net saw Mrs. Watkins' grandson begging on the street; people jeering at him; the boy weeping in despair. By morning she was more tired than when she went to bed. She decided to skip her water aerobics class, didn't have the energy.

When Ruth came over, she looked just as sleep deprived.

"Did you eat anything?" Net asked.

Ruth shook he head.

"Sit," Net poured coffee and put out bran muffins she had bought the previous day.

"You didn't sleep well either, huh?"

"Not much. I wish we had never gone to that lecture."

"So do I."

They drank coffee, nibbled on muffins and stared out the window. The overcast sky heralded more rain. The ground was still dry and the farmers were complaining. But in the mood she was in, Net needed sunshine and clear skies.

"Let's take a good look at this thing now," Ruth said in her practical manner.

"Okay." Net cleared the table and they set out the applications.

Ruth read aloud. "This is a non-profit organization formed for the betterment of the environment. If you are interested in more information, fill out the application and mail it in the post paid envelope. A member of our staff will contact you."

"What do they want to know?"

A deep furrow appeared between Ruth's eyes as she read: "Name, address, sex, age, marital status, leisure activities. Why would they want that information?"

Net shook her head and, stared at the piece of paper in front of her. Her eyes met Ruth's.

"Last night I dreamt of Mrs. Watkins' disabled grandson all night. I feel I have to find out more about these people for his sake."

"You're not actually going to fill this out, are you?" Her friend's voice rose in disbelief.

"Maybe some of it, but I'm curious as to what they'll say on the phone. I'll have to pray to St. Anthony about this."

Ruth grabbed her hand. "Why don't you talk it over with your son? After all, he is a lawyer."

"Huh. He'll tell me to stay out of it." The furrow between Net's eyes deepened. "Ruth, you're good with computers. Why don't we look up this organization and see what it says." She looked expectantly at her friend.

"Why didn't I think of that? They must have a web site."

Net had no idea what a web site was but she felt certain that Ruth knew what to do.

"Let's walk over to the activity center right now," Ruth said excitedly. "They have a number of computers there."

Without another word, they hurried out the door and decided to drive; it would be quicker. Net had grabbed her purse and car keys as they left the townhouse. She opened the garage door with the key pad, they got into the car, and were at the main building in minutes.

"Where are you two going in such a hurry?" Margo Brewster asked as the women made their way down the hall.

"I'm going to give Net a lesson on how to use the computer," quick thinking Ruth said.

"Wonderful," Margo cooed. "It keeps the brain cells active."

Net gave her a half smile. The woman was so condescending that sometimes she wanted to put the *Malocchio* on her.

They sat down at a terminal and Ruth powered up the machine.

"Why does it take so long?" Net asked impatiently.

"Like everything else, it has to warm up. There, now we have the icons." Skillfully she used the mouse to access the Internet. "Here goes." She typed in Society for the Fifth Beneficence. A message appeared saying the requested name could not be found.

"Hmm." Ruth scowled. "If they're a legitimate environmental organization, they should be on the Net." She then typed in environmental organizations. As she scrolled down the list, she found no reference to the Society.

"That's very strange. I'll try Brother Rupert." The name brought up numerous people named Rupert so and so but not the one they were searching for.

"How about Andrew Marcus?" Net suggested.

Ruth typed in the name and got results.

Andrew Marcus: PHD in psychology, professor of genealogy ... A long list of credentials followed.

"Dio mio, I had no idea," Net exclaimed. "What's a man like that doing involved with that Society?"

"We don't know that he is involved," Ruth said, "only that he's teaching genealogy classes. Maybe he had nothing to do with selling our names. I think we should give him the benefit of the doubt until we know more."

"Does that mean you're going to fill out the form?" Net asked.

"I don't think so and neither should you. Please," she grabbed Net's arm, "don't do anything foolish."

"I won't." Net gave her a sheepish grin. "Not to worry."

* * *

The following day was the scheduled genealogy class. Net was still bristling over the call from Professor Marcus. She decided to confront him face to face after the class.

She waited around in the library, pretending to look at the books. She pulled out one after another then settled in a chair and began thumbing through a travel book. She kept an eye on the closed door, waiting for the class to end.

When the door finally opened she watched the folks file out, some talking, others appearing bored. What a dull class, she thought. When Cassandra Dolton exited the room, she held the book up to cover her face. She could hear her talking with Professor Marcus. What if they walked out together? Damn!

Then she heard him say, "You go on, Cassandra, I have to see Miss Brewster for a moment."

She jumped up, placed the book on the table, and followed him. "Professor Marcus, may I have word with you?"

He turned and gave her a gracious smile. "Mrs. Petrone, what a pleasure."

"I've been thinking over what you said. Sorry I was rude."

"Come, dear lady, let's sit in this alcove where we can have some privacy." He led her to two comfortable chairs facing each other.

"I must apologize for being so tactless. I know I brought back painful memories."

She sighed and folded her hands in her lap to stop their trembling. "You certainly did." She raised her eyes to his and, for a moment, thought she saw a look of understanding. "Just ... how would you go about attempting to find my daughter when the police failed?"

He hesitated for a moment and rubbed his chin. "There are certain people who specialize in this sort of search."

"But we *did* hire private investigators and they found no trace."

"How do I put this without sounding indelicate?" Again he rubbed his chin. "I'm sure they went through the proper channels."

"Of course."

He paused for a moment. "I'm referring to those with non-official contacts."

Net frowned. "What do you mean by that?"

"Your daughter had a history of taking drugs, am I right?"

Net lowered her eyes and nodded.

"There is a network of former drug addicts who help find these people. It's a dangerous business, but they have contacts the police know nothing about." The expression on his face appeared serious and sincere.

"If it's dangerous, why do they do it? For money?"

"No. Because of their history, they try to save others. Their motives are altruistic you might say. I know I'm throwing some heavy stuff at you. Another thing you might consider is that some people with a past they wish to forget, take on an entirely new identity, closing the door on their former lives. Your daughter may have done just that. Give it some thought. Here is my private number." He handed her a card with nothing but a phone number printed on it. "Call me if you want my help."

He rose, gave her a slight bow, and left.

Net sat for a long time, staring at nothing, her mind in a whirl.

Chapter 12

Rupert sat behind the massive mahogany desk, a furrow between his piercing eyes, a pile of papers in front of him.

"What's bothering you?" Sandra Dolton asked, caressing his hand.

"I haven't been able to settle that Watkins will. The sons are claiming their mother was coerced into signing. Supposedly she wrote another will and hid it somewhere in the house. So far, it hasn't been found." The furrow deepened as he wiped his hands over his face.

"I don't trust that woman who bought the townhouse," Sandra said sitting down in an overstuffed chair. "She started the genealogy class but dropped out after the first session. I didn't like the way she looked at me."

"It may be just your imagination." Then he thought for a moment. A smile crossed his face. "I have the perfect person to keep an eye on her."

"And who is that, may I ask?"

"Our new recruit, the one who calls herself Sister Varena." He remembered the plain mousy looking woman begging him to admit her into his inner circle. She was obviously enamoured of him.

"That one. She thinks she's in love with you," Sandra said, sarcasm dripping from her voice.

"My dear, the two strongest emotions are love and hate. She may be useful to us if I play my cards right."

Her eyes narrowed. "Just make sure you remember who your most loyal follower is. And besides, I know all your secrets."

The expression on her face left no doubts in his mind. He rose from behind the desk and gripped both her hands in his. "I'm well aware of that, my love. Don't worry, when it's time to disappear, we will do it smoothly and covertly. I am in the process of putting the wheels in motion. It will be just the two of us." His steely eyes bored into hers in a hypnotic fashion until she melted into his arms.

Chapter 13

When Net returned home and saw the blinking light on the answering machine, she almost didn't want to know who it was. Two messages. She sighed, plopped into a chair and pressed the button.

"Ma, how about coming over for dinner Sunday?" She heard her son's excited voice. "We brought baby Diane home yesterday and she's growing already. Melissa's parents are coming, too. Call me."

So that's what they named the baby. With everything that had been going on, she hadn't even asked. It wasn't an Italian name, but then, Melissa wasn't Italian. She gave her head a shake. Of course she would go, get all this nonsense off her mind. But Vince would know something was bothering her. Being a lawyer, he was very perceptive. She sighed, could always fall back on her knee surgery.

The next message was from Sam. "Hi, Doll, just wanted to ask about the new baby and find out how you're doin'. Give me a call."

Net leaned her head against the chair back. Sam was the last person she wanted to talk to right now. He would ask endless questions that she wasn't prepared to answer. She would call him later—much later.

She bit the bullet and called Melissa, heard the baby's lusty cry in the background, and confirmed the date and time for Sunday. Then, on second thought, she got directions to their new home.

Oh boy, this will be a housewarming as well as a welcome to the new baby. Better go shopping. That will certainly occupy my mind. Ruth was volunteering at the animal shelter so Net took herself off to the Orland Park Mall. Better take my cane, she thought. The nurse had told her at her eight week checkup to continue using the cane for a while.

As she drove to the mall, Professor Marcus's words replayed in her mind. Should she talk it over with Vince? Not a good idea. Maybe Sam? That wasn't wise, either. She would discuss it with levelheaded Ruth the first chance she got.

I don't feel like shopping, she thought, and gave a little laugh. What woman did not want to shop? It was in the female genes. She found a parking slot near Macy's entrance. That seemed to indicate that she would find what she wanted in that store instead of traipsing the entire mall. What was she looking for? Net had no idea. I'll just look around until something shouts at me.

After an hour of browsing, she had bought a few things for the baby and a card in which she would enclose a generous check. As she walked through house wares, a modern print of a still life caught her eye. Just the thing for a new house. She glanced at the price and determined that it was affordable, Net handed over her credit card and the saleswoman graciously wrapped the print and fixed a handle for easy carrying.

Net thanked her and, feeling the strain on her knee, began to hobble toward the exit. Suddenly the hairs on the back of her neck bristled. She felt a presence behind her. But when she turned around, she saw a few women browsing through the clothing racks, but no one seemed familiar nor threatening. She thought about slipping the hatpin from her purse, and then almost laughed out loud. What possible protection could that thing give her? But this was the second time this had happened. Was she going bonkers or was someone following her?

Trembling, she hurried to the car as quickly as she was able, and deposited her packages. She glanced around numerous times, got in, and drove home as fast as the speed limit allowed. She kept watching the rearview mirror, but no cars appeared suspect. Net didn't like it at all. Something was going on and she had to find out what it was.

* * *

Ruth's car had just pulled into her garage. Good, Net thought, she's home. She pulled into the driveway directly behind her, feeling a compelling need to talk to her friend.

Ruth turned and gave her a questioning look.

"I have to talk to you," Net called from the open window. "Do you have a minute?"

"Sure, come on." Ruth waved her in.

Net turned off the ignition, got out, and made sure the car was locked, although that precaution wasn't necessary in this guarded complex. Exhaustion slowed her step as she followed Ruth into the house.

"What's the matter with you? You're pale and look like you're about to pass out." She grabbed Net's arm and led her to a chair.

Net closed her eyes and leaned her head back taking slow deep breaths.

With a practiced eye, Ruth slipped a footstool under her friend's feet. "Your leg is starting to swell. What have you been doing?"

"Got any brandy?" Net whispered.

Ruth frowned at her. "Brandy? Will you please tell me what's up?"

"Okay. Let me rest a minute."

"I'll make some herbal tea."

Net wasn't fond of tea but she knew Ruth drank it all day long.

By the time Ruth returned carrying a tray with two mugs of tea, sugar, and cream, Net had composed herself. "You didn't have to bring it in here. I can walk to the kitchen."

"Stay right where you are," her friend commanded as she placed the tray on the coffee table. "I don't have any cookies so you'll have to do without." Ruth sat on a chair facing her. "You want sugar and cream?"

"Just a little sugar." After Net took a sip and decided it wasn't too bad, she met Ruth's discerning eye.

"Are you ready to tell me what's got you so upset?"

"I think someone's watching me."

"Watching you, whatever for?"

"I have no idea." Net took a deep breath and another swallow of tea. "I was at the mall and, as I was leaving, I felt someone behind me. You know, how the hairs on the back of your neck stand up? It happened last week, too, at the activity center. I *know* someone was watching me, but when I turned around both times, no one was there." She took another sip of tea.

Ruth frowned. "You have an overactive imagination, my friend. That doesn't prove anything. There's something else, isn't there?"

Net put down the mug and fiddled with the *corno* around her neck. "I spoke with Professor Marcus after the genealogy class this morning."

"I didn't see you there," Ruth said.

"I was in the library, waited 'till everyone left, then went up to him." With some emotion, she proceeded to tell Ruth about the discussion. "What do you think I should do?"

"Drop the whole thing!" Ruth almost shouted. "Don't even think of getting involved with something like that. Besides sounding illegal, it may be dangerous." Her voice softened as she took Net's hand. "I know how much you want to find your daughter. I'm sure I'd feel the same way if I were in your place, but I don't think this is the way to go about it."

Net rubbed her eyes then her cheeks. "I suppose you're right. Now I'd better go home and lie down. I'm kind of tired."

"What were you doing at the mall without me?" Ruth asked.

Net explained about the visit on Sunday. "How about coming with me?" She knew her friend had no family in the area and was pretty much a loner. She spent her spare time volunteering in soup kitchens and animal shelters. The two women had become close since Net moved in.

Ruth hesitated. "I don't know."

"Come on. Italian families like big groups. The more the merrier. If it makes you feel better, I'll ask my daughter-in-law."

"Okay, but I'll have to bring a gift."

"No you don't." Net knew how she would feel if she turned up empty handed. "Bring a couple of bottles of wine, one white and one red."

"All right. Let me know what your daughter-in-law says."

Net thanked Ruth for listening then drove into her own garage. She scanned the entire area before alighting from the car. As the garage door descended, she realized she had neglected to tell Ruth that she intended to fill out the application for the Society for the Fifth Beneficence. When exactly had she made that decision? Something compelled her to do it. What would Ruth have to say about that?

Vince beamed as Melissa walked into the room. She greeted the women and then retreated to the great room so as not to disturb the baby.

"What's this great room?" Net asked, her brow furrowing.

"Most of the modern houses don't have living rooms anymore," Melissa explained. "There's a kitchen and dining area opening onto this large space."

Furniture was strategically placed to afford a small enclave where people could sit and converse. More space provided a view of the wooded area behind the house through long wide windows.

Net shook her head in wonder. She would never feel at home in these cavernous rooms.

As if reading her mind, Vince said, "Ma, it takes some getting used to after the small rooms in the old houses, but we like the spaciousness." He smiled at Melissa and slipped his arm around her waist.

"We have a few things in the car," Ruth said.

"I'll help you." Vince led the way as Net settled herself in an armchair and gazed out the window.

Vince and Melissa fussed over the impressionistic still life and decided the foyer would be the best place for it. Vince lightly tapped a nail in the wall and hung the picture.

"It looks great," Melissa exclaimed. "Thanks so much, Net."

Net still felt uncomfortable with her daughter-in-law calling her by her first name. She always used 'Mom' when addressing Joe's mother, but she finally accepted it as the modern way, along with so many other changes.

Jim and Marge Pauling, Melissa's parents, arrived shortly. They parked beside Ruth's car in the roomy driveway. Again Dominic ran out to greet them.

Net had met them a number of times, but they had nothing in common. The Paulings were a nice enough couple but were involved in their country club and played endless games of golf. Besides, they were fifteen years her junior.

Vince introduced them to Ruth then gave them a tour of the house. Jim piled a number of packages in the foyer. Net's eyebrows raised. One gift wasn't enough for these two. As Marge began discussing her golf game with Melissa, Net felt out of place and— old.

She and Ruth retreated to the garden and sat on a bench watching Dominic play on his swing set.

"Look at how high I can go," he called out.

After a short time Marge came out. "Oh, here you are. I must apologize for monopolizing my daughter but I was so excited by my golf score in the tournament yesterday, I just had to tell her all about it. Do either of you play golf?" She sat next to Net, her expensive perfume wafting through the air.

"I used to play," Ruth said. "Long ago. I've lost interest in the game lately. Guess I'm too old."

"Nonsense, one is never too old for golf. What about you, Net?"

"I never learned. Joe and I were more involved with community affairs back in Melrose Park. We never joined a country club." She gave the woman a condescending smile.

When Vince came outside, Net asked, "Did you send an announcement to your Aunt Molly?"

He wrinkled his brow. "I'm sure Melissa did. She was in charge of that stuff."

"Did she respond?" Net persisted.

Vince shrugged. "Have no idea. Ask Melissa."

Net pursed her lips. That sister of mine. I'll give her a call this week. She should at least send a gift. She's probably out cavorting with one of her gentleman friends.

At that moment Melissa called everyone in to lunch. She served a sumptuous meal of roast pork, baked potatoes, fresh green beans and salad.

After dinner, Vince and his father-in-law went outside to play ball with Dominic. While Melissa nursed the baby, the women sat in the great room making small talk. Marge looked out the window and bit the side of her lip.

"Is something wrong, Mom?" Melissa asked. "You seem preoccupied."

"I was just thinking about a woman in our bridge club. She died of a heart attack last week—just like that." She snapped her fingers and looked bewildered. "She was fine one minute and gone the next." She took a tissue from her pocket and wiped her eyes.

"Did she have a history of heart trouble?" Melissa asked.

"No, but she did have asthma. Used one of those inhalers."

"That's strange," Net said. "Did they do an autopsy?"

"I really don't know. Never thought to ask. Her body was cremated."

"Wasn't the family curious about what caused her death?" Net asked.

"I have no idea," Marge said. "The memorial service was for family only. The members of the bridge club were totally excluded." A tear sneaked down her cheek. "We had known her for such a long time." She sighed and sat back. "It didn't seem right."

Melissa put the baby on her shoulder, patted her back until a loud burp made them all laugh.

"That's a shame, Mom," Melissa continued. "I know how close you are to all those women."

"Yes, we're a good group. But lately Nora was becoming distant and withdrawn. She even talked about dropping out."

"Why?" her daughter asked, putting the baby to the other breast.

"She was vague about her future plans. Said something about a society for the betterment of the environment. It was soon after that her personality started changing."

Net perked up. "What was the name of the society?"

Marge shrugged. "She didn't tell us. All she said was that its tenets were secret and to be shared by the members only. Why do you ask?"

Net and Ruth exchanged glances, then Net decided to tell them about Mrs. Watkins. "The woman who owned the townhouse I bought died suddenly of a heart attack. She, too, joined a society dedicated to saving the environment. She changed her will and left everything to the society and died shortly after that."

"Oh my God!" Marge said. "I wonder if Nora did the same thing?"

"What's all this talk about secret societies," Vince asked walking into the room.

"Huh," Net said, "that one not only has an eagle eye but he's got sonar like a bat. Picks up everything."

"Vince," Melissa said, "one of Mom's bridge friends joined a secret society and so did the woman who owned your mother's townhouse. They both died suddenly."

Reluctantly Net told them about her visit from George Watkins and his search for the missing will.

Vince shook his finger at his mother. "You stay out of it. It sounds highly illegal—crooks bilking old ladies out of their life savings. When we moved you into that townhouse, Ma, there was nothing there but that buffet in the dining room. You said you searched it and didn't find anything so—end of story." He gave her a stern look like a parent reprimanding a child.

"So now my son is scolding me." Net folded her arms across her chest and turned her head away. "But someone should put a stop to these people."

"I'm sorry, Ma. I just don't want you getting involved with crooks. We see it every day at the office, older people taken in by con men and scams. They usually have smarmy lawyers and everything appears to be legal until something happens and the whole operation is exposed."

Net gave her son an indignant stare. "Young man I do not consider myself old and I'm not signing anything without your approval. Does that make you happy?"

"Italian women can be so obstinate," Vince grumbled. Then he turned to Melissa and smiled. "That's why I married an English girl." He kissed his wife, picked up the sleeping baby from her arms, and placed her gently in the bassinet.

* * *

Later, as Net and Ruth drove home, Ruth said, "I really enjoyed the day with your family. They're so friendly and warm. And Melissa's parents are nice, too."

"See? I told you they'd welcome you." She hesitated a moment and then voiced what was on both of their minds. "What do you think of that woman in Marge's bridge club and the secret society? Could it be the same one?" Her voice dropped at the last sentence.

"It does seem odd," Ruth agreed. "And she died suddenly, just like Mrs. Watkins."

"Hmm." Net ruminated. "Something sounds wrong. I thought that in cases of sudden death like that an autopsy was required."

Ruth shrugged. "Well, some religions forbid so called 'desecration' of the body. So, if a doctor signs the death certificate, it's okay. They can always call it heart failure."

"Hmm," Net muttered again. "But lots of things can cause heart failure. I was reading in one of my mysteries that some substances leave no trace so the real cause of death is never determined."

"You read too many of those mysteries."

"But," Net continued, "I would love to know if that woman changed her will and left everything to the society."

"Don't get involved in something that may be dangerous. I swear you should write mysteries yourself with that vivid imagination."

Net crossed her arms and nodded. "Maybe I will."

Chapter 15

Net sat staring at the form in front of her. Should she get involved? She had always dreamed of playing an amateur sleuth, but now that the opportunity presented itself, she was wary. This was definitely no game. What if she got in trouble? Worse yet—danger. These people played for keeps. I should just mind my own business, she thought. But now that she had recovered from her surgery and was back into a routine, life seemed dull.

Again she looked at the form, but before she could make a single stroke of the pen, the doorbell rang.

"It's probably Ruth," she muttered getting up from the chair. "Coming," she called. When she looked through the peep-hole it wasn't Ruth but her niece, Lena, or *Lane* as she called herself.

Net opened the door to the young girl wearing jeans so tight that Net thought the seams would split at any moment. She tried not to frown at the skimpy top revealing her navel. Then she looked at the blond curls, the blue-gray eyes, and the dimpled smile. She welcomed her niece with a hug and a smack on the cheek. "Where have you been, naughty one? Why haven't you called your old aunt?"

Lane returned the hug and walked into the living room. "Sorry, Aunt, but I've been trying to sort out my life." She glanced around the room, walked to the bay windows and looked at the pond outside.

"This is a pretty nice place," she said as Net showed her around.

"Come on, we'll sit in the kitchen and you can tell me what's on your mind."

Lane followed her into the kitchen and straddled one of the chairs, leaning her chin on the backrest.

"Is that any way for a lady to sit?" Net scolded. "Young people today have no proper manners."

"Oh Aunt Net, who cares about manners. I don't know what to do with my life." She put her forehead down against the back of the chair and gave a deep sigh.

"Don't be so melodramatic. You're just like your mother," Net said, rolling her eyes. "Here, have some milk and a slice of this chocolate cake I made, and let it all out. I'm listening."

Lane turned around in the chair, took a generous swallow of milk, and a bite of the rich layer cake. "This is good." She sighed and looked into Net's eyes. "You know I want desperately to be an artist, even studied commercial art in school, but I'm getting nowhere." She gazed out the window and seemed to be in another world.

"You know how authors claim to have writer's block? Well I have artist's block. I want to come up with a unique idea, but nothing works. I'm stagnating." She took another bite of cake and chewed slowly.

"You have a job, don't you?" her aunt asked.

"Yeah, if you call it that. I work in an art supply store for peanuts. Oh sure, they hang some of my stuff in the window, but nothing is selling." She seemed ready to cry.

"There's something else, isn't there?" Net asked leaning forward.

"I broke up with my boyfriend." She sniffed and brushed away a tear.

"How come?"

"I found out he had another girl on the side. What a jerk!"

"Then you're better off without him. A pretty girl like you shouldn't have any trouble finding a nice boy."

"Maybe I don't want a *nice* boy. I should be like my mother and just sleep around."

Net put her knuckles on the table and stood up. "Lena Andreoli, don't you dare talk like that. You'll never be like your mother."

Lane's nostrils flared. "Aunt Nettie, or should I call you Antoinette, don't call me Lena."

Net winced.

"We made a deal, remember? You call me Lane and I'll call you Aunt Net."

Net sat down, a frown creasing her brow. "All right, *Lane* Anderson." She emphasized the first name.

They sat for a moment, neither one saying a word. Then Lane glanced at the form on the edge of the table. "Hey, what's this? The Society for the Fifth Beneficence? What the hell is that?"

Net grabbed it out of her hand. "Nothing. It was left in the mailbox. I was just going to throw it in the recycling."

"Well I hope so. It sounds spooky."

"By the way," Net said, eager to change the subject, "the former owner left some things in the garage. Her son didn't want them. I thought you might be able to use them, in a still life or something."

The girl heaved a sigh. "Let's take a look. It's probably junk."

Net led her into the garage where a small box sat next to the garbage can. "In that box. Pick it up and take it into the kitchen."

Without much enthusiasm Lane picked up the box and carried it to the kitchen table. The first thing that caught her eye was the goblet. "This looks kinda cool." She held it up to the light and turned it around. Then she looked inside. "There's some kind of markings inside. Did you see them?"

Net shook her head. "To tell you the truth I wasn't much interested."

"And there are markings on the bottom, too. It could be like, a signature of whoever made it. You know, this might be valuable."

"I doubt it." Net shook her head. "Mr. Watkins would have known if his mother had something of value."

"Anyway," Lane replied, "it'll look cool in a still life." She pulled out the other items. "I like this jug with the broken handle and this music box."

"I thought you might. Take them and see what you can come up with. You're a bright girl."

"Thanks for the vote of confidence." She kissed Net on the cheek, picked up the box, and walked to the front door. "I'll let you know if I paint a masterpiece."

"You do that." Net watched her deposit the box in the trunk of an old car, its sides rusting and the tires almost bare. She shook her head and waved as she watched her niece drive away.

* * *

Net returned to the kitchen and put the dishes in the sink. Her eye caught the form for the Society. She read it over, again, then put it down. She would give it more thought.

That night she dreamed of Mrs. Watson and her disabled grandson again. Then suddenly Marge and her bridge group appeared talking about Nora, the woman who died so suddenly.

Net woke feeling distressed and not at all rested. Again she examined the form. If she did send it in, she would definitely leave out her income level and other personal information. Those were none of anyone's business. But the ringing of the phone pulled her away from such thoughts.

"Hello."

"Hi, Doll, what time do you want me to pick you up?"

"Oh, hello Sam." She had totally forgotten that he was taking her to the Lincoln Park Conservatory. He was the last person she wanted to see right now. He would sense that something was troubling her and she was afraid she would tell him the entire story.

"Net? Are you all right?" His concerned tone snapped her out of her dilemma.

"Oh sure. I just didn't sleep too well last night. A day out is just what I need. How about eleven?"

"Sounds good. See you then."

No sooner had Net put down the phone than the doorbell rang. "Oh God, now what?" she muttered shuffling to answer it. Squinting through the peep-hole she saw Ruth standing there dressed in a rust-colored outfit. She opened the door and tried to smile, but her facial muscles refused to cooperate.

"Good morning," Ruth said, giving her friend a critical look. "What's wrong?"

"Why is it that my emotions are always printed all over my face like the pages of a book?" She sighed. "Didn't sleep too well; promised to spend the day with Sam and he'll quiz me just like you."

"Where are you going?"

"Lincoln Park Conservatory."

"That's a beautiful place," Ruth answered, a hint of envy in her voice. "And on a gorgeous day like this, you can forget all your worries and just enjoy the flowers."

"Good advice. And where are you going all spiffy looking?" Net asked.

"Today is the last genealogy class. Professor Marcus hinted that he might present something special this time. Probably just cookies and tea."

"Have you really gotten much out of that class?"

Ruth bit her lip and thought for a moment. "Not as much as I would like, but I have learned how to research my past and, who knows, I may keep it up."

"Enjoy yourself," Net said half-heartedly.

"I'd tell you to do the same thing, but, by the look on your face, that will take some doing." She smiled and gave her friend a hug. "Why don't we connect later and talk about our day?"

"Okay. See you tonight."

Chapter 16

When Sam arrived, Net greeted him with as much enthusiasm as she could muster. She had put on a colorful print tunic over black slacks. A careful makeup job and a pair of pearl earrings completed the picture.

Sam, of course, fussed over her and told her she was beautiful. She blushed at his sincere flattery.

"Sam, you old devil, you always knew how to make the girls feel special."

"That's not true," he said. "Only one is special." He smiled, still able to exert a boyish charm, even though his curly hair was mostly gray and wrinkles lined his cheeks and forehead. She knew the smile was genuine.

When they reached the Conservatory, Net remarked at how well maintained the building was even though it was over one hundred years old. They roamed through the palm house, the fernery, and the tropical house. There was no special showing of seasonal plants but each room had its own charm. Some new plants caught Net's eye and she spent time examining their names and countries of origin. Finally they both decided it was past time for lunch.

"Let's try that new café down the street," Sam said. "Somebody told me the food was good."

Net agreed and, after they had settled in a booth and placed their order, Net grew serious.

"What's on your mind?" Sam asked. "I can always tell when something's bothering you."

"I know," she admitted with a sigh. After a long pause, she told him what Professor Marcus had said about his contacts and his willingness to attempt to locate Donna.

Sam slowly shook his head. "Net, it's time to face the truth. You've been living on hopes and dreams for too long. You've got to accept the fact that Donna's not coming back. You don't really know if she's even alive."

"No! She is alive. I feel it. And, someday, I'll see her again." She took a tissue from her purse and wiped a tear from her eye.

"Okay, sorry I said anything." Sam's voice mirrored his frustration and just a little annoyance.

Net realized how foolish she sounded to someone else, but she was convinced. "Let's not talk about it, Sam. Sorry I brought it up."

Their lunch order arrived and they ate their sandwiches and drank their coffee over small talk. She told him about Lane's visit and her irritation with her sister, Molly, and Sam brought her up to date on the changes that were happening in the old neighborhood.

* * *

That evening Ruth came over for a chat. "So, how was your day with Sam?"

Net shrugged. "Okay. He's always hinting at a relationship. I just don't feel that way about him, never did. I hate to hurt his feelings, but I've told him time and time again that I feel like we're brother and sister."

"You can't blame him for trying. Obviously he's in love with you and always has been."

"I know." Net fussed around the kitchen and pursed her lips. "I told him what Professor Marcus said about searching for Donna."

"You did?" Ruth gave her friend a dubious look. "Do you think that was wise?"

"No, he thought I was foolish for holding on to hopes and dreams." She hesitated a moment then lowered her head. "Maybe he's right."

"Speaking of Professor Marcus, he approached me after the meeting and a nicely catered lunch, I must say."

"Oh?" Net's curiosity was piqued.

"He asked about you. Seemed concerned for some reason. He wants you to call him." She handed Net a business card.

"Did he say why?"

"No, just that it was important."

Net examined the card: Professor Andrew Marcus, Genealogy Expert, and a phone number. Nothing more.

"Well, I'm not interested in searching my past. I have enough to think about the present."

"Are you going to call him?"

"I'll consider it." She hesitated for a moment then decided not to tell Ruth that she had made up her mind to fill out the form for the Society for the Fifth Beneficence. She felt compelled to investigate these people. Somehow she felt a distinct possibility that Mrs. Watkins's and Nora's deaths were somehow connected with that group.

* * *

After Ruth left and, with no further procrastination, Net filled out the form, omitting the personal information, walked to the mailbox, and dropped it in. There. Done. No turning back. She would wait and see what happened next. The Society might just ignore her as a potential member because she failed to provide all the requested information. But at least she had tried.

Chapter 17

A week passed and Net had no reply from the Society. She decided to put it out of her mind and concentrate on other things, but bizarre dreams invaded her sleep. No matter how much she tried to ignore them, she felt that she was supposed to do something. But what? She had no idea.

The phone rang just as Net was sitting down to breakfast. *Why don't people leave me alone? Now my toast will get cold.*

"Hello," she said, none too cordially.

"Aunt Net." Her niece almost shouted through the line. "I have good news."

Net smiled at the girl's exuberance. "So, did you meet a rich handsome prince?"

"No," Lane answered, "but I think I broke through that artist's block I was telling you about. I put that goblet and the music box in a still life arrangement and it looks great! I polished the goblet and it shines like some kind of precious metal."

Net grunted. "It's your artistic imagination, my dear. But if it gives you inspiration, that's all that matters."

"Oh yes," the girl continued. "I've already blocked in the painting and I feel deep inside that it will be the best thing I've ever done."

"Good to hear. You must show it to me when it's finished."

"I will. And thanks, Aunt Net, for helping me."

Net shook her head as she went back to her cold coffee and toast. She took a swallow, dumped it down the sink, and poured a fresh cup. At that moment the doorbell rang. "Am I to have no peace this morning?" she grumbled as she went to answer it.

A smiling Ruth greeted her. "Hope I'm not disturbing you," she said.

"Come and have some breakfast." Net walked into the kitchen, poured another cup of coffee and put two fresh slices of bread in the toaster.

"I'm really excited about that beginning yoga class we signed up for, aren't you?"

"Yeah, I think I need to get involved in something new. Toast?"

"I've already eaten but I think I can handle one slice. What kind of jam is that?"

"Gooseberry," Net answered. "Try it. It has a very distinctive flavor."

They chatted about everyday affairs, and then Net blurted out, "I filled in that form for the Society."

"You what?"

"I mailed it last week." She held up her hands to stop her friend's protest. "Hear me out before you say anything. I've been having dreams about Mrs. Watkins and that Nora. It's as if they're trying to tell me something. It's eerie, Ruth." She blew out a heavy breath, grabbed her *corno*, and looked around as if expecting to see someone or something.

"I can't believe you did that without consulting me." Ruth seemed concerned and also a little annoyed. "Have they responded?"

"Nope. I guess, since I didn't give them all my personal information, they decided I'm not an appropriate candidate for their fancy society."

Ruth grabbed Net's hand. "Please don't follow up on it. I have bad feelings about those people."

Net waved her off. "I won't. I've decided to put it out of my mind and concentrate on other things, this beginning yoga class for one. I hope my knee is healed enough to go through those moves."

"It's chair yoga," Ruth said. "Most of the moves are with the upper body."

Then she told Ruth about Lane's call, the baby's progress, and every other mundane topic she could think of.

I should never have told her about mailing that membership form, she thought when Ruth left. Now she'll quiz me every chance she gets.

* * *

That same afternoon Net received a call from a man with a slight accent she couldn't identify.

"Antoinette Petrone, please," he said rolling the "r".

Net winced at the sound of her name. "This is she."

"Ah, Ms. Petrone, my name is Armond and I'm calling from the Society for the Fifth Beneficence."

Oh, oh, she thought, now I have to make a decision.

"We received your application for membership, but it is incomplete."

I guess I'm supposed to respond to that. "Yes, that's all the information I'm willing to give out about myself. Do you have a problem with that?" Might as well be aggressive, she thought, though the palms of her hands were beginning to perspire.

"Not at all, dear lady. Many of our members are hesitant to share personal information. That is not a problem. I am calling to invite you to our next meeting, Friday evening at 7 PM." He gave her an address in Orland Park.

Net hesitated. Now that she actually had the opportunity to do some investigating, she was getting cold feet.

"I'll have to check my calendar. I'm not sure if I have that evening free."

"Not a problem. If you can make it, we would be delighted to meet with you. Goodbye ... for now."

She heard the disconnect, then the dial tone. Why did he hesitate before he said 'for now'? Was I imagining something? she chided herself. I'll think about it.

She walked into the bedroom, spotted the statue of St. Anthony sitting on the dresser, a serene expression on his face. She considered asking his advice then laughed out loud. He didn't help me find my Donna, so what makes me think he'll help me make this decision. She frowned and left the room.

* * *

Wind and rain on Friday gave Net the perfect excuse to avoid going to that meeting, but the previous night she had such a vivid dream that Mrs. Watkins seemed to be right there, in her bedroom. The woman was trying to communicate with Net, to tell her something, but a barrier existed that she couldn't break through.

"That's it," Net told herself with determination. "I am going to that meeting—just one—and see what this is all about. What harm can it do?"

When Ruth asked her to go to the movies with her, Net said she was going to Vince's house. She hated to lie, but she couldn't tell her friend the truth. She might tell her after the fact or, not at all.

She felt nervous as she dressed in a conservative business suit. She must maintain control at all times. She would refuse to give them any more information about herself.

When Net reached her destination her hands were trembling. She grabbed the *corno* hanging around her neck and muttered a prayer for strength and protection. The building had obviously been a small movie theater that had been renovated. Something told her to turn the car around and leave right then but the vision of Mrs. Watkins and her disabled grandson urged her on.

Hesitantly she walked to the entrance just as two other women arrived. They were dressed in expensive looking attire and Net noticed the heavy gold rings on the gnarled fingers of one of them. She nodded and followed them inside.

The smell of incense filled the foyer. It wasn't overpowering, just a pleasant woodsy scent. A man in a long white robe greeted them.

"Welcome, Sister," he said with a slight nod of his head. He handed her a program and ushered her into the auditorium. She was surprised to see that the seats had been removed and replaced by rectangular tables with eight chairs around each. Lush beige carpeting covered the floor. Net sat at one of the rear tables where she felt she would be able to leave unobserved if she chose.

She began to relax as she examined the people seated around her. The front tables had filled up first. She was surprised at the number there, mostly women, but also a few men. She judged their ages to be mostly fifty and older. There were no young people that she could discern. That fact alone set off an alarm bell in her head.

If this organization was dedicated to saving the environment, why were no young people involved? They were the next generation, the ones who should be the most concerned, but they were not the ones with the money. Something wasn't right.

As she scanned the room, her heartbeat accelerated as she spotted a familiar couple standing next to the stage: Professor Andrew Marcus and Sandra Dolton.

So, the genealogy class was just a ruse to get the names of people who might have more than a few dollars to donate to this organization. Net became more suspicious by the moment. She grabbed her *corno* and slowly extended her second and fifth fingers on the table to ward off the *Malocchio*, the Evil Eye.

Chapter 18

Ruth was disappointed in the movie. She found the story weak, the acting only fair, and too many special effects. That's the way movies are today, she thought—all car chases, explosions, and noise. After an hour she got up and left. She walked through the huge multiplex and glanced at the other titles. She could easily go into any one of them, but nothing grabbed her interest.

As she made her way to the car she suddenly remembered that this was the last day to sign up for the outing at Navy Pier. She and Net had discussed it, but made no decision. I wonder if Net's home yet? Ruth drove toward the complex without stopping at the store, which she had previously intended to do, and pulled into her garage.

The sky was darkening as she hurried into the house. She grabbed the phone and punched in Net's number. It rang until the answering machine picked up.

"Oh darn," she said aloud. I can call her at Vince's house. I'm sure she won't mind. She searched her phone book until she found the number and punched it in.

Hello," a male voice answered.

"Hello, Vince? This is Ruth Borden, your mother's friend."

"Oh, hi, how are you," he answered, a surprised tone to his voice.

"Just fine. And how is that baby doing?"

"Growing like a weed. All she does is eat and sleep, and she's prettier every day."

Ruth heard the note of pride in his voice and smiled. "Is your mom still there?"

"No, Ma's not here. What made you think she was?"

"I thought she told me she was going to your house." Ruth wondered momentarily if she had misunderstood.

"I haven't seen her since last week. Is anything wrong?" Vince asked.

"No, no. I must have gotten the date wrong. Just wanted to ask her something. She's probably shopping."

"Yeah, she does like to shop. Stop by the next time Ma comes over and see the baby," he said.

"I will, thanks. Goodbye."

Ruth replaced the phone on the charger and picked up a book. I'll call again in a little while, she told herself. She probably did go to the mall. But she couldn't concentrate on reading. Something bothered her. Net wouldn't go to that meeting alone, would she? Did she lie to me?

Ruth paced, tried Net's phone again, then decided to sign them up for the Navy Pier outing. She walked out the door and toward the main building. She was disturbed by the thought that her friend might be getting into something dangerous.

* * *

Net was startled to see the lights dim. Then she watched everyone settling back in their chairs as a tinkling bell sounded. It was a pleasant sound and, along with the incense that had gotten stronger, seemed to promote relaxation and a feeling of well being. She took a deep breath, sat back, and waited.

Brother Rupert walked to center stage wearing, not the expensive suit he had worn at the lecture, but a long white robe similar to the one worn by the greeter at the door. A pale blue spotlight bathed him in an ethereal light. The audience burst into animated applause. He stood still, smiled for a few moments, then held up his hands to silence the crowd.

"Welcome Brothers and Sisters and any newcomers and visitors to our family." More applause. Net felt as though he was looking right at her. Silly, she thought, I'm in the back and it's dark in here. But she did feel somewhat uncomfortable.

"As you know," he continued, "our God ordained mission is to work toward saving the environment. In a few moments I will show you a video of what is happening to our planet. I must warn you that some of these scenes are disturbing, but we must be aware of this desecration and do all in our power to stop it." He stood still, arms hanging down, head bowed.

Everyone in the audience stood up and, again, applauded. So as not to be singled out, Net also stood and half-heartedly clapped.

Brother Rupert held up his hands. "Before the film we shall have our customary cup of tea."

The lights came up half way and people materialized carrying trays with cups and saucers. They placed a cup of steaming liquid before each person and muttered some sort of incantation. Net watched those around her as they appeared to enjoy the drink. She lifted the cup to her nose and inhaled a bitter aroma.

I'd better give this a try, she thought, or I'll never know what's going on here. She took a sip. It was hot, but not enough to burn her mouth. The taste was foreign to her, bitter but not repulsive. She took a swallow then put the cup down. Her tongue and the inside of her mouth tingled unpleasantly.

That's enough of that, she thought pushing the cup away. She watched the others in the audience apparently relishing the drink and nodding for more as people came around with pots.

"You're not drinking your tea," a soft voice said. Net turned to see a woman in a white robe smiling at her. Her eyes stared at Net but didn't seem to be looking at her. The smile was forced.

"I don't care for tea, thank you. I prefer coffee."

"Oh, but this is a very special blend. You'll get used to it after a while." The pasted on smile persisted.

"I don't care for it, thank you," Net said forcefully.

Without another word, the woman moved on and continued refilling cups.

How strange. She reminded Net of a robot. A feeling of foreboding gripped her. She wished she had never come and promised herself she wouldn't return. She turned and searched for the nearest exit, but someone wearing a robe manned each door. Somehow she felt that they wouldn't allow her to leave.

Again the lights dimmed, a screen lowered, and the video began. As with the last one she had seen, it depicted severe weather changes, oil spills, drought, starvation—all the warnings everyone had been seeing for a number of years.

But the reaction of the audience startled her. Women began moaning and crying. Even the men reached out their arms and cried out, "Stop this desecration!" Someone yelled, "Oh, no ..."

What's happening to these people? Net wondered. As soon as the video finished, Brother Rupert appeared again, this time bathed in a red light. He began to chant, softly at first, then louder. The audience chimed in until the cacophony was too much to bear. Net put her hands over her ears and again searched for a means of escape. She saw one door unguarded. Unobtrusively she slipped from her chair and made her way into the foyer. She breathed a sigh of relief as she hurried to the entrance.

"Are you leaving so soon?"

She jumped at the sound of a voice behind her. The man who had greeted her stood there with the same pasted on smile and vacant look in his eyes as the woman who had poured the tea.

"Ah, I'm not feeling well," she said inching toward the door.

"Do come back again, please."

"Yes, yes, I will." She bounded out the door, took a deep breath of the fresh evening air and ran to her car.

* * *

Net was still unnerved as she walked into her house. She poured a small glass of brandy and took a sip. Immediately she began to cough. Why are people always drinking alcohol to calm their nerves? She took a couple of deep breaths, another sip, and felt herself beginning to relax.

The sound of the doorbell jarred her. Who in the world? Did someone follow her home? Now I'm becoming paranoid, she thought, as she peered out the peephole. She was surprised to see Ruth standing there.

"Hi," she said opening the door and trying to keep her voice as calm as possible.

"Net, where have you been? I've worried myself into a frenzy." Ruth barged in and shut the door behind her.

"I thought you were going to the movies," Net said.

"I didn't like the film. Then I remembered we hadn't signed up for the trip to Navy Pier. I tried to call you at Vince's house, but he said he hadn't seen you since last week." Her voice rose with each sentence.

"I forgot all about the outing."

"You went to that meeting, didn't you?" By now Ruth's tone was accusing.

"Sit down and stop getting all flustered," Net said, grabbing her friend's arm and sitting her down on the sofa. Then she sat across from her. "Yes, I went to the meeting. I had to find out what it was all about. And who do you think were there? Our friends Dr. Marcus and Sandra Dolton. They didn't see me, though." She pursed her lips and gave her head a slight nod.

Ruth began to calm down. "I knew it, stubborn Italian that you are. You would go there by yourself."

"Well I'm back in one piece and you worried for nothing." Trying to change the subject she asked, "Did you sign us up for the outing?" She raised her eyebrows in a question.

"Yes, I did." Ruth took a deep breath and sat back.

"I hope you didn't say anything to Vince about the meeting."

"No, I didn't. Now tell me all about it."

For the next twenty minutes Net related the entire experience. "The way those people reacted was so strange. The video was essentially the same one we saw at that church, remember?"

"Yes, I do. So what was different to cause such an emotional outburst?"

"I've been going over and over it in my mind and I think it must have been some kind of mass hypnosis. His voice is mesmerizing. Unless—it was something in the tea."

"It didn't affect you though."

"No, but I guess I wasn't primed for it or something. I just don't know. Then again, I only took a sip. Hmm."

"Net," Ruth grabbed her friend's hand, "I don't trust those people with that puzzling name that makes absolutely no sense. They seem to be designed to put their members in danger.

You're not going back, are you?"

She simply looked at her friend and didn't answer.

Chapter 19

Net was still shaken the following day. Since she hadn't stayed until the end of the 'performance', she had no idea when the next meeting would be held, so she tried to put the entire experience out of her mind.

She regularly attended her water aerobics classes, enjoyed the outing at Navy Pier with Ruth, and even accompanied her to some of her volunteer programs. As the days passed, the Society for the Fifth Beneficence was relegated to the recesses of her mind.

A few days later she received an animated phone call from Lane. "Aunt Net, you'll never believe what happened."

"Since I'm not a mind reader, you'd better tell me."

"I did the most fantastic painting using that goblet and the old music box you gave me. And," she hesitated for effect, "it was accepted in a very prestigious show. What do you think about that?"

"*Brava!* I think it's great. And when is this show?"

"In two weeks. I'll send you an announcement and one to Vince and Melissa. I'll even send one to my mother." Her voice dropped at the mention of Net's sister.

"She'd better come or I'll put the *Malocchio* on her," Net said playfully. She knew how much this meant to her niece. Against her better judgment, she decided to call her sister, Molly, and urge her to put in an appearance.

After she finished talking to Lane, she sat back and analyzed the situation. The girl had been so excited, it brought tears to Net's eyes. "Oh that sister of mine," Net said aloud through gritted teeth. She looked up the number and placed the call. After seven rings she got the answering machine, left a message and hung up. Would Molly call back? Maybe yes, maybe no.

A few days later Net received the announcement for the opening of the show. Her eyebrows rose when she saw the address on North Michigan Avenue, a very high rent district. Still no call from Molly. She was probably on a trip with her latest fling. Molly went through men like a kid through candy.

Net called Sam and he said he would be delighted to escort her and Ruth to this prestigious event. On the day of the reception, Net dressed in a brand new black and white dress. She fussed over the neckline that ended in a V exposing a little too much cleavage as far as she was concerned.

When Ruth came over, Net asked her opinion.

"These days women show their navels with jewels embedded in them and wear pants so tight that you're waiting for the seams to split. Don't worry about the neckline. It's a lovely dress and it complements your figure."

Net preened. Ruth wore a plain black sheath with a thick silver chain around the high neckline. Her earrings were small silver balls suspended from thin chains. Her makeup accentuated her high cheekbones and generous mouth. She certainly was a striking woman.

It wasn't long before Sam arrived dressed in a navy blue suit with a red and white tie. Net thought he looked ready for the Fourth of July as she gave him a welcome hug.

"Am I a lucky man to be escorting two such beautiful women tonight." He bowed theatrically and led them to the car.

Before she left, Net scanned the area. Ever since she attended that meeting, she had been feeling antsy, as though someone or something was watching her. She shook those thoughts from her head and decided to enjoy the evening.

* * *

As they drove down Michigan Avenue, Net marveled at the beautiful plantings in the median strip dividing the street. The annuals put on a magnificent display. Tall grasses swayed in the breeze.

Sam stopped the car in front of the gallery and let the women out. "I'll park and meet you inside."

"He is a gentleman," Ruth said watching him turn the corner.

"Oh yes, he's one of the kindest and most thoughtful men I've ever known," Net agreed.

"And he's crazy about you."

Net heaved a sigh. "I know." She turned to Ruth. "But I don't feel that way about him."

"He knows that, too," Ruth said. "Life is so strange. Why can't we love the people who love us?" A look of pain crossed her face.

Net wondered what was in her past. Ruth was a very private person. They had never shared their deepest secrets. They only spoke about their pasts in generalities. Maybe it was better that way.

"My, look at the crowd of people," she said eager to change the subject. "Let's go in and look for Lane." Net felt excitement building inside her, happy with her niece's accomplishments.

The gallery was tastefully hung with paintings, well spaced so that observers could examine each one individually.

"It looks like there are two or three rooms," Net said. She picked up a brochure lying on an entry table. "This should give us some idea of where to look."

"Maybe we'd better wait for Sam," Ruth suggested. "He won't know where we are."

"You're right. Let's go outside and study this brochure."

They walked out into the balmy evening and stood off to one side. As Net examined the brochure her eyes widened. "Look at these prices!"

Each painting listed the name of the artist, the medium, and the price. They started with the better known artists whose work was displayed in the first room. The prices were all in the thousands. The second room held sculpture works. Some of the bronzes were in the tens of thousands. The third room displayed the work of the newer artists. Lane's painting was listed with a price of $750. Not too bad, Net thought. But, of course, the gallery would take a nice chunk of anything that sold. This was a prestigious place.

"Here comes Sam," Ruth said, waving him over.

"Are you ladies ready?" he asked taking each one by the arm.

"Indeed we are. Let's start in the third room. That's where Lane will be," Net suggested.

They gradually made their way through the crowds of people gathering around certain works. The second room wasn't as crowded. Net stopped suddenly and stared at a man and woman who appeared to be discussing a piece of sculpture with the artist.

"What's the matter?" Sam asked.

"Oh, nothing. I thought I recognized someone, but I was mistaken." She glanced at Ruth who stared at the two then gave her a slight nod.

The third room was more crowded than the others. Here were more affordable works.

"There's Lane, over there," Net said excitedly.

She recognized the items in the still life: the goblet and the music box along with an old book, lying on its side. The colors were muted to give the impression of age and serenity. The balance was pleasing to the eye. She felt proud of her niece as tears welled up in her eyes.

Lane wore a long purple dress that she had probably bought at a thrift store. It fit her perfectly and complemented her light brown wavy hair. Her earrings almost reached her shoulders. Around her neck hung a pendant that Net recognized as something Molly had given her. It was a little gaudy but she knew the girl was hoping her mother would show up.

When the couple she had been talking with moved on, Net hurried up to Lane and hugged her tight.

"Oh Aunt Net, I can't believe this is really happening. A banker is interested in my painting and he might actually buy it!" She had some difficulty restraining her excitement.

"That's wonderful. I knew you could do it. You remember my friend Ruth and, of course, Sam."

They greeted her and congratulated her on her budding new career.

"The gallery owner said I can hang another painting at their next show." Lane literally bubbled over. "Vince and Melissa were here earlier. They couldn't stay because the baby sitter had to leave by seven. But it was nice of them to come."

Net noticed the girl searching the crowd. She knew she was looking for her mother. Damn you, Molly, you'd better show up, she thought.

"We're going to look around, dear, but we'll be back."

"Go ahead. There's lots of neat stuff."

Net pulled Ruth aside. "Did you recognize that man talking to that sculptor?"

"He looked like Brother Rupert, right?"

"Uh huh, and I wonder who the woman was. Collecting money for the environment, phooey. They're con artists."

"Maybe they're art lovers," Ruth said.

"Art lovers go to museums not galleries that sell work at exorbitant prices. Look at this list. None of these sculptures sells for less than $5000." Net gritted her teeth.

"Here comes Sam," Ruth said. "Get that look off your face."

"There's food over there," he said munching on a cracker with some type of spread and holding a plastic champagne glass. "Come on, girls, before it's all gone."

Unobtrusively Net tried to watch Brother Rupert, or whatever his real name was, and his lady friend. She saw them walk into an office followed by a man wearing an Armani suit and shoes polished to such a sheen that some of the surrounding colors reflected off of them.

"Hey Net," Sam nudged her shoulder, "Isn't that Molly?"

Net turned to see her sister making a grand entrance followed by a short rotund man with a balding head. His clothes reflected wealth. Molly wore a bright red suit with a hat to match. She made sure no one would miss her.

"Where is my daughter?" she asked, a little too loud.

One of the staff came up to her. "Whom are you looking for, Madame?"

"Why Lane Anderson, of course," she demanded.

The woman consulted the brochure and indicated the third room.

"Why isn't she in the front?" Molly demanded.

"I don't know, Madame. I didn't hang the show."

At that moment Net intervened. "Hello, sister dear." She gave Molly a half-hearted hug with air kisses and received the same in return.

Molly turned to the man behind her. "This is Gordon Masters. My *older* sister, Net Petrone." She accentuated the word older.

Ruth and Sam came up and were properly introduced. Then Net led the way into the third room. They saw Lane surrounded by a group of young people apparently asking her questions.

"Where in God's name did she get that dress?" Molly asked.

"Please." Net took her sister's arm. "This is her night. Don't spoil it."

"All right. You know, she should have been *your* daughter instead of mine." With those words Molly held out her arms and walked to Lane with a theatrical embrace.

Net had all she could do to contain herself.

"Easy," Sam said. "She's a phony, but, at least she showed up."

* * *

As she lay in bed that night, Net reviewed the evening in her mind. She was happy for Lane and at least her sister had behaved well. But she couldn't get the picture of Brother Rupert and his companion out of her mind. They were obviously contemplating buying that expensive sculpture. Why? It wasn't anything of a religious nature or environmentally appropriate. Were they independently wealthy or were they using the funds from the Society? Should she ignore the entire situation or try to investigate the Society in depth?

What would her favorite amateur sleuth do?

Chapter 20

For the next few weeks life returned to normal. Net and Ruth went on another outing to downtown Chicago and had a great time. The group went to Millenium Park and laughed at the Crown Fountain with its screen of changing faces, a real tourist attraction. They marveled at the Cloud Gate, also referred to as "The Bean', because of its shape. They all gazed upwards at their reflections in the gleaming stainless steel structure. Net sat on one of the benches while some of the others explored the gardens. She was feeling some aching in her knee and thought better of doing too much walking.

Later they lunched at an outdoor café and watched droves of people walking by: children running and shouting, parents scolding, and older folks strolling along. It was a perfect mid-summer day: a cloudless sky, temperatures in the upper seventies, and a refreshing breeze blowing in from the lake.

When Net walked into her townhouse, she breathed a satisfied sigh and plopped down on the sofa. Even though they had taken a bus, they had done a lot of walking and the confusion alone was tiresome.

"Eh," she said aloud, "I'm not as young as I used to be. I wish I had more energy."

She sat still for a few moments. It was then that she noticed the light blinking on the answering machine. She reached over and depressed the button.

"Mrs. Petrone, this is Andrew Marcus calling. I must speak to you on an urgent matter. Please call me."

At first she was frightened then became angry. "What does that man want? To tell me how he can find my daughter? To open old wounds and let them bleed again?" she shouted aloud.

She got up and paced. The enjoyable day was now replaced by the picture of him with that Dolton woman at the meeting. She had tried to forget it, but now it resurfaced. In her mind she saw the audience reacting in such a bizarre way to the video. Then she visualized old Mrs. Watkins in the audience.

"*Madonna mia,* what shall I do? Should I go back and see if I can find out what's going on there? Or am I just an old fool living vicariously through the books I read?"

She vacillated between calling Marcus and ignoring him. He said it was important. She knew she wouldn't rest until she found out what he wanted.

Where did she put his card? She searched through her top dresser drawer where she tossed things that she might someday need. After twenty minutes of throwing out useless papers and cards she found it.

She looked at the phone and hesitated before picking it up and punching in the numbers. It rang five times and she was ready to disconnect when Marcus answered.

"Mrs. Petrone, I'm so glad you called." His voice was smooth as glass.

Net frowned. That damned caller ID. She would have to find out how to block it. "What do you want?" Her tone was far from friendly.

"To warn you. I saw you at the meeting of the Society for the Fifth Beneficence."

For a moment fear gripped her. "What about it? I was curious, that's all."

"Stay away from there. It may seem harmless but there are ruthless people controlling it," he said with emphasis in his voice.

She felt a chill run up her spine. "Then what are *you* doing there?"

He hesitated for a moment. "I have my reasons. Please, don't go there again. It may put you in danger." With those words he disconnected the call.

Now Net was more curious than ever.

Should she tell Ruth about the call? She paced the floor, muttering in Italian when another call broke her indecision. Someone from the administrator's office told her that one of the residents had died in her sleep. It was to be expected. This was a community of old people, she told herself. Someone died on a regular basis.

* * *

"Net, are you going to the memorial service?" Ruth asked the following day.

Net shrugged. "I didn't even know the woman. Are you going?"

"Uh huh, I usually do because we all live in the same area."

"All right. I'll go with you." She put aside the phone call from Marcus for the time being. She'd think about it later.

The chapel was almost full. Apparently the woman was well liked. Light streamed in through the vibrant stained glass windows and soft music played in the background. Net found it comforting.

Afterwards they greeted the family members and had light refreshments. An eight by ten portrait of the deceased sat on one end of the table. Net glanced at it then turned back and studied it. Underneath was her name: Alice Martin, followed by her dates of birth and death. She had seen that woman somewhere. Of course, she told herself, probably at one of the social functions. No, it was somewhere else, but she couldn't remember where.

My memory, she mused. Oh well, it will come to me sooner or later. It doesn't really matter anyway.

As she and Ruth milled around munching cookies and sipping punch, Net heard bits of conversation: "a very pious woman"— "went to services every Sunday"—"loved Brother Rupert."

That was it. Net had seen her at the meeting of the Society. She was sure of it. As Ruth conversed with one of the other residents, Net went up to the family to offer her condolences.

"This was not unexpected," the daughter said. "Mother's heart was very bad. In fact the doctors were surprised she lived this long, poor dear. We'll miss her." She wiped a tear from her eye.

"I'm sure you will." She thought of Joe. Her heart still ached for him.

"I know this is a bad time, but may I ask you a question?"

"What is it?"

"Did your mother belong to the Society for the Fifth Beneficence?"

The woman frowned. "Not that I know of. She never mentioned it. Why do you ask?"

"I thought I saw her at a meeting. Never mind. I must have been mistaken." Net moved away as someone else approached the daughter.

"Are you ready to go?" Ruth asked coming up to Net.

"Yes, let's get out of here."

They walked out into the warm evening. A soft breeze blew through the trees. "It's perfect, isn't it?" Ruth purred, breathing deeply. "Net? Are you listening to me?"

"Huh? Oh yes, beautiful."

"Okay, what's on your mind." Ruth pulled her down on a bench and stared at her.

Net fiddled with her purse then looked into Ruth's eyes. "I'm sure I saw that woman at the meeting of the Society."

Ruth frowned. "Maybe, but so what?"

"I wonder if she signed over all her worldly goods to those people." Net pursed her lips and returned her friend's stare.

"You won't let it go, will you."

"I can't. There's something else I haven't told you." She recounted the phone call from Andrew Marcus.

Ruth's look turned to one of concern. "Please listen to his warning and stay away from that place."

"I don't intend to go back," she answered, but wasn't entirely sure.

"I wish we had never gone to that lecture," Ruth said.

"So do I, but we did. And, I bought Mrs. Watkins' townhouse. I can still see the distraught expression on her son's face. I'll never forget it."

Chapter 21

"Damn!" Rupert paced from one end of the room to the other. "That woman was primed and ready to sign. What was her name?"

"Mrs. Martin," Sandra answered and shrugged. "These people are on the edge, that's why we choose them, remember? It's not the first time one of them died of *natural* causes before they signed the new will. It happens." She walked behind him, pushed him down into a chair, and began to massage his shoulders. "Relax. There will be others."

"Umm. That feels good. But right now I need some comfort." He pulled her onto his lap and kissed her neck, her lips. Then he took her hand and led her into the bedroom.

She made all the right moves, knew exactly how to control him. As she pretended to respond the way he liked, she thought of her plans. She had been careful to keep duplicates of everything. They were in a safety deposit box that he knew nothing about. If he so much as indicated that he intended to leave her behind, she would nail him to the wall.

Chapter 22

When she woke the following morning, Net promised herself that she would tend to her own life and enjoy her grandchildren. She empathized with Mr. Watkins but could do nothing to help him. She had scoured the house and found no trace of the missing will. After all, she wasn't an amateur sleuth like the characters in the novels she read so avidly. She was an older woman trying to adjust to the radical changes in her life.

The ringing phone startled her. I hope this is good news, she thought, grasping the *corno* around her neck.

"Hi, Ma," came Vince's welcoming voice. "I hope you remember about the ranch." His tone was half joking.

"Of course I remember," she said irately. "Do you think I'm getting senile or something?" God, I did forget, she thought. With all this business of the Society and the will, she had put the vacation with her family right out of her mind.

"I'll pick you up Friday morning about ten o'clock," he said. "Check-in is at three and it's a five hour drive. See you then."

After she put the phone down Net allowed herself a few moments of nostalgia. Trail's End Ranch in Wisconsin held so many pleasant memories for her. As a child, her father took the entire family there for a month in the heat of summer. At that time it was rather small, with just a few cabins.

Years later she and Joe went there with Vince and Donna. The place had grown considerably and was extremely popular as a family retreat. The cabins still held their rustic charm, and meals were served in a communal dining room. Net remembered the ringing of the dinner bell and everyone making their way to the main house.

To her the highlight of the trip was always the breakfast rides in the early mornings. All those able to ride a horse met at the barn and were assigned their steeds; the very young and the older folks rode in a horse-drawn wagon. They made their way into the woods on a twenty minute ride to an area set with picnic tables. Two robust women cooked at a huge steam table: bacon, sausage, eggs, hot cakes, and French toast, with juice, milk, and coffee to drink. She remembered smelling the coffee well before they arrived.

Her last trip there was a romantic weekend with Joe a year before he died. It was a particularly colorful fall. They canoed down the river, went on a hayride, ate buffalo burgers, and made love on a rug before the fireplace. It was magic. Tears streamed down her cheeks as she remembered that time. She could almost smell her husband's scent.

"Oh Joe, why did you leave me?" she pleaded out loud. She had asked that question so often but could still not reconcile herself to the loss.

"Net, Net, are you there?" Ruth's voice came through the open kitchen window.

"Come in, Ruth. I'm here." She grabbed a tissue and blew her nose.

"You seemed to be a million miles away. I called and you didn't respond."

"Eh, I was remembering—too much." She grabbed a tissue and blew her nose.

"You weren't still thinking about that Society, were you?" Ruth asked.

"No. I was remembering my last trip to Trail's End Ranch with Joe." She let out a deep sigh and gave her head a slight shake.

"That's right. You're going there with Vince and the family. When is that?"

"Leaving Friday. He just called to remind me. To tell you the truth, with all this stuff going on, I almost forgot."

"It will be good for you to get away for a while—forget about that will and the Society, and Professor Marcus." Ruth gave her head a vigorous nod.

"That's just what I want to do, go away and leave all this nonsense behind." She reached over and took a plate of coconut macaroons off the counter. "Try one of these."

"Mmm, they're good. Where did you get them?" Ruth picked up a second one.

"It's a funny thing. They were sent from a local bakery with a note saying 'sweets to the sweet'."

"Who sent them?"

"There was no signature but I'm sure it was Sam. It's so like him to say something trite like that." Net munched on another one. "I'll call and thank him."

"You know you should be nicer to him," Ruth said. "He's such a dear and he's always there for you."

"I know, but every time I'm with him I think of the past, and Joe is always between us."

* * *

Friday came too soon. Net busied herself with packing and instructions for Ruth to take in her mail and water her plants. She forgot all about calling Sam, and thought about it only when she was in the car with her family. Oh well, she thought. I'll call him when I get back, and put it out of her mind along with everything else. She brought along two new mysteries by her favorite author and prepared for an enjoyable week.

Net sat in the front with Vince while Melissa took the back seat to tend to their children. Aside from a few, "are we there yets?" from Dominic, the ride was pleasant. The weather remained warm and sunny.

* * *

The cabins were much larger than Net remembered. There were three bedrooms, two baths and air conditioning. "They've certainly upgraded this place," she said as she walked around the spacious rooms.

"It's great," Melissa said.

"Can I ride a horse?" Dominic asked. He ran around the room slapping his backside and pretending to be astride a horse.

"Okay, Buddy," Vince said. "As soon as we get settled, it's off to the barn. Anybody want to come?" He looked from Melissa to Net.

"I have to feed the baby," his wife said.

104

Net shook her head. "I don't think I'm up to riding at this stage of my life. I'm going to walk around the grounds and see what's changed."

* * *

Later Net took her cane, walked down the hill to the barn, and watched as Dominic sat astride a horse. One of the wranglers led him around the paddock. The expression of accomplishment on his face tugged at her heart. She remembered Vince doing the same thing.

"Grandma, look at me," he called.

"I see you and you look great." She raised her camera and took a picture. With a pang she remembered how she and Joe had ridden on the trail. He was a natural on horseback while she never felt quite stable.

Soon the boy ran up to her hardly able to contain his excitement. "I'm gonna ride a horse tomorrow on the breakfast ride." He pushed out his chest and lifted his head with pride. "Dad, can I have one of those western hats?"

Vince laughed. "Sure. I suppose they sell them at the Country Store. We'll get one after supper." He glanced at his watch. "The dinner bell is going to ring soon so let's go back to the cabin and get washed up."

"Okay. Boy am I hungry," the boy said, running on ahead.

Net and Vince exchanged a smile. "He loves it," Vince said.

"Just like you when you were his age," Net said swallowing the lump in her throat. She was glad she had her cane. The hill seemed steeper than it had been the last time she was here. Of course, she was much younger then.

A few minutes later the clanging of the dinner bell propelled everyone into the main building where a long dining room faced the barn and pastures. They were assigned a table which they would occupy for their entire stay.

The supper of pork chops, mashed potatoes, corn and apple pie was tasty and filling. Dominic rubbed his belly and let out a sigh of contentment. "I'm full."

"You should be," his mother said. "Two helpings of mashed potatoes and an extra piece of pie." Melissa smiled at her son and put the baby on her shoulder.

"Let me take her," Net said, "so you can finish eating."

Melissa gratefully handed the infant to Net. She looked down into the large blue eyes and the dimpled cheeks, so like her Donnatella. Net cuddled her and kissed the downy head as the baby cooed in return.

Oh, Donna, where are you? She wondered. Have you come back to me in this baby? She sighed. Am I being a fool still looking for you? She would probably never know.

After dinner they all went down to the Country Store which was comprised of a bar, a store with clothing and souvenirs, and a game room.

Net remembered drinking hot buttered rum after she and Joe had been out in the crisp fall air. The place was filled with memories. If Joe were here now, would he get involved with the Society? What would he think about the recent deaths? He was a man of principle and would want to see justice done.

Dominic's voice pulled her out of her reverie. "Mom, Gram, how do you like my hat?" The boy came up to them sporting a western style straw hat.

"It's great," his mother said.

"I'm gonna wear it on the breakfast ride tomorrow. Dad, can we go fishing now?"

Vince nodded. "Okay, let's go get our gear. See you ladies later." He followed his son out the door and waved to the women.

"He's such a good father," Melissa said.

"He had a great role model. Joe was just like him," Net said with a heavy sigh.

"You really miss him, don't you."

"Every minute of every day."

Chapter 23

The following morning the breakfast ride was all that Net remembered. She rode in the wagon carrying baby Diane so Melissa could ride with Vince and Dominic. Watching them gave her as much joy as if she had been on horseback herself.

She breathed in the scent of the morning dew and the earth. The majestic pines had been planted in straight rows before Net was born. Now they towered a hundred feet into the air. She relished every moment realizing that this might be her last trip here.

Suddenly the buzzing of the mosquitoes caught her attention. She covered the baby's hands and face with the netting she had brought as she watched the horses' tails swishing back and forth in a fruitless effort to rid themselves of the pests.

The smell of frying bacon and fresh coffee wafted through the woods. Her salivary glands responded filling her mouth with saliva. They would soon be there. The horses knew it, too, and began to canter.

When they arrived Melissa took the baby and Vince helped his mother down from the wagon. Dominic was jumping up and down with excitement. "Look at all that food!" he shouted. "I'm starving."

"You go ahead with your father. Your Mom and I will be right behind you." Net turned to Melissa. "Why don't you make yourself a plate while I hold the baby. Then we can switch." Melissa hesitated. "Go, go," she urged.

"Okay." She handed the child to Net who sat on a bench and cooed to the little one. She was rewarded with smiles and baby sounds.

Later, after Dominic had finished his second plateful of food, he finally admitted he had enough.

"Everything does taste better in the fresh air," Melissa agreed. "This is nice. I'm glad we came."

Net smiled with satisfaction. The trip had been her idea and Melissa was less than enthusiastic. When they returned to the barn, the wrangler told them they were putting out the buffalo feed if they wanted to watch.

Melissa chose to return to the cabin. Diane was fussy and needed a change of diaper and a feeding.

Net, Vince and Dominic walked to the fenced in area where bales of hay were distributed. A huge water trough sat on one side.

A number of years ago, the ranch owners had purchased a few buffalo. They thrived in the area and had grown to a large heard. To keep the heard manageable, the owners sold some, and slaughtered a few to make burgers. Every Wednesday night was buffalo burger night.

"Listen," Vince said. "Here they come."

The thundering hooves of the huge beasts running toward them made the earth tremble. Dominic inched closer to his father. A large bull was the first to arrive. His massive head moved from side to side as he plunged it into the water trough. When he finally lifted his head, he looked directly at the people watching him. Water dripped from his beard. His eyes appeared wise as if he knew how majestic he was.

The bull glanced at the cows. They stopped as if he sent a silent signal. Then he moved on toward the hay and began to feed. Only when he finished did the rest of the heard dare to touch the hay.

"You see," Vince told his son. "That big one is the leader. He always eats first."

"What would happen if one of the other ones would try to eat, too?" Dominic asked.

"Look at the size of that head. He'd plough right into the other buffalo."

Dominic nodded and took his father's hand.

Net smiled. Vince was so patient with the boy, just like Joe.

* * *

By Wednesday, Net was beginning to tire. She looked up at the darkening sky portending the predicted thunderstorm. How would they occupy Dominic? His boundless energy was exhausting. Right now he and Vince were at the swimming pool. She curled up in a comfy chair and began reading her book while Melissa tended to the baby.

Was that someone knocking at the door? There it was again, a knock, harder this time. "I'll get it," Net said putting her book down.

She opened the door to a young boy holding a piece of paper in his hand. "Message for Mrs. Petrone," he piped.

"I'll take it. Just a minute." She hurried to her purse, took out a dollar bill, and handed it to him.

"Thanks, Ma'am." He turned and ran off, waving the bill in his hand.

"Who was that?" Melissa called from the bedroom.

Net didn't answer. Her eyes were glued to the note as she read it a second time.

"What is it?" Melissa walked up to her, the baby on her shoulder.

"It's from my neighbor, Ruth. I'm to call her as soon as possible." She looked up. "Something must have happened." Net squeezed the *corno* hanging around her neck for protection.

"My cell phone is charged," Melissa said. "Use it."

"All right." Net examined the phone in confusion.

Melissa pushed a button. "Now it's activated. Just punch in the numbers."

Net's hand shook as she slowly pressed the numbers. The phone was so small that she had to repeat the process because she pushed the wrong button.

Finally a ring tone. "Hello."

"Ruth, it's Net. What's wrong?"

"Oh God, there's been a rash of break-ins in the townhouses and one of them was yours."

"*The Malocchio*," Net muttered. Her knees turned rubbery as she reached for a chair. "What did they take?"

"I'm not sure, but you have to make out a police report. Did you have any money anywhere?"

"I think there was a couple hundred dollars in the dresser drawer."

"Well, I'm sure that's gone," Ruth said. "Is there any way you can come home?"

"Sure. I'll make arrangements and call you back."

"You're as white as a sheet," Melissa said. "What was that about a break-in?"

"Someone broke into some of the townhouses in the complex and one was mine."

"I thought that was a gated community."

"It is, partially. The gates are only down at night." Net sat back breathing hard and feeling violated. Nothing like this happened when she lived in Melrose Park. She had to get home right away, but how?

"I'm going up to the office and find out if there's a train from one of the neighboring towns."

"Vince can drive you home," Melissa offered.

"And leave you alone with the two children? No. Let me see what I can do." She was out the door as the first raindrops began to fall.

When Net returned, Vince and Dominic were back. Lightning streaked across the sky and thunder rent the air.

"Ma, you're soaked." Vince grabbed a towel and rubbed her dripping hair. "Melissa told me what happened. What did you find out?"

She let out a sigh and sank into a chair. "There's not much public transportation around here. The closest station is fifty miles away."

"I know just how to handle this." Vince picked up the cell phone and punched in some numbers. "Hi Sam, Vince Petrone."

Net shook her head.

Vince frowned at his mother and walked into the bedroom.

"You can't involve Sam," she protested, as she tried to follow him.

Melissa stopped her. "Sam will do anything for you, and this is an emergency."

Net held her head in her hands. *"Madonna mia,* what a mess."

"Okay," Vince said returning to the living room, "Sam is leaving right away. He'll stay overnight and you can be on your way first thing in the morning."

"Is Uncle Sam gonna sleep in my room? I get the top bunk." Dominic said. "Maybe he can go on the breakfast ride with us."

"No, Dom," his father said. "He's coming to take Grandma home. There's a problem with her house."

"Did it fall down?"

"No, silly," his mother said. "Now come on, let's play one of those board games we brought along."

Net felt so helpless She stared out the window at the rain falling in sheets. God bless Sam. She promised to be be nicer to him from now on and try to leave the past behind.

Chapter 24

Net stared anxiously out the cabin window as the storm showed no signs of moving on. She winced with each crack of thunder, visualizing Sam driving through the downpour.

"Stop looking out the window, Ma," Vince said. "It won't get him here any sooner. Come on and play Monopoly with us."

She sighed, hated board games, but reluctantly took a seat beside Dominic and joined in the game.

Sam didn't arrive until after nine. Vince had given him accurate directions, and they were all relieved to see his car inch its way up the muddy road to their cabin.

"Here comes Uncle Sam," Dominic shouted excitedly. He had been allowed to wait up because Sam was special to all of them.

Vince opened the door and ushered the exhausted man inside.

"Not a night for driving," Sam said good naturedly. "Had to keep the speed down."

"Oh Sam," Net said giving him a warm hug. "This is above and beyond." She gazed into his tired eyes and saw only love.

"Anything for you, Doll." He hugged her back and greeted the rest of the family.

* * *

The storm raged throughout the night. Net lay awake wondering if it was some sort of omen. What would she find when she reached her townhouse? How had anyone gotten into a gated community? Suddenly she felt vulnerable. As she pondered the situation, Net thought of the amateur sleuths in the books she read. Perhaps she would follow their example and try to learn the reason for the break in. There was always a reason.

* * *

"Sam, I can't thank you enough for driving all the way out here." The sun shone and warmed the rain-washed earth as they made their way back to Chicago.

"I told you a long time ago that I'll do anything for you." He reached over and squeezed her hand. "No strings attached."

She felt tears sting the back of her eyes. She couldn't respond for fear she would burst out crying.

The ride was long and tedious, but Sam played a number of CDs of Italian crooners. He even sang along with some of them. He had a pleasant voice and Net smiled. He did have a way of lifting her spirits.

When they reached the townhouse, Net saw Ruth run outside. She hurried over to the car. The women embraced each other. Net felt herself trembling as she clung to her friend.

"Hello, Sam," Ruth said shaking his hand. "It was good of you to bring Net home."

He shrugged. "No problem."

"Can we go inside?" Net asked, unsure of the procedure.

"Oh yes. The police are finished with their investigation and want a list of anything that's missing. The intruders entered all three houses through the rear bedroom windows. They've been boarded up until they can be replaced."

Net shivered. Nothing like this happened in her old house. Would she ever feel safe again? As they walked inside she recoiled at the sight of her belongings strewn about the room.

"They were looking for something," Sam said.

Ruth nodded. "The police think it was money. The intruders only took money from each house."

Net hurried to her bedroom and checked the second dresser drawer where she kept spare money. The envelope was empty. "Yeah, they took the bills I had in here."

"How much?" Sam asked balling his fists and frowning.

"Only a couple of hundred."

"How about jewelry?" Ruth asked.

Net opened her jewelry box but nothing was missing. "Did they take anything else from the others?"

Ruth shook her head. "Only cash. The police think it might have been drug addicts."

Sam walked from room to room. "I don't think so. If they found cash you would think they'd leave right away instead of searching through all these drawers and cabinets." He shook his head. "I got a feeling they were looking for something specific. These were experienced thieves. They knew how to get in and out without alerting anyone. Something doesn't smell right."

Net felt a chill up her spine. The will—could they be searching for that? But why break into the other townhouses? She grabbed her *corno*. Of course, as a cover. She had read enough mystery and detective stories to make that obvious. She decided to keep her suspicions to herself for now. "I'm getting an alarm system," she declared.

"Good idea." Sam put his arm protectively around her.

"Oh, the administrator wants to talk to you," Ruth said.

"All right." She examined the mess around her. It would take all day to sort it out.

"Don't worry, I'll help you," Sam said as if reading her mind. "Go talk to the big wigs then we'll tackle this job."

* * *

After calling Vince and telling him everything was under control, she and Sam began the task of cleaning up. Two hours of sorting and pitching exhausted them both. Net finally convinced Sam that she could finish the job herself. He agreed and left with a promise to call the following day.

I have to do something nice for him, she thought. But I don't know what. I'll think of something. For now she decided that she, too, needed a rest. With a book and her reading glasses, she stretched out on the sofa and was asleep within minutes.

* * *

An hour later, Net woke but didn't feel rested. She glanced around the living room, with a nagging sensation of doubt that this had been a random break in. No, the intruders were searching for something specific and it had to be the will. She was convinced that the other two houses had been a cover up.

I'll call George Watkins, she told herself as she forced her weary body off the sofa. Now where did I put his card? In the phone book, of course. She found it tucked in the page with the Ws.

What am I going to say to him? Shall I tell him about the other women who died suddenly? That I went to a meeting of the Society? Oh why didn't I mind my own business. Then she became angry and indignant. But this *is* my business now that my home has been invaded. With determination she punched in the number. He answered on the second ring.

"Mr. Watkins, this is Net Petrone calling. Do you remember me? I bought your mother's townhouse."

"Of course I remember you. It's nice of you to call. Have you found anything that might help us?" There was a note of desperation in his voice.

She took a deep breath and proceeded to tell him about the break in and the other women who died. For some reason she decided to omit her visit to the Society.

"Mrs. Petrone, do you really believe that whoever broke into your home was looking for the missing will?"

"I do."

"How can you be sure?"

"Let's just call it woman's intuition."

He hesitated for a moment. "You must be careful. You might be in danger."

"For what reason? The intruders turned my house upside down. They took the money I had in my dresser drawer but nothing else. I told you before, Mr. Watkins, the will, if there ever was one, is not in this house."

He let out a frustrated sigh. "My attorney is contesting the current one. We're attempting to prove that mother was coerced into signing it. But without the witnesses or a doctor's affidavit that she was not of sound mind, we're on shaky ground. The best we can do right now is stall them and hope the will turns up."

"I'm really sorry," Net said. "But I thought you should know about what happened. How is your nephew getting along?" Net felt compelled to ask.

There was a long pause, before he said, "While Mom was living she paid for help three days a week. That gave Myra, my sister-in-law, some time to herself.

"Luke is a sweet kid and very bright, but like I told you, he has trouble communicating. His speech is garbled. He can walk with assistance but he falls a lot." His voice became husky and he paused.

"I'm afraid the added burden is affecting the entire family, especially Myra."

Net knew there was a lot more he wanted to say but didn't. How would she cope with such a situation?

"I'm sorry for burdening you with my family problems. Thank you for your efforts, but don't trouble yourself further. I'm afraid it's a losing proposition. My brother and I have pretty much resigned ourselves to that fact. I'll help him as much as I can. Goodbye and, be careful."

Net shook her head. A real life mystery and she was helpless to solve it. Her next call was to the security company. The salesman promised to come the following day. The broken window would be replaced that afternoon.

There was something else she was supposed to do, now what was it? I hate this forgetting things. She walked from room to room in an attempt to spark a memory. She had spoken to Vince earlier and assured him that everything was all right. Sam had called her, too.

It was something else. She walked into the kitchen and remembered the macaroons. Yes, the bakery. She looked up the number and placed the call.

"Whole Grain Bakery, you order it and we deliver. How may I help you?" a pleasant musical voice asked.

"Hello, my name is Net Petrone. I received a box of coconut macaroons last week from your bakery."

"Was anything wrong with them?" the woman asked. "Did you receive them in good condition?"

"Oh, they were fine. I simply don't know who sent them. Can you look up that order and tell me whose name was on it?"

The woman laughed. "Certainly, Ma'am. What is your name again and your address?"

Net gave her the information and waited. She glanced out the window at the beautiful sunny afternoon. I should take a walk, she thought.

"Oh, Ma'am, there was no name on the order but yours. I remember specifically that the gentleman wanted to remain anonymous." She giggled. "It seems you may have a secret admirer."

Net frowned. "What did he look like?"

"Hmm, let me think. Nothing specific except that he had very light blue eyes and was rather tall. In fact, he was in again just this morning with another order."

Net became irate. She didn't like this game at all. "Don't even bother to send them because I won't accept the package."

"But it's already on the truck. I'm sorry you're upset, Ma'am."

"You tell that person the next time he comes in, that I will not accept anymore gifts unless he identifies himself."

"Oh, I certainly will. What about today's order?"

"What kind are they?" Net asked sheepishly.

"Double chocolate, our cookie of the week."

"I suppose it's okay, but don't send any more. Is that clear?"

"Perfectly. Thank you for calling."

After she ended the call, Net sat back, perplexed, trying to identify the man. The description certainly didn't fit Sam. Besides, when she had asked, he claimed he knew nothing about the cookies.

I'll ask Ruth, she mused as she picked up the phone again. But before she placed the call, Ruth was at her door.

"Net," she called as she knocked. "May I come in?"

No one was more welcome at that moment than Ruth. "Where are you going dressed to the nines?" Ruth wore a long flowered skirt and a gauzy white blouse. Her hair, as usual, was coifed to perfection.

"I'm just on my way out and thought I'd check on you before I left. Going to a luncheon fund raiser for the Animal Welfare League."

Net shook her head and laughed. "I swear, sometimes I think you're the sole support of those charities."

Ruth grinned. "You okay?"

"Just tired. By the way, I want to ask you something." Net told Ruth about her call to the bakery and the description of the man.

Ruth screwed up her face and thought. "Doesn't sound like anyone I know."

"Why in the world would some stranger be sending *me* cookies?" Net asked, more to herself than to Ruth.

"I haven't the vaguest idea. On another note, I saw the men replacing the windows on the other townhouses. They should get to yours soon. Will you be all right?"

"Of course. Enjoy yourself. I'll see you tomorrow."

Net sat for a long time pondering the dilemma. As wild as it seemed, was it possible someone from the Society trying to lure her back? But, then, why not identify himself?

"This is too much," she said aloud. "I don't want to be an amateur sleuth. I'm just going to let the whole thing go."

Chapter 25

"I think you should carry a can of pepper spray at all times," Ruth said. They sat in Net's kitchen reading the instructions for setting the new security system.

Net breathed a deep sigh. She did still have the hatpin, but realized it wasn't a reliable weapon. "Now where would I buy pepper spray?"

"Why don't you ask Vince, or, better yet, Sam. I'm sure he would get you one."

Nat shook her head. "You're bound and determined to push me and Sam together, aren't you?"

Ruth cocked her head. "He's the best friend you have, and you'd better remember that."

"Humph!" Net folded her arms across her chest and said nothing, but she knew that Ruth was right.

* * *

Net tried to put all thoughts of pepper spray and disturbances out of her mind and kept herself involved in the many activities provided for the residents of the complex. She spent time with her grandchildren as often as she could. But at the back of her mind lingered the suspicion that the break-in was more than it seemed.

She kept her alarm activated at all times and was careful to inspect the area whenever she left the house. Sometimes she felt as if she were being followed but couldn't pin point anyone specific.

"You read too many mysteries," she kept telling herself, but she couldn't shake off the feeling.

A few weeks passed without incident and she began to relax. No more cookies arrived nor any other packages she hadn't ordered. Maybe it was all over and she could forget about the unusual happenings in her life—until she picked up the morning newspaper.

The headlines were nothing new—more fighting in the Middle East—more Americans killed. "I can't read this stuff," she muttered turning the pages. She almost missed it, then looked again. Goose bumps crawled up her arms as she scanned the short article.

Skeletal Remains Found

The skeletal remains of what appears to be a teen-aged female were found by workers digging in a vacant lot destined to be converted into a wildflower garden in Melrose Park. The crime lab is examining the remains to determine cause of death and to identify the victim.

Net sat—frozen. Could this be her Donnatella? They had been through this so many times when she first went missing; had viewed so many victims of violent death. But none of them was her Donna. Was the nightmare about to resurface? She must call Vince and ask him what to do, but not now. All she could do was stare out the window, her mind in a daze. She wanted to shut out the world and forget the past and the present.

* * *

Later Net dragged herself off the sofa where she had laid down. She was surprised to see that the sun had made its way low in the sky. Had she fallen asleep? Been in a trance? Or just retreated from reality? With trembling fingers she punched in Vince's number.

After five rings a distraught sounding Melissa answered. "Hello."

"I hope I'm not calling at a bad time," Net said hearing crying in the background.

"There's never a good time these days," her daughter-in-law said. "Vince is so involved in a case that he doesn't come home until nine or ten every night. Dominic is having a temper tantrum right now and Diane is hungry." She took a deep breath. "Sorry to unload on you."

"Do you want me to come over and give you a hand?" Net suddenly put her concerns aside.

"Thanks, you're a dear, but my mom and dad are on their way. We're having pizza. You're welcome to join us if you like."

Net knew it was an afterthought and decided to decline. "I appreciate the invitation, but I have some errands to run. Just called to say hi. We'll talk later."

The last thing she wanted right now was to engage in small talk with Melissa's parents. They were lovely people but lived in a whole different world.

Ruth, she thought; she'd understand. But Ruth had gone to visit her son in Colorado, would be gone for two weeks. She had urged Net to go with her, but she had refused. She didn't want to leave her home unattended. She still had the feeling that someone was watching her. It was unnerving.

Now as the sun set over a golden evening, Net felt more alone than she had in a long time. "Oh Joe, I miss you so much." It would be a long night.

* * *

The next morning, Net paced as she drank her third cup of coffee. All night bizarre dreams had invaded her sleep with Sam coming to her rescue. Was she destined to rely on this good man for the rest of her life?

With Vince tied up in court and Ruth away, she knew she couldn't face this alone. What about Lane? Maybe she would be some help. She thought about it for a few minutes then decided the girl was not the right choice, and certainly, not Molly. She hadn't spoken to her since the art exhibit. That left Sam. She picked up the phone three times and put it down again.

Aimlessly she walked into the bedroom and glared at the statue of St. Anthony sitting benignly on the dresser. "I've been asking you for years to help me find my Donna. Is this the answer? It's not the one I've prayed for." With those words she threw herself on the bed and sobbed.

* * *

With trembling fingers, Net punched in the numbers on the phone.

"Hi, Doll," Sam's cheery voice answered.

That damned caller ID, she thought. No one has any privacy anymore. "Hello Sam." She tried to sound positive but knew she was failing miserably.

"What's wrong?" he asked. "I can tell by your voice."

"I need a favor."

"Anything. Just name it."

In halting tones, Net told him about the article in the newspaper.

"Yeah," he said, "I saw it, too. What do you want to do?"

"I don't know. I tried to call Vince, but he's tied up with a trial and comes home late every night." She hesitated a few moments. "So I called you. Thought you would know what to do."

"Hmm, I been thinking ever since I read about the remains found in Melrose Park. Do you remember the name of that detective who worked on Donna's case? He might be able to help, if he's still around."

Net grabbed her forehead. "Oh *Dio*, what was his name? I thought I would never forget it. Let me search through some old papers. I'll call you back."

"Remember," he said, "I'm right here, always."

"I know, Sam, I know."

After replacing the phone on the charger, Net walked into the bedroom and glared at the statue of St. Anthony. She pursed her lips and blurted out, "All right, St. Anthony, you've been no damn help to me so far." She clapped her hands over her mouth. Oh *Dio*, she thought, I shouldn't be swearing at a saint. Her superstitious nature took hold as she made the sign of the cross three times and begged forgiveness.

Then she began again. "Please, just this once, help me to remember the name of that detective." She sat down on the bed and closed her eyes trying to make her mind a blank. After five minutes, no name flashed across the screen of her brain.

She sighed, shook her head and went to the bottom drawer of the dresser where she kept important papers. Before she could grab hold of the knobs, the name "Clarence" popped into her head. That was it! Detective Clarence Dobbs. "Thank you, St. Anthony, thank you."

She called Sam and gave him the name.

"So you found it, huh?" he asked.

She snickered. "Actually, St. Anthony told me. I haven't been very respectful to him lately. I'll have to do better."

Sam didn't answer for a moment. "Okay, let me see what I can find out. I've still got a few connections with the Melrose Park Police. I'll call you back."

"Thanks, Sam, you're a jewel."

After she terminated the call, Net decided to take a walk. Sam wouldn't be calling back any time soon and she couldn't sit here and brood. She activated the alarm, made sure she had her key, and double locked the door. She walked out into the late afternoon and breathed in the fresh air. She sauntered over to the pond where she could watch the ducks. A graceful swan moved back and forth in a mesmerizing dance. For a time she was able to clear her mind and simply enjoy nature. But how long was it going to last?

Chapter 27

As she walked back to the townhouse, Net heard a blaring sound. What was it? A siren of some kind? As she got closer she realized it was coming from her house—the alarm! She hurried as fast as her knee would allow and when she opened the door, the sound was deafening. She clasped her hands over her ears then realized she had to key in the code. After she punched in the numbers, the sound abruptly stopped.

Her entire body trembled as she began searching for whatever had triggered the alarm. Before she knew it, a police car stopped in front of her house.

"Ma'am, are you all right?" a uniform clad officer asked, as Net opened the door. "We were alerted by the alarm company."

"I—I don't know what happened. I was walking home and heard it," she stammered.

"Step aside," he said kindly, "and we'll search the house." Another officer alighted from the car and was walking toward the back of the house examining the windows.

Net sat on a bench in the front, feeling a chill of foreboding. At that moment the security car belonging to the complex pulled up. She repeated her story and he joined the police in their search.

When the three men returned, the one in charge was holding something in his hand. "This was thrown through the kitchen window." He held up a hard baseball. "Are there young people in this community?"

Net shook her head. "No one under fifty. Maybe someone had grandchildren visiting?" She didn't believe her own words.

The officer looked at the security guard. "This is a gated community, isn't it?"

The man sputtered. "Yes it is, but the gates are open until dusk. That's when we lock up and have a guard checking identities of anyone who comes in."

"So," the policeman continued, "until then, anyone who wishes has access to this area."

"Uh, yes, that's so." The guard appeared flustered. "We don't have the funds to keep the place locked at all times."

The officer turned back to Net. "We'll canvas the area and ask if anyone had young people visiting." He hesitated as Net shifted from one foot to the other. "Is there any reason anyone would be harassing you, Ma'am?"

In halting tones she told him about the break in and the theft of money, but she refrained from mentioning the will or the Society.

He turned to the security officer and the three spoke in hushed tones for a few minutes. Then the two policemen left to begin ringing doorbells.

"Mrs. Petrone, I can't tell you how distressed we are that this has happened so soon after the break in," the security man said.

"I thought this was a safe place to live," she said trying desperately to control the tremor in her voice.

Uttering profuse apologies, he got in his car and drove away. The police returned shortly and told her that no one had visitors that day. They attributed the broken window to an act of vandalism, but Net knew better. It was a warning.

As she walked into the kitchen, she turned on all the lights in the house. The bottle of brandy sat on the counter. Without even pouring it into a glass, she took a generous swig and ended up sputtering all over herself.

She almost dropped the bottle as the ringing of the phone jarred her.

"Hello?" She forced her voice to sound as normal as possible.

"Net?" Melissa said. "Are you all right? I was out in the backyard and when I returned there was a call from the security company saying your alarm was going off."

"Oh, it was a short. Everything is fine," she lied.

"I was a little worried after that break in you had. If I couldn't contact you, I was going to call Vince."

"No, no, don't bother him. He has his work to do. The security system will be repaired later today."

After she put the phone down, Net went into the bedroom and said to the statue of St. Anthony, "I have to ask forgiveness for lying to my daughter-in-law. But I can't involve my family in all this. Please, help me find the strength." She crossed herself three times and plopped in a lounge chair staring at the darkening sky.

* * *

After the window was securely boarded up, Net spent the evening watching a TV movie, but remembered none of it when she turned it off at ten o'clock. She climbed into bed with a book and read until midnight, but didn't remember the plot.

She fell asleep from sheer exhaustion and was surprised when she opened her eyes to a bright morning. The clock said eight AM. She had slept the night through. That hadn't happened in a long time.

"I wish Ruth were home," she said aloud, as she shuffled into the kitchen to start breakfast. Glancing at the calendar, she noted that her friend should be back in three days. The women had become so close that they were more like sisters than friends. Net treasured the relationship. Her own sister was so distant that sometimes she even forgot they were related.

She whittled away the morning, rearranging dust on the furniture and vacuuming, chores she disliked intensely. But it was a way to pass the time. She willed Sam to call her with some news. Would she tell him about the baseball through the window? Better not. Sometime today a new window would be installed, so she had to stay home. The feeling of confinement made her uncomfortable. It must be terrible to be house-bound, she thought. It had never entered her mind until now.

"Fool," she muttered, "I think I'll bake a cake." She had lost five pounds and felt a treat was in order. As she was assembling the ingredients, the phone rang. She snatched it from the charger with an anxious, "Hello."

"Hi, Doll," Sam said. "I was hoping you'd be home."

"Any news?" she asked without any small talk.

"I did find Clarence Dobbs. The old coot is still around. He's retired, of course, but never got over the fact that he failed to find Donna." Sam let out a breath while Net held hers.

"He read the article and is going to look into it. Said he'll get back to me in a day or two."

Net had been hoping for more, but she should be grateful for that much. "Thanks, Sam, I can always depend on you."

"You sound kind'a depressed," he said. "Want to go someplace?"

"I can't. One of my kitchen windows has a crack in it, needs to be replaced, and the men are coming sometime today."

"How did that happen?" he asked.

"I don't know. Shoddy workmanship, I guess. Just call me as soon as you hear from Dobbs."

"You can count on it," he said.

* * *

After the window repair was completed, Net decided to go out. "I can't be a prisoner in my own house," she said aloud. "I have my hatpin for protection."

She laughed at the vision of a lone woman protecting herself from an attacker with a hatpin. She decided then and there to ask Sam to get her a can of pepper spray. She must be prepared for the unexpected. But who would want to do her harm, and why? She hadn't gone back to any meetings of the Society, but she couldn't get over the feeling that someone was watching her. In the back of her mind lay the sneaking suspicion that these people may still believe the will was someplace in the house. They may even think that she had found it. A shiver went through her.

Nonsense. She was going out to enjoy what was left of the day. Perhaps take in a movie or do some shopping at the mall. She made sure to secure the house. After examining the surrounding area, she convinced herself that no one was around. With a sigh of relief she drove out of the complex and headed for the mall.

She saw a dark blue car pull out of a side street, but thought nothing of it.

Chapter 28

Andrew Marcus let himself into the building that was the temporary home of the Society for the Fifth Beneficence. Rupert had told all his minions that he planned to build a magnificent new building powered by solar energy as a tribute to their environmental mission. Marcus knew better, knew that Rupert had a totally different agenda.

He felt certain that no one would be around at this hour of the night, nearly one AM. Quickly and quietly he searched the offices but couldn't find the information he sought. As he approached Rupert's office, he saw light coming from under the closed door. He heard raised voices from the room but only caught a few words. He flattened himself against the wall and listened.

"Don't like it ..." a woman's voice said. He recognized Sandra Dolton.

"Nothing to worry about ..." Rupert's placating tone.

"She's trying ... in love with you ... trouble ..." Sandra again.

"Soon ... won't need her ... dispose ..."

Marcus had heard enough. He let himself out the same way he came in and drove away without turning on the headlights, until he was safely on a main thoroughfare. He thought about the few words he had heard. So, Sandra Dolton and Rupert were an item. He had suspected for some time, but they were always discreet.

Who was the other woman Sandra had referred to? He had no idea. But from the little he heard, this woman was expendable. As soon as she was no longer needed, she would meet with a natural or accidental demise. That was Rupert's M.O. No possible connection to him or his organization.

Marcus's hands tightened on the steering wheel as he headed for home, frustrated that he hadn't found the proof he sought.

Chapter 29

Sam was as good as his word. The following day Net received a call from him.

"Dobbs still has some connections," he said. "The remains have been taken to the state police crime lab. He said it didn't appear that the girl died a–natural death." He paused.

Net winced at his words–remains–unnatural death–murder. She didn't want to hear any gruesome details. She had conjured enough in her head already.

"So, what's next?" she asked.

"They'll do a DNA analysis and try to identify her. He said you can have your DNA analyzed for comparison."

Net's breath came in short gasps. Did she really want to know? As long as there was no actual proof, Donna was still alive in her mind.

"Net, are you there?"

"Yeah, Sam, just a little nervous."

"Sure. I understand. Dobbs said we can have your DNA sample taken at the Melrose Park police station since the remains were found in their jurisdiction. He still knows some of the guys there. They'll fill out the paperwork and send it to the state crime lab. He said he'll meet us there."

Net's hands were shaking as they terminated their conversation and she set down the phone. She sat in a chair, frozen, staring at nothing. When Donna first went missing, she and Joe had looked at so many dead girls that she thought she would go mad. Later they did dental comparisons. Not this time. The remains were too old. Maybe the teeth were gone. Maybe ...

She burst into tears. "Oh *Dio,* give me my Donna, either dead or alive. Let me bury her next to Joe or let me hold her in my arms and tell her I forgive her for whatever she did." Net cried until no more tears came. Then, like an automaton, she walked into the kitchen to fix something to eat, but found herself staring out the window, her mind a blank.

* * *

On the appointed day, Net was awake with the dawn. The sun climbed up in a clear blue sky, the kind of day that should have made her spirits soar. But not today. All she could think of was the visit to the police station.

They're only going to swab the inside of my cheek, she told herself. No big deal. It should take a couple of minutes. But that's not what bothered her. It meant that another missing girl's remains had been found. And some eager loved ones were waiting for an identification, just as she was.

By the time Sam got there, she had worked herself into a frenzy of nerves. She jumped at the sound of the doorbell even though she saw his car pull into the driveway. "All right," she said aloud. "Get a hold of yourself." She took three deep abdominal breaths through her nose and slowly let them out through her mouth. "Better." She patted her hair in place and opened the door.

"Hi Doll." Sam grabbed her and planted a kiss on her cheek. "Hey, are you okay? You're shaking."

She clutched at him as he circled her in his arms. "Oh, Sam. I'm a wreck. What if it *is* Donna?"

He patted her on the back as she began to sob. "We been here before, you know. And it was always somebody else." He sat her down on the sofa, grabbed a tissue from the box on the end table and wiped her tears.

"I almost wish it is Donna," he said. "Then you can lay her to rest, once and for all."

She didn't answer; knew he was right. But in her heart, Donna was alive and well—somewhere. She couldn't give up that hope.

"Come on," he said. "Let's get this over with, and then I'll take you out to lunch."

131

She took three more deep breaths, nodded and got off the sofa. Sam's arm around her felt reassuring. After going through her security routine, they walked out of the house and got in the car.

During the ride to Melrose Park Sam tried to make small talk, but Net was barely responding. Then he hit her with something that made her sit up and take notice.

"Did you hear that Kiddieland is closing?"

"Closing?" She stared at him, her mouth gaping open. "Why? When?"

"I read it in the paper. I guess the owners had enough of the business and their kids aren't interested in upgrading. After all, it's about eighty years old."

"But we went there when we were kids," Net said, a catch in her voice. "Remember how the three of us sat on the tilt-a-whirl, me in the middle?" She could see the small amusement park on the corner of North Avenue and 5th; remembered her father taking her and Molly there as children. Joe and Sam usually came with them.

She and Joe had taken Vince and Donna there when they were little. It was an institution. It couldn't close. Mired in nostalgia, she hadn't noticed Sam pull into a parking spot.

"We're here," he said, gripping her hand.

He helped her out of the car, his arm circling her waist. As they walked into the new modern building that had replaced the old one, she momentarily held back. Then, with a sigh of resignation, let Sam take over.

They walked into an airy reception room with chairs lining the walls. A grizzled old man got up from one and walked toward them. His limp was familiar. Clarence Dobbs had aged considerably in twenty years but Net recognized him.

"Mrs. Petrone," he said in a voice hoarse from years of smoking. His handshake was still strong and reassuring, as it had been on their first meeting so long ago. Small, smoky blue eyes smiled along with tobacco-stained teeth.

He turned to Sam and shook his hand. "How are ya, Sam? God, where have the years gone? You and me are old but this little lady is pretty as ever."

Net felt herself blush at his words. He had a way of putting people at ease.

He took them over to three chairs and had them sit down. "Now, this is how it works. A technician will swab the inside of your cheek, Mrs. Petrone, and I'll personally see that the sample gets to the state crime lab with the proper paperwork. You know, sometimes stuff gets lost, especially on old cases." He took a breath and rubbed his hand over a face that bore the map of many years of hard living.

Net sat on the edge of her chair as she listened.

He let out a sigh and continued. "Now one thing you gotta realize. This body has been buried for a long time. Sometimes," he hesitated, "sometimes they can't get enough DNA to make an accurate match. And, there's a big backlog of cases, so this can take months. I'll do what I can to give it priority, still know some guys, but I suggest you try to put it out of your mind and get on with your life."

Net closed her eyes and nodded as Sam squeezed her hand.

"Okay," Dobbs said. "Ready?"

"Yes."

He spoke with the receptionist and they were ushered into a small laboratory. A technician wrote down the pertinent information then donned a pair of latex gloves and took out a sterile swab.

"This will only take a moment," she said. "I'm going to take some cells from the inside of your cheek." She smiled in an attempt to put Net at ease. "Open your mouth, please."

Net felt as if her lips were glued together. Her mouth was so dry she had difficulty opening it. Before she realized what the technician was doing, she heard the words, "All done." Net had felt nothing.

Sam took her arm and led her out of the room. She was drained of every ounce of energy. He sat her in a chair and spoke with Dobbs for a few moments. Suddenly, as if someone were telling her, Net realized the detective would be the perfect person to get her the pepper spray.

Sam excused himself to use the rest room. "Too much coffee," he said with a grin.

This was her chance. She grabbed Dobbs by the arm. "I must talk to you privately."

"Is something wrong?" he asked, his face a mask of concern.

"Yes, but Sam mustn't know about this. Please," she pleaded, "give me your phone number and I'll call you. It'll take some explaining."

"Sure, sure." He handed her a card that she shoved in her pocket just as Sam was returning. Dobbs continued to examine her with some concern.

"Want some lunch?" Sam asked the two of them.

Net shook her head. "I'm not hungry."

"I gotta meet somebody," Dobbs said. He turned to Net and held her hand for a moment. "Remember what I said. Try to put it out of your mind. I'll be in touch."

The men shook hands and Sam led Net to the car.

"You want to go home?" he asked.

She turned to him. "No. Take me to your house, please. I don't want to be alone."

"Sure, anything you say." He started the car and headed home.

* * *

For the remainder of the afternoon, Net and Sam watched old movies. It kept her mind occupied. He fixed a simple meal of linguine with clam sauce, complimented with a salad and a glass of white wine.

"What time do you want me to take you home?" Sam asked.

Net turned anxious eyes to him. "I don't want to go home."

"Do you want to go to Vince's house?"

She shook her head. Had no desire to explain her depressed mood to anyone, least of all her son.

"Can I stay here with you, Sam?"

His eyes opened wide. "Sure. I got plenty of room, even got a new toothbrush you can use." He gave her a wide grin.

"You're a jewel. You know me so well and you don't ask questions, just put up with my moods. What would I do without you?" She wiped a tear escaping from her eye.

"I'll always be here for you, Doll. Told you that a million times." He kissed the top of her head and walked out of the room.

Net sat, her thoughts mired in a world of doubt and grief. I have to let her go, she told herself. If the remains are Donna's I'll bury them on Joe's grave. But in her heart she kept hoping the results would be negative. She had to keep her mind occupied for the next few weeks. But what about the other problem that had taken over her life? Clarence Dobbs might be just the person to help her.

* * *

Later that night Sam settled her in the guestroom fussing like an old *Nona*. "Are you comfortable?" he asked for the third time.

She laid tucked in bed, wearing a pair of his pajamas; a glass of water on the bedside table; soft music playing on the radio. "I'm fine. Now go to bed and let's both get some sleep. It's been an exhausting day."

"Sure." He kissed her on the forehead and went to the door. "Call if you need me," he said, reluctantly, walking out and closing the door behind him.

Net lay for a long time in a state of limbo willing her mind to be still, to blot out all thoughts and to visualize a peaceful place. She finally fell into a fitful sleep, but fearful dreams made her cry out. "Joe, Joe, where are you?"

The door opened softly and Sam entered the room.

"Joe," she called out pitifully.

Sam sat on the side of the bed and took her in his arms. "Shush, it's okay. I'm here." He caressed her cheek and patted her back.

"Why did you leave me?" she muttered clutching at him.

"I'm here. I'm here. Go to sleep. Everything's all right."

She mumbled something and began breathing deeply. Sam laid her down gently and watched until he thought she was asleep.

"Oh Net," he whispered. "I love you so much. I want to be with you always. If you could only love me, just a little." A tear dripped down on her cheek. He gently kissed it away, smoothed her hair, and quietly left the room.

But Net wasn't asleep. She had heard every word he said and it broke her heart.

Chapter 30

Net tried to resume her worry-free lifestyle. But Sam's words kept playing over and over in her head. Then there were the DNA results. She knew it would take months. She had to call Detective Dobbs and share the information about the Society with him. Maybe he could look into it.

When Ruth returned from her trip, Net practically fell into her friend's arms. She told her everything that had happened. She did omit Sam's intimate declaration of love. That was for her alone to sort out.

"Oh Net, I'm so sorry I wasn't here for you." Ruth grabbed her hand and gave it a squeeze.

"I'm not a child. Should be able to handle these things myself." Net sniffed.

"I'm glad Sam was there," Ruth said.

"Me, too. He's like 'Old Faithful,' predictable and reliable." Net smiled at her friend. "Let's do something fun."

"Okay," Ruth responded. "I think there's an outing, but can't remember where. We'll go check the bulletin board."

There wasn't much going on that day so they decided on a book review by an author neither one of them had ever heard of. It was scheduled for two that afternoon. Each returned to her townhouse with promises to meet up in time for the presentation.

* * *

Net picked up the mail before she unlocked her door. She paid no attention to the bundle of catalogues and the pleas for donations. But one envelope stood out from the rest. She pulled her hand away as she studied the familiar stationary with her name written in calligraphy.

"That damned Society!" she shouted out loud. She debated whether to throw it away unopened or take a peek inside. Her curious nature won out. Cautiously she opened the envelope and read the message.

You are invited to a special meeting for the Society of the Fifth Beneficence.

To be held Sunday, July 24, at (the address was the same as the last time).

Brother Rupert has recently returned from the field.

He has a disturbing message for all those concerned about the environment.

We hope you will attend.

She tossed it aside and made a cup of herbal tea. Then she recalled the bitter brew served at the last meeting. With a shudder, she dumped it down the drain and poured a glass of orange juice instead.

I can't tell Ruth about this, she thought. She'll have a fit if she even thinks I'm contemplating going back there. The vision of Mrs. Watkins' disabled grandson kept creeping into her mind.

If there really was another will, where could she have hidden it? Net had scoured the house for loose boards in the cabinets. She had walked through every room in the townhouse searching for hiding places, but found none.

She thought of the woman in the assisted living section who said she had signed a paper for Ella Watkins, but when they had questioned her further, she said she signed everything, even the Declaration of Independence. Definitely not a credible witness.

I'll call Dobbs, she told herself, pulling his card off the refrigerator where she had attached it with a magnet. She hesitated for a moment, and then punched in the numbers.

He answered on the third ring. "Dobbs here."

"Detective, this is Net Petrone."

"Oh, dear lady, I've been worrying about you since our meeting. Do you want to tell me what's bothering you?"

"Yes, but not over the phone. Can we meet somewhere?"

She heard him let out a breath. "Can it wait until next week? I have to go out of town on family business."

Net felt deflated, but she couldn't expect people to be at her beck and call. "Sure, next week is fine. And, can you get me a can of pepper spray?"

His voice took on a note of concern. "Why?"

"Well, there was a break in and I'd feel better if I had some kind of protection."

"Do you have an alarm system?" he asked.

"Oh yes I do. Keep it activated all the time," she assured him.

"Well, you're probably over reacting, but I'll get you one. Listen, I gotta meet somebody. I'll call you as soon as I get back in town and we can talk."

"Thanks, but, please, don't tell Sam."

"Gotcha. Bye now."

Net shook her head as she replaced the phone. He probably thinks I'm a crazy old lady but I have to talk to someone with connections.

* * *

When the evening of the meeting of the Society arrived, Net was still vacillating over whether to go. Ruth had gone to a meeting of one of her many charities. She had asked Net to go with her, but she declined. Net took that as a sign that she should go to one more meeting of the Society. This will be the last one, she promised herself.

The evening was warm and muggy. Humidity hung in the air like a heavy blanket. The meteorologists predicted rain later that night. That would probably make it worse.

Net dressed conservatively. She didn't want them to think she was a wealthy widow. She wore a loose black top over lightweight gray slacks. Her ever-present *corno* hung around her neck.

As she parked her car, she had a feeling of foreboding. Am I doing the right thing or being a foolish old woman? It's really none of my affair. But something pushed her forward as if an unseen presence was guiding her. Could it be the spirit of Mrs. Watkins? She felt a chill as she gripped the gold horn around her neck.

When she entered the building she noticed the same smell of incense permeating the foyer. A warning bell went off in her head and she was ready to turn around and leave when a white robed figure greeted her.

"Welcome, Sister," he said in a soft mesmerizing voice. He handed her a program and ushered her into the auditorium.

Too late now, she told herself. The room was exactly as the last time. Tables for eight were set up around the room. Again she chose a seat near the door, in case she decided to make a quick exit.

The incense scent was stronger here, almost cloying. Before she knew what was happening, white robed figures came to the tables depositing a cup of tea before each person.

"Oh, I love this tea," a woman whispered to her companion. "Don't you?"

Net didn't hear the response but the woman sitting beside her urged her to drink.

"It's bitter," Net said after taking a sip. "Don't they provide a sweetener of some kind?"

"Oh, no," the woman answered. "That would interfere with its healing properties. You get used to it very quickly. It comes all the way from the Orient. Go on," she urged. 'Drink."

Net raised the cup to her lips and took another sip. She felt her lips and tongue begin to tingle and then get numb. No more of this for me, she thought. She played with the cup and pretended to drink, but began to wonder where she could dump it, unnoticed.

She searched for any sign of Andrew Marcus or Cassandra Dolton, but they didn't seem to be there, at least, not in plain view.

Before long a woman Net hadn't seen previously came onstage. She, too, wore a long white robe. Her brown hair hung loosely down to her shoulders and she wore no makeup. Her face was plain and devoid of any expression. She reminded Net of a character from *The Stepford Wives.*

"Dear friends," she began in a robotic sounding voice. "Our beloved Brother Rupert is here tonight with a report directly from the fields where our people are laboring ceaselessly to stop the rape of our environment. He has a special message just for you." With those words she extended her hand as brother Rupert came onstage to a standing ovation of applause and shouts of, "savior", "saint"…

He bowed his head and held his right hand over his heart until the room grew quiet. He, too, wore a long white robe with a bright red sash tied around his waist.

"Brothers and Sisters, I come to you tonight with a message of both hope and despair. This red sash around my waist represents blood, the blood of our planet." He hesitated for effect.

Without realizing what she was doing, Net kept taking small sips of tea. It didn't taste so bad after a while. The minions went around quietly refilling the tea cups, including Net's.

Rupert continued, his arms outstretched. "I have just returned from an extensive tour of the rain forests of South America. Loggers are felling trees at an alarming rate. The native people are helpless to stop them. They have made a deal with the government to strip the trees and turn the lush earth into farmland.

"What's wrong with that? You ask. The rain forests are a crucial part of our Eco-systems. Strip these bare, and the wildlife that inhabits them becomes extinct. Strip them bare, and the nutrients in the soil soon become used up by farming. Then they will move on to the next area until the entire rain forest dies. The effects will be catastrophic!"

Groans from the audience.

"We will now show you a graphic video of this destruction. Then, my friends, it's up to you to decide how you can help in this endeavor." He bowed again and left the stage to more shouts and applause.

A screen descended from the ceiling; the room darkened; and the show began. The images were the same that Net had seen many times before on television, but something was different. She felt as though she was part of the actual rain forest. She almost reached out her hand to touch a magnificent tree. Others in the room did the same thing.

Was this in 3D? No, she reasoned, one had to wear glasses to have that affect. She couldn't understand the change.

As loggers cleared swaths of forest and bulldozers dug up the earth, she heard people around her moaning and crying. Then she realized that she, too, was weeping. What was happening?

When her fingers wrapped around the teacup, she stopped herself. That was it—the tea. There must be something in this stuff to cause such a vivid reaction in the entire audience. She pulled her eyes away from the screen and studied the people around her. Some were swaying back and forth, others shouting, "Stop this!"

She struggled to keep her rational mind in control but her eyes kept wandering back to the video. As it showed more devastation, the audience became more agitated. Net shook her head to try and clear it. How much of this stuff did I drink? She asked herself. She looked around for a way of escape, but the doors were closed and each was manned by a robed figure.

Could she feign illness? No, the less attention she drew to herself, the better. Then an idea struggled though the fog of her mind. What if she could take a sample of this tea and have it analyzed? She couldn't ask for some. That would be too blatant.

Unobtrusively she opened her purse and searched for anything that might be useful. She pulled out a handkerchief and slipped one end in the teacup. When it was thoroughly soaked, she pondered what she could wrap it in. She always carried a zip lock baggie with almonds and raisins for a quick snack. As she searched her purse, a figure materialized beside her.

"It seems you've had a mishap," a soft voice said.

Net stared at the white robed figure. Where had be come from?

"Let me get you a fresh cup," he said.

"It's all right," she protested. "I'm quite finished."

"Then I'll just take this away." With those words he whisked away the cup with the handkerchief inside and melted into the crowd.

Damn, she thought. There goes the evidence along with my nice linen handkerchief.

Her eyes drifted once more to the screen. Now animals were disappearing from the rain forest because their habitat was being destroyed. Suddenly a woman screamed and cried in loud wracking sobs. Net felt tears streaming down her own face. No matter how much she tried to control her emotions, it was impossible.

She kept her eyes averted as much as possible and attempted to study the reaction of the audience. The shouts and weeping grew louder until the video ended.

Net took a deep breath and blew it out her mouth; then another. She was drained. The lights came up and most people attempted to compose themselves. But one woman bedecked with jewelry and wearing an expensive looking outfit continued to sob and leaned on the man next to her in a half faint.

Two of the robed figures helped her to her feet and led her to the front of the auditorium and down a side passage.

"Where are they taking her?" Net asked the woman beside her.

"She's ready to pledge," she answered in a monotone.

"Pledge what?"

The woman gazed at Net through glazed eyes. "Everything," she sighed. Then she closed her eyes and her head sank down on her breast.

Net searched for a sign indicating restrooms. She needed to splash water on her face to bring herself out of the effects of the tea.

At that moment figures appeared with another beverage.

"I don't care for anything else to drink, thank you," Net said.

"You must drink this," the man said literally forcing her to swallow a few ounces of something that tasted like juice.

She coughed, and indignantly demanded, "Where are the restrooms?"

He pointed to the same hallway where they took the woman. Net got up, and, holding on to a wall, made her way in the direction he had indicated. Within a few minute her mind began to clear and she realized the juice was some sort of antidote to whatever was in the tea. Of course, they couldn't have people driving under the influence of drugs.

As she made her way toward the signs with male and female figures on the doors, she heard voices coming from one of the rooms.

"Are you ready to give all to the cause?" Brother Rupert asked.

"Yes, yes. Where do I sign?"

Net's eyes opened wide as she flattened herself against the wall. So that was it. They doped these people up and had them sign away all their money, and then they suddenly died of a heart attack. How convenient.

As she backed away from the door as quietly as possible, a hand suddenly clasped over her mouth and an arm around her waist. "Hush," a voice whispered as the person dragged her into a darkened room.

Chapter 31

Net struggled as she let out a low moan.

"Quiet," the soft voice whispered in her ear, "or we're both dead."

Those words shocked her into the realization that she was in real danger. As her eyes adjusted to the dark, she was just able to make out a window at the back of the room.

"Now, if you promise not to make a sound, I'll let you go," the voice said.

It sounded somewhat familiar. Net nodded, as she felt the hands release her. She turned and recognized Andrew Marcus. He held an index finger to his lips.

Through the wall they could just hear subdued voices but were unable to make out the words. Marcus tip-toed to the window and quietly slid it open. He grabbed Net's hand and pulled her toward it.

"But ..." she said.

"Hush. You must leave—now!"

She nodded again. He sat her on the sill and helped her swing her legs over the side. As she looked down, she saw that it was only a couple of feet.

"Go," he said. "And never come back here."

She jumped down, lost her balance and sat on a thorn bush. She grimaced but made no sound. Marcus handed down her purse, closed the window and was lost in the darkened room.

My God, she thought as she painfully extricated herself from the bush. What am I dealing with? She looked around attempting to orient herself. The parking lot had to be on the other side of the building.

Carefully she crept through the low growth of shrubbery to the corner. Peeking around, she saw the lot still filled with cars. People were beginning to emerge from the entrance and it would be simple to join them unobserved.

Her mind had cleared but her nerves were frazzled by her experience. Her heart pounded so hard that she felt as though it would jump right out of her chest. But, of course, that was impossible. She took another deep breath through her nose and let it slowly out of her mouth. Better. After a few more, she was able to think.

I'll just blend in with the crowd, she thought as she inched her way through the bushes. The branches seemed to reach out, thorns grabbing at her clothing. She made the sign of the cross three times, and inched her way between the others. She didn't feel safe until she was in her car with the doors locked. Even then, she felt eyes watching her.

Have to get out of here. But there was a queue moving slowly to the one exit lane. As she waited her turn, her eyes darted back and forth watching the other cars moving slowly along. From the corner of her eye she saw a woman being escorted from a side door. Wasn't she the one who was carrying on so? The one bedecked with jewelry? Net squinted. Yes, she was certain it was the same woman. Someone half carried her to a black Cadillac and helped her into the back seat while another woman got behind the wheel.

The car joined the line directly behind Net. I wonder what will happen to her now? She thought. It's none of my business. I'm going straight home and follow Marcus's advice and stay away from this place. But her mind kept replaying the scene: heard the woman groaning, someone asking her if she was ready to sign. Would she, too, die shortly of a heart attack?

Net watched the car directly behind her. Did she dare follow it and try to find out where they were taking the woman? Perhaps get her address and warn her?

No, she told herself. It might be dangerous. Why should I risk my life for a total stranger? Because she's a fellow human being and these people have to be stopped. As she continued rationalizing with herself, she allowed the black car to overtake her as soon as she left the parking lot.

She tried to read the license plate number but couldn't keep her eyes on the road at the same time. How do they do it in the movies? She asked herself. Stay back; let someone cut in front; don't make them suspicious. She was being foolhardy but it didn't seem so difficult. She kept her distance and totally ignored the traffic behind her.

After a short ride, the Cadillac tuned into a subdivision with mini-mansions behind lush manicured lawns and colorful flower borders. Net vacillated for a moment, and then followed. She noticed a blue sedan continue down the street but made nothing of it. She slowed down as the Cadillac turned into a driveway. Net squinted at the number on the house—1461. I must remember that, she thought as she picked up speed. She drove down for a while as if she were searching for an address, caught the name of the street, St. James Place, and turned down another lane.

She kept repeating 1461 St. James Place over and over. Before she realized it, she was lost in a maze of cul-de-sacs and winding roads. She attempted to back track but couldn't find St. James Place. After twisting and turning endlessly, she finally spotted a main thoroughfare. Carefully she turned out of the subdivision and onto the street.

"That's enough sleuthing for me," she said aloud, letting out a deep breath. "I'm going straight home."

As she headed for Harlem Avenue she spotted a blue sedan behind her. She noticed a dent in the front bumper. Was it the same one she had seen earlier? Could it be following her?

She picked up speed and so did the other car. "*Madonna mia!* What do I do now?" If I speed, maybe a police car will spot me, she reasoned. Since the area was filled with forest preserves and there were no places of business along this section, that seemed like her only alternative. She pounced on the gas pedal and was jolted back as the car took off.

The speedometer climbed to sixty—sixty-five—seventy—seventy-five. Her hands became numb as she gripped the wheel. She had always stayed well within the speed limit, had never received a speeding ticket in her life. Now she wished with all her heart that a patrol car would stop her.

Little traffic barred her way as she careened down the street, her pursuer close behind. Suddenly from a side street a patrol car emerged, lights flashing, siren screaming.

"Oh, thank God!" she shouted as she pulled over to the side followed by the police.

"Officer, I'm so relieved to see you," she said, opening her window and smiling at the swaggering young policeman approaching her.

"Lady, do you know how fast you were going?" he asked, a deep frown forming between his eyes.

"Yes, yes, I do, but I was trying to get away from that blue car."

"What car?"

"The one right behind me. Surely you saw him. He was following me," Net insisted.

"The only car I saw, Lady, was yours. Now let's see your driver's license and registration."

Net looked around in confusion. What happened to the blue car? It was right behind her. It couldn't disappear into thin air. Had she imagined it? Was the effect of the tea playing tricks on her?

"Lady, license and registration," the policeman repeated in a less than friendly tone.

"All right." She fiddled in her purse and produced the requested cards.

"Stay right where you are," the officer said, as he returned to his car to look up her record.

Where does he think I'm going? Net thought. And what could have happened to the blue car? She examined the area behind her and caught a glimpse of a gravel road almost obscured by a copse of trees. So that's where he went.

"Okay, Mrs. Petrone, your record's clean but I have to give you a ticket. I clocked you at eighty in a fifty-five mile zone." He stood there, ticket book in hand and a deep frown on his face.

"Yes, I understand. But there *was* a car following me."

"Sure, sure. You look like a nice lady. Now watch your speed and go home." He handed her the ticket and returned to the patrol car.

Net waited until he pulled out then followed him at a safe distance until she reached the intersection where she turned off. She watched cautiously, but no one was behind her for the rest of her journey.

When she pulled into the garage, she sat in the car shaking, until, with deep breaths and a few prayers, she managed to compose herself. When she walked into the house, the first thing she did was to write down the address of the woman—1461 St. James Place. But what town was it? She couldn't worry about that now.

Then she grabbed the bottle of brandy and poured herself half a water glass full.

Chapter 32

When Net woke the next morning she felt as though the previous evening had been a bad dream. Then she spied the $150.00 ticket sitting on her dresser and everything came back to her. It was true. Those people were scam artists, but worse than that, she was sure they were murderers. That woman from last night was in danger, she was certain of that. But how did they do it to mimic a heart attack? As far as she knew, none of the women who had died suddenly had been autopsied. But most of them had histories of previous health problems. Of course, from reading all those murder mysteries she knew there were poisons that left no trace in the body.

What to do? How could she warn that woman? She knew where she lived but that might be too risky. What about talking it over with Ruth? She knew exactly how her friend would react. No, not Ruth. And she surely couldn't go to Vince with the whole thing. He would be furious with her. And Dobbs was out of town. Marcus? No, she still wasn't sure about him.

Perhaps she should call Mr. Watkins and tell him about it. The more she thought about it, the better she liked that idea.

* * *

Later when Ruth called and asked if Net was going to the concert by a church group that afternoon at the activity center, Net gave her a lame excuse. Whether Ruth believed her or not was irrelevant. There was no way she could face her friend without blurting out the entire experience. And that was something she did not intend to do.

Net vacillated most of the morning. Every half-hour she looked out the window searching for the blue car. Hopefully that would be the end of it, but her common sense told her otherwise.

By mid-afternoon, after taking a walk, then sitting by the pond and watching the ducks and swans glide majestically back and forth, she had made her decision. She would call George Watkins. She went inside, picked up the phone and punched in the numbers.

He answered on the second ring. "George Watkins." His voice sounded strained.

"Mr. Watkins, this is Net Petrone. Do you remember me?"

"Of course I do, Mrs. Petrone. You're not calling to tell me you found the will by any chance?"

"I'm afraid not, but I do want to talk with you. I think I may have gotten myself in trouble."

Immediately his voice took on a note of concern. "What kind of trouble, and what can I do to help you?"

"It concerns that Society. I don't want to discuss it over the phone. Can we meet somewhere?"

"Certainly. I hope you haven't done something on my account. I would never forgive myself for involving you." By now his voice rose a few decibels.

"No, no. Let's meet and I'll tell you all about it." At this point she was sorry she had called, but it was too late now.

They decided on a coffee shop in Orland Park, a neighboring suburb. "I can be there in an hour," he said. "Is that convenient for you?"

"Yes, I'll be there."

Net breathed a sigh of relief. Now she was about to involve another innocent party in this mess. Was she doing the right thing?

* * *

As she drove to the coffee shop, Net kept her eye on the rear view mirror. Was that blue car following her? No, it turned off after a couple of blocks.

"Oh God, I'm getting paranoid," she mumbled. "Somebody must have put the *Malocchio* on me." Her mind conjured up a picture of Cassandra Dolton. "I'll have to find a *strega* to remove it." She knew how ridiculous that sounded, but her grandmother had believed that a good witch could remove the curse. Who was she to say otherwise. But where could she find one? Certainly not in the yellow pages.

Net parked off to the side so that her car was not visible from inside the shop. She thought she recognized George Watkins' car but couldn't be sure. After all, she had only seen it once.

When she entered the shop, Net immediately recognized the man. He had an iced drink in front of him and searched anxiously around. She responded to his wave and walked up to the table. He stood and held out a chair for her. A gentleman, she thought. Not many of those left. She ordered a lemonade, then came right to the point.

"I went to two meetings of that Society and I'm convinced that they are somehow responsible for the deaths of your mother and at least one other woman that I heard about. A third may be in danger." Without realizing what she was doing, she began tearing her paper napkin into little bits.

"Mrs. Petrone, you must *not* go back there, under any circumstances. I won't have you risking your life for my problems." George Watkins was adamant. His eyes mirrored deep concern.

Net went on to tell him about the tea, Andrew Marcus, and her wild ride and encounter with the police. After telling him everything, she felt a little better. After all, sharing the burden was relieving oneself of half, or so she rationalized. She then gave him the address of the woman she had followed and asked if he could find out her name and phone number.

"That's easy enough. I'll do it as soon as I get back to the office and I'll call the woman myself. But I do not want you to involve yourself any further. Is that clear?"

"Very clear. My best friend says the same thing and so does Andrew Marcus."

Promise?" he persisted.

"Promise."

"But it might be better if I called the woman because I was at the meeting and heard what they said. She might believe me rather than you." Net held her *corno* all the while she was talking.

"I wish you wouldn't do that," he cautioned. "If these people are as ruthless as you think, who knows what they might do."

Net felt the fingers of fear crawl up her spine at his words. She knew he was right. But she had to warn that woman, couldn't live with herself if she didn't.

He let out a deep sigh and gazed off into the distance.

"You seem upset about something else, Mr. Watkins," Net observed as she studied the furrowed brow.

"I don't want to burden you further with my problems, but my nephew is in the hospital," he blurted out.

"What happened?"

He shook his head. "He developed a bedsore from sitting too long in his wheelchair and it became infected." He rubbed his hands and slowly shook his head back and forth.

"Oh Lord." Net visualized the boy unable to help himself, dependent on the diligent care of others. In this case it seemed there was a lack of concern. "Where was his mother?"

"Huh. She's gotten involved with an off-beat church group. Says she needs socialization with other women. She spends less and less time at home these days." He rested his elbows on the table and held his head as if it were too heavy to support itself.

"I've been helping my brother as much as I can but I'm not a rich man and the sort of help they need doesn't come cheap. We're investigating a volunteer group through my church that may be able to send someone out temporarily. But that doesn't solve the problem, not by a long shot." He let out a sound that almost sounded like a sob, and turned his head away.

"I've taken up enough of your time. Now please, remember what I said. Stay out of this."

"I will," Net said. This time she meant it.

* * *

An hour later George Watkins called back with the woman's name and phone number. She was Felicia Morganson.

"That name rings a bell," Net said. "I've heard it somewhere before."

"It should. Morganson Investments is a very successful company and I believe she's the matriarch. Her husband died some years ago and left her a small fortune. Her sons run the business now."

"You've been doing some sleuthing yourself," Net said, smiling.

"When I found out the woman's name, I wanted to confirm that she was the same Morganson," he said.

"So now what?" Net asked hoping he would have some ideas.

Silence for a moment before he spoke. "Since I'm a businessman and my mother was duped by these people, I feel honor bound to alert the sons. I've already put in a call to the company and stated that it was urgent I speak to one of them. I'm waiting for a call back now."

"Okay," Net said. "What shall I do?"

"Nothing," he said emphatically. "Stay out of this. Leave it to the family. After all, it's their inheritance she may have signed away." His voice softened. "You've done more than enough, Mrs. Petrone. Please don't put yourself in any more danger."

"You're right. I'll do just that. But you will let me know what happens?"

"I will. Now go about your business and try to forget my problems. Goodbye and thank you."

Net heard the final note in his voice and the disconnect, but she continued to hold the phone to her ear. She looked at the number for Mrs. Morganson, and punched it in. Immediately she grabbed her *corno* and uttered a prayer.

After six rings, Net disconnected. She didn't want the answering machine to kick in. It might identify her phone number and she certainly didn't want that. The woman must be out. That was either a good sign or a bad one, depending on the significance of the word "out". She tried calling numerous times throughout the day but got the same result. Finally she decided to wait for George Watkins' call. There was nothing else she could do.

Chapter 33

Net felt relieved that she made the promise to George Watkins. She would remove herself from the entire situation and get on with her life. No more adventures for her that would put her in danger.

A knock at the door pulled her out of her reverie. She glanced out the window at the welcoming sight of her friend, Ruth.

"We haven't had a good coffee-klatch in a long time," Ruth said as Net let her in. As usual she looked like a gracious lady belonging in an expensive mansion.

"You have a new hairdo," Net observed leading her friend into the kitchen.

"Since I cut it short, I decided to get a perm." She patted the saucy curls that framed her narrow face. "You like it?"

"Anything looks good on you," Net said laughing. Ruth's clear skin, sparkling eyes and regal posture belied her seventy years. Even though she was dressed in slacks and a loose fitting print top, she looked ready for any occasion.

"I swear," Net said examining her friend rather enviously, "no matter what you wear you always look like you stepped off the cover of a magazine titled, *Aging Graciously.*"

A slight blush spread across Ruth's cheeks. "You're exaggerating, but it sounds nice any way."

As the women settled down at the kitchen table with coffee and cookies, Net felt Ruth's eyes boring into her.

"What have you been doing while I've been busy at the animal shelter?" she asked.

"Oh this and that." Net avoided her friend's gaze but knew she wasn't good at subterfuge.

"Don't give me evasive answers. I've tried to call you and left messages on your machine that you haven't returned. Now, what's up?" Ruth tapped her fingers on the table. "I'm not leaving here until you tell me. I would love to hear that you've been with Sam making mad passionate love, but I know that's not the case." She continued tapping her fingers.

Net let out a heavy breath. "All right, but you're not going to like it." She poured more coffee in their cups, settled back and told Ruth the whole story beginning with her second visit to the society, the encounter with the police, and ending with her visit with George Watkins.

"Oh my God!" Ruth grabbed Net's hand and squeezed it. "I thought you were going to stay out of that entire business. Are you trying to get yourself killed?"

"Don't be so melodramatic," Net said. "I'm finished with the whole affair. George Watkins is going to contact the woman's sons and take it from there. And, when Detective Dobbs returns, I'll tell him everything. He still has connections. Then my conscience will be clear that I've done all I can."

"Promise me that." Ruth said.

"I promise."

The two sat for a while, neither saying a word.

"I was thinking of spending a few days with Vince and Melissa, just to get my mind off this business," Net said after a few minutes.

"That's a great idea. Now let me tell you something exciting." Ruth's eyes shone like a child with a secret.

Net didn't feel as though she needed any more excitement, but went along with her friend. "What is it?"

"How about going on a cruise?" She pulled out a colorful brochure from her pocket and laid it on the table.

Net's eyes flew open as she saw the picture of the huge cruise ship, five decks high. Her stomach began to rumble and do flip-flops.

Ruth apparently didn't notice her reaction and continued talking about the cruise. "We fly into Athens, board the ship, and stop at numerous ports on the Mediterranean including Monaco. Twelve days of sailing and sight seeing. How does that grab you?" She examined Net's pale face. "Are you all right?"

Net closed her eyes and swallowed hard. She said in a small voice, "No cruises for me. I get sea sick on a row boat."

Ruth laughed. "There's a huge difference between a cruise ship and a row boat. You don't even know the thing is moving."

Net took a deep breath, closed her eyes for a moment, and bit down on her lower lip. "Let me tell you about my honeymoon." She sat back and shook her head.

"Joe and I planned a great trip to Italy. We were going to visit Florence, Venice, Rome, and Naples. I was so eager to see Pompeii and Herculaneum. I read about them voraciously. We were to fly to New York and change planes at La Guardia." She gazed out the window, her face wreathed in regret.

"What happened?" Ruth asked leaning forward.

"I had never been on a plane before. As soon as I saw the massive thing my knees almost buckled under me. Joe had to practically carry me on board. I remember telling him I couldn't do it. I made a complete fool of myself. He was so sweet and encouraging that I decided to do it for him. But as soon as the plane took off, I started vomiting. I don't know how many barf bags I used. Whenever the plane hit some turbulence I thought I would die. That hour and a half flight seemed like forever." She wiped the perspiration that dotted her forehead.

"Needless to say, we never made it to Italy. Spent our honeymoon in New York City going to plays, the Met, museums and shopping. Joe was an angel. If he was disappointed, he never showed it. I was the one disgusted with myself. I had so wanted to see Italy. He offered to take me to a doctor and get some medication, but I flatly refused. We came home on a train." She let out a deep sigh. I haven't been on a plane since and, at this stage of my life, I don't intend to." She gave her head a vigorous nod and folded her hands on the table in a determined gesture.

"I can't believe that you've never done anything to conquer your fear: hypnosis, psychotherapy, positive reinforcement. There's so much help out there these days." Ruth's tone was disbelieving.

"Nope. No deal. I'm not getting on a plane or a cruise ship. That's that. If I can't get to my destination by car or train, I simply won't go."

Ruth slowly shook her head. "If you're that adamant, I won't bring it up again. Some of the other ladies are interested, but I thought you might enjoy the trip."

The ringing of the doorbell precluded any response by Net.

"Now who is that?" she asked, annoyance audible in her voice.

Ever wary these days, she peeked out the window to see the truck from a local florist. She recognized the name as the establishment that always delivered flowers Sam sent her. She had neglected him lately. Would have to call and thank him, maybe invite him over for dinner. Opening the door with a smile, she scribbled her name on the required line, took the bouquet, and thanked the man.

"Flowers," she announced as she returned to the kitchen.

"Who sent them?" Ruth asked.

"Probably Sam. It's the same florists he used before." She unwrapped the bouquet of summer blossoms and grabbed a vase from the shelf.

Ruth arranged them tastefully, put in the packet of preservative, and filled the vase with water. Net frowned as she searched for a card. None. A chill gripped her. First cookies and now flowers.

Net examined the arrangement. "Ruth, do these flowers smell strange to you?"

Her friend sniffed. "I've never smelled that scent before. It's very sweet, almost like some type of cleaning fluid. Certainly doesn't smell like anything I recognize. What do you think it is?"

"I don't know but I'm calling the florist right now." She moved the strange smelling flowers onto the counter next to the open window. Then, with shaking hands, she grabbed the phone book and thumbed through the names of florists.

The sunshine slowly disappeared as the sky clouded over and a distant rumble of thunder marred the previously lovely morning. Net shivered. She punched in the numbers and spoke to the woman who answered.

"I received a delivery of flowers with no card. Can you tell me who ordered them?"

"Certainly. Sorry about that. Your name and address, please?"

Net gave her the information and waited. A frown crossed her face as she watched Ruth closely examining the flowers and wrinkling up her nose.

When the woman came back on the line she sounded perplexed. "There's no record of the sender. Now that I recall, the lady said it was a surprise and you would understand. I thought that strange, but she paid in cash and I saw no need to question her about it."

Net's frown deepened. A woman? "What did she look like?"

A pause. "I can't really recall. We were busy at the time, but there was nothing striking that I remember except that she was a brunette. She did keep rubbing her forehead as though she had a headache."

Net continued. "There's a strange odor about these flowers, something I don't recognize."

"Oh yes," the woman said. "She gave me a pack of special preservative. Said it gave the bouquet longer freshness. It was a commercial packet, the same as we sometimes use. So I saw no harm to it." By now the woman's voice sounded concerned.

"If that woman comes in again," Net said adamantly, "or anyone else unwilling to identify themselves, tell them I will not accept any more gifts. Do I make myself clear?" She pursed her lips and tugged at her *corno*.

"Yes, Ma'am. I'm so sorry if you're dissatisfied."

"It's not your fault. Someone is playing a sick joke and I refuse to go along with it." She put the phone back on the charger and turned to Ruth. "Are you getting a headache?"

"Yes," Ruth answered rubbing her hand across her forehead. "I'm feeling a little sick to my stomach, too."

"So am I." Quickly Net opened the patio door and put the vase of flowers outside. "There's something in this water. Get one of the big garbage bags from under the sink."

Net found an empty jar and a pair of disposable gloves and went outside followed by Ruth. "Hold the garbage bag open, but don't touch anything." Gingerly she picked up the flowers and shoved them into the bag. Then she poured some of the water into the jar and closed it tightly. She dumped the rest of the water onto the cement walk then she put the vase in the bag also.

"Seal it up," she told Ruth.

"What's going on?" her friend asked in concern.

"I'm not sure, but we have to have all this analyzed by somebody. I'm sure that packet of preservative was tampered with.

Come on. Leave everything out here and we'll scrub our hands and faces and open all the windows."

No matter what she had said to George Watkins, the Society for the Fifth Beneficence wasn't finished with her yet.

Chapter 34

"What are you going to do?" Ruth asked, fear reflected in her eyes.

"I'm not sure. Since Dobbs is away, maybe I should call Marcus. He's involved with these people but I don't think he's one of them. I have a feeling he has a hidden agenda."

"Oh, Net. Be careful. Can you trust him?"

Net shrugged. "I'll have to."

"I think you should call Vince and tell him about the whole affair. He'll know the proper people to contact," Ruth said.

Net shook her head. "I'd never hear the end of it. He'd call me a meddling old fool and lecture me no end. I've gone this far, I feel that I have to see it through."

"What about Sam?' Ruth persisted.

"I can't worry that dear man. He would become over protective and be here all the time."

"Is that so bad?" Ruth wouldn't let up.

"I don't want to involve anyone else. If these people went after Sam or any member of my family, I'd never forgive myself. No, Marcus is my only recourse."

"By the way," she asked Ruth, "how is your headache?"

"It's gone—just like that," Ruth answered, a puzzled expression on her face.

"So is mine. I think whatever was in that packet was meant to be a warning. I'm calling Marcus, now."

Ruth hovered over her friend as Net took the card from the counter, picked up the phone, and placed the call.

After three rings he answered. "Mrs. Petrone, has something happened?"

"Yes. I must talk to you. I believe these people from that organization are warning me."

"This is not a secure line," he said. "I'll come to your house later, say nine this evening? I want to be sure I'm not followed. But what time do they close the gates?"

"Around dusk. During the summer they've been leaving them open a little longer. But you had better come by eight."

Ruth had her ear as close to the phone as she could and heard some of his responses. She shook her head and mouthed 'no'.

"All right," Net said, ignoring her friend. "I'll expect you." He immediately disconnected and Net let out an audible breath.

"Oh dear, I wish you wouldn't," Ruth said grabbing Net's hand.

"I must know what's going on before another woman is murdered," she said.

"I'll be here with you," Ruth insisted.

"Absolutely not. I don't want you involved. I have my alarm that I can activate if necessary. Now go home and let me think this through."

"Call me as soon as he leaves," Ruth demanded.

"I will. Now I think I need to lie down for a while."

After Ruth left, Net activated her alarm system and closed all the venetian blinds. She was annoyed that the one covering the picture window in the living room did not close all the way. *What's wrong with this thing?* She fiddled with it until she just left it halfway open. *I'll get maintenance to look at it tomorrow.* She went into the bedroom, said a prayer to St. Anthony, and collapsed on the bed.

* * *

She was awakened from a deep sleep by a ringing sound. *What was it? Her groggy mind began to surface. What time is it?* She wondered. *The phone, that's what was ringing.*

Picking it up, she managed a sleepy, "Hello."

"Ma," Vince's voice called over the instrument. "You okay?"

"Oh Vince, I was just taking a little nap. I'm—I'm fine."

"You sure? You don't sound right," he persisted.

"I said I'm fine and that's what I meant." She was wide awake now and had to reassure her son. "There's so much going on around here that an old lady gets tired."

"All right. I've been so busy with that trial that I'm tied up 24/7. I just took a minute to call you. Why don't you go spend some time with Melissa and the kids?"

"I will, dear. In fact I was thinking of going over there tomorrow," she lied.

"Good. I gotta go. My partner's waving to me. Bye, Ma."

"Bye." She clutched the phone and let out a breath. "Whew, that was close. I swear that boy is like a bloodhound. If he so much as gets a whiff of trouble, he'll be relentless." She paced as she talked to herself. "I'd better call Melissa and make good on my promise."

Before she could make the call, the phone rang again. She gaped at the instrument in her hand as if it were a living thing. Hesitantly she pushed the talk button. "Hello?"

"Hi Doll. Been thinking about you. I called a couple of times, but you weren't home."

"Hello Sam. Funny, I didn't get any messages."

"I didn't leave any. Everything all right?"

Everybody was concerned about her welfare. No, she was embroiled in a mess of murderers and threats. But could she tell that to Sam?

"Yes, I'm fine. Vince just called asking the same thing. Why wouldn't I be?"

"Well, after that break-in and that business about …" he hesitated for a moment. "You know, the DNA sample. I thought you might need some cheering up."

She grimaced. That's exactly what she didn't need. Sam was as bad as Vince. He'd know for sure that something was wrong.

"I'm not depressed. There are so many programs going on here that they keep me busy."

"Oh." The disappointment in his voice was audible. "Remember that old theater we used to go to when we were teenagers?"

"I remember." God, she thought, that was another lifetime.

"Well they've remodeled it and are putting on plays instead of movies. There's one there now about an Italian family that's supposed to be really funny. Some friends of mine saw it. Would you like to go?"

Maybe that was what she needed—laughter. "Sure, Sam, sounds like fun."

"Great! I'll get tickets for Saturday night. Are you free?"

"Yes, Saturday will be fine." As long as I'm still alive, she thought, and shivered.

"Swell. We can go to Mama Gina's for dinner and then the play, like old times."

Old times, she thought. If she could only bring them back. "What time shall I be ready?"

"I'll pick you up at five thirty. The play starts at seven."

"Why don't I drive out there and meet you at the restaurant? It's a long way for you to go back and forth."

"Oh no. A gentleman always picks up a lady. See you then."

"All right. Bye."

Might as well call Melissa while the phone is still hot in my hand. She placed the call and was invited to lunch with her daughter-in-law and grandchildren. After she replaced the phone, Net sat back on the sofa, exhausted. Am I a good enough actress to reassure the people who care about me? She wondered. No way will I let them know what's going on and possibly put them in danger.

* * *

As the sun inched across the sky on a beautiful mid-summer evening, Net paced and watched the clock as the hands crept slowly around the face. Am I doing the right thing? She asked herself over and over again. Joe, why aren't you here to advise me? Fool. If he were here, she wouldn't be in this predicament. He would take care of her. He always did. Now she had to make decisions on her own and wasn't sure at all if she was making the right ones.

From the west window she watched the colors streak across the sky: reds, pinks, purples. Net shivered. She made sure the doors were locked and bolted, the alarm was on, and all the blinds were closed.

She settled in a corner of the sofa, picked up a book, and stuck the hatpin along the spine. A lot of good that will do, she thought, but, one never knows. She began to read but the words had no meaning. She read the same paragraph over and over until, in frustration, she closed the book.

I'd better have some supper, she thought, but her stomach contracted at the thought. Got to keep my strength up. As she walked into the kitchen, the phone rang. Net froze. Was it Marcus calling to cancel? Or maybe Ruth? Hesitantly she picked up the ringing instrument. "Hello."

No answer, only breathing on the other end.

"Hello, who is it?" she repeated. Then the disconnect.

Her knees buckled as she sank into a chair. Was it a wrong number or a warning? "*Madonna!*" she moaned clutching her *corno*, the *Malocchio*. She leaned her head back as stars danced before her eyes. Then anger stirred up her Italian temperament.

"I refuse to let these people intimidate me," she shouted aloud as if the words could float on the air and reach the offenders. Bracing herself, Net put down the phone, walked into the kitchen and, with shaking hands, poured an ounce of brandy. She swallowed it in one gulp then ran to the sink for a glass of water to sooth her burning throat.

I can't get sloshed, she thought. Have to keep my wits about me. Her hands were no longer shaking as she made herself a cheese sandwich and forced it down with another glass of water. Not much of a supper. Her mother would have been ashamed of her, a good Italian housewife eating a cheese sandwich and nothing more—no salad, no greens. But her mother was never in such a predicament. She lived a simple life cooking and keeping house for her family. Net envied that life. But she was here in this strange situation and had to see its end. The word *end* made her shiver again.

After swallowing the last bite, she glanced at the clock—seven thirty. A half hour before Marcus was scheduled to arrive. She turned on the television and watched the nature channel—animals devouring each other. She switched to the health channel where a pathologist was performing an autopsy. As she switched from one station to another, everything shouted violence. Finally she settled for cartoons. At least Tweety Bird always managed to save himself.

Finally the hands of the clock inched toward eight. It was still light out, but the sky was darkening. Net turned off all the lights except for a small table lamp in the corner of the living room. She turned off the television, held her book with the hatpin, head sticking out, and waited.

At five minutes after the hour she heard something. Peering between the blinds, she saw a dark car making its way slowly down the street. Its lights were off giving it a foreboding appearance. The car stopped on the gravel along the pond well way from her house. A figure emerged dressed in dark clothes and carefully made his way to her door.

Net's throat went dry as she heard the soft knock. "Yes?" she asked through the closed door.

"It's me, Marcus."

She unlocked the door and he quickly entered and bolted it behind him.

"Just what is all this cloak and dagger business?" Net whispered.

"Sh." He held his finger to his lips. "Do you have a room with no windows?" he asked so softly she hardly heard him.

"Dining room." She led the way through the house lit only by the small lamp in the living room.

"Good," he said seeming to relax a bit. "I can only stay a short time. I'm quite sure I wasn't followed but I can't be certain."

She told him about the flowers, her call to the florist, and the headaches. "Are you going to tell me what's going on?" she demanded.

"I'll take the flowers as well as the water they're in and have everything analyzed," he said without answering her question. "But I think they were sent as a warning. Whatever you do, if you receive any food or drink of *any* kind, *don't touch it.* I can't emphasize that enough."

"Is that the way they killed those women who signed their savings over to the Society?"

"It's complicated. The less you know the better." They stood huddled in a corner of the darkened room.

"Just who are you?" Net asked. "You're obviously playing both sides of the fence. What's your stake in all this?"

"I'll tell you in due time. I'm a private investigator working undercover. That's all I can say for now. If they find out, I'm a dead man."

"Oh!" Net drew back and grabbed her *corno.*

"You *must* stay away from the Society and, above all, *do not* try to contact Mrs. Morganson. It may already be too late." His voice dropped as he let out a deep sigh.

"Oh my God, these people have to be stopped." She wrung her hands together and began muttering in Italian.

"I do intend to stop them," Marcus said forcefully. "But you must not interfere. Is that clear?"

"Yes."

"Get the flowers then I'll leave before they lock the gates. Don't call me. I'll contact you."

Without another word, Net slipped out onto the patio to retrieve the garbage bag she had put there earlier. The patio was empty. She searched but found nothing. Locking the door, she turned to Marcus. "It's gone."

"Was anyone around when you put the bag outside?"

Net thought. "Only the grounds crew cutting the grass. They may have presumed it was garbage and taken it away."

"Perhaps. Then again, these people are very careful about leaving evidence around. They may have been watching you."

Net trembled. "What do we do now?"

"Nothing," he said. "I have to lay low for a while to avoid suspicion. You go about your usual routine and after a while they may realize you're not a threat to their plan."

"I'll do anything you say."

"Good. Turn off that lamp and bolt the door as soon as I slip out."

"Be careful," Net cautioned.

Before she realized it, he was gone. She peeked through the blinds and watched as he quietly started his car and crept slowly down the street without turning on his lights. She bolted the door and set the alarm, then went into the kitchen and grabbed the bottle of brandy.

Before she could take a sip, the ringing of the phone rattled her so that she spilled the liqueur down her blouse. With trepidation she picked it up. "Hello?" she whispered.

"Net," Ruth's voice came over the instrument. "I thought you were going to call me. Are you all right? I was watching from the window. What is going on?" Her voice rose with every word.

"I can't talk now. I'm drinking brandy. This is all too weird. Come over in the morning and I'll tell you everything. Now I'm going to get drunk." She put down the phone, poured more brandy and carried the glass into the bedroom. Before she could down the first swallow, she lay back on the bed and passed out.

Chapter 35

Again Net slept poorly. Every time the refrigerator kicked in, she thought someone was trying to open her door. By morning she was glad to see daylight, but was just as tired as she had been the night before. Perhaps she should cancel lunch with Melissa and the children. No. Marcus told her to go on with her life as if nothing unusual had happened and that was what she intended to do.

First she had to contend with Ruth. Dragging herself out of bed, she showered and washed her hair, then dressed in bright colors. The reflection staring back at her in the mirror appeared haggard. Makeup might help.

Yawning, she grabbed the blush, eyeliner and lipstick and, through glazed eyes, did a fair job. The result was passable but it wouldn't fool Ruth, not for a minute.

Mechanically Net filled the coffeepot and switched it on. Then she put a plate of muffins on the table and was just about to sit down when the doorbell rang. Net sighed, stood up straight, and attempted to put on a cheerful face. She opened the door to an anxious Ruth.

"Are you okay? What happened last night? All your lights were off and I was worried sick." The words came spilling out as Ruth embraced her friend.

"One question at a time," Net said as she led Ruth into the kitchen. She went through the ritual of pouring coffee and offering Ruth a muffin. "Sit and I'll tell you everything."

After a brief pause, Net related the entire episode beginning with Marcus's silent entry and ending with the same exit.

Ruth gazed with wide eyes and her mouth agape as Net finished and shook her head. "The *Malocchio*, that's what it is," Net muttered.

"What are you going to do?" Ruth asked, a tremor in her voice.

"Just what he said. I can't afford to meddle in this business. These people are murderers and won't let anyone stand in their way. I don't want to put Marcus in any danger either." She looked at her empty cup and felt bile rising in her throat. Enough of that.

Her brow furrowed. "One thing puzzles me, though. Did you notice anyone, the grounds crew or anybody else, take that garbage bag off my patio?"

Ruth thought for a moment. "No, it wasn't trash pickup yesterday and I don't remember seeing anyone. But, then, it's not unusual to see a workman walking around with a bag of garbage."

Net nodded. "So, it could have been one of the men tidying up, or ..." She left the sentence unfinished.

"Now what?" Ruth asked, her face ashen.

"I'm going to see Melissa and the children and act like everything is fine."

"How are you going to do that? You look like hell, even with the makeup."

Net shrugged. "Eh, if she says anything I'll tell her that I didn't feel well for a few days. It won't really be a lie. I've been practically scared to death."

As she led her friend to the door, she repeated Marcus's words. "If I go on with my life and stay away from that Society, they'll eventually realize that I'm not a threat and leave me alone."

The women exchanged glances. Neither one believed it for a minute.

* * *

Net tried to calm her mind and visualize her visit with the grandchildren. Kids had a way of making folks forget all their cares, at least for a little while. She made sure no one was following her as she drove to an Italian bakery tucked away in a strip mall. She purchased some of her favorite pastries, knew Vince would appreciate them when he came home from a long day in court.

The sight of Dominic and Melissa's beaming faces erased all thoughts of danger and subterfuge. She handed her daughter-in-law the pastries and was assaulted by her grandson.

"Look at my new train, Grandma." Dominic jumped around grasping her hand and pulling her toward the playroom.

"My goodness, let me catch my breath." She laughed. It felt so good. It had been a long time since anything had given her joy and merriment. The baby was asleep and Net ached to hold her in her arms.

"I'll get lunch ready while he shows off his train with all the bells and whistles," Melissa said.

Net played with her grandson and when Diane awoke, she held her and kissed the soft pudgy cheek. At almost two months the child was laughing and reaching for Net's *corno*.

"Eh, you know what's special, huh? There's enough Italian in you that you recognize protection. Grandma will get you one when you're older." She held the baby close and remembered, with an aching heart, holding her own daughter so many years ago.

"Grandma, you're not watching me," Dominic scolded.

"I'm watching, I'm watching. Can't I play with both of you at once?"

"Lunch is ready," Melissa called. "Dominic, go wash your hands."

"Why do I always have to wash my hands?" He stomped toward the bathroom.

"That boy." Melissa shook her head. "Always contrary."

"It's the age," Net said. "If you told him never to wash his hands, he'd probably be in there every few minutes with soap and water."

They laughed as they went into the sparkling kitchen with all the modern conveniences. Net remembered her first kitchen in a small Melrose Park apartment. It had an old stove, a refrigerator and a sink—no dishwasher, no microwave, no convection oven. Why did each generation seem to need more?

Melissa nursed the baby as Net and Dominic sat down and began eating premade sandwiches with the crust cut off the bread. She wanted to ask what was wrong with the crust but decided to keep her opinions to herself.

They made small talk, Melissa describing Dominic's school programs and Net mentioned all the programs at the senior center.

"How are your parents?" Net asked.

"Oh fine: playing golf almost every day that the weather permits. Mom is still active with her bridge club. Now they're all talking about some sort of Evangelist preaching about saving the environment."

Net froze. She felt the blood drain from her face.

"Why Net, what's wrong?" Melissa asked, concern in her voice. "You're so pale. Are you ill?"

It took Net a few minutes to regain her composure. "What's the man's name?" she asked.

Melissa furrowed her brow. "Ah, Brother something or other. It's not a common name."

"Is it Brother Rupert?"

"Yes, I believe it is. Why do you ask?"

"Melissa." Net placed her hands on the table and sat forward. "Tell your mother and her friends to stay away from that man."

"For heaven's sakes, why?"

"He's a con artist. Some women from the center got involved with him and his Society and were talked into handing over their life savings to 'save the environment'". She said nothing of the suspicious deaths.

"You seem adamant about this," Melissa said, as she placed the baby in the bouncy chair.

"Oh I am. Please, stay away from that man." Oh God, how can I warn her of the danger without blurting out the whole sordid mess? Net wondered.

"All right. I'll tell Mom what you said."

"If she wants to call me, give her my number," Net said.

Later Net choked down a half of one of the pastries. She cooed over the baby and joined her grandson in a board game. But she couldn't wait to leave, knew she was sending out negative vibes and could see that she had upset her daughter-in-law.

With the excuse that she had errands to run, she left as soon as possible. She worried about Melissa's mother and her friends and knew that she would get a call from her son very soon.

* * *

When the phone rang that evening, Net knew it would be Vince. She wasn't surprised at the irate tone in his voice.

"Ma, what's all this warning about this Brother—Rufus—or whatever his name is? Have you gotten yourself mixed up in some sort of scam?"

"No, no. Don't get all excited. I just wanted Melissa to warn her mother that the whole organization is a way to extort money from wealthy widows." Again she failed to mention the sudden deaths of said widows.

"And just how do you know that?"

"It happened to a few ladies living here in this complex. That's how I know." She was becoming annoyed with him.

"Are you sure you're not involved?" he persisted.

"Vince, have I ever lied to you?" She made the sign of the cross and asked forgiveness.

He hesitated for a minute. "Okay, I'll warn Melissa's mother and you be sure to stay away from those people. I'll also have some friends of mine in the fraud department check into this guy and his organization."

"You do that. And, let me know what you find out."

"Why do you want to know?"

Just curious, that's all."

Chapter 36

When Clarence Dobbs finally called, he told Net to meet him at Centennial Park in Orland. It would be filled with mothers and children and seemed like a safe place to talk.

Net parked her dark gray Honda Civic between two SUVs. It appeared to nestle comfortable and protected. Fool, she thought. Cars can't protect each other. But at least it didn't stand out like something painted fire-engine red.

She found a secluded park bench well away from the pool area. In the background the muted sounds of children laughing and shouting filled the air. How carefree, she thought, and longed for the days when her children were young and she sat with other mothers in a place like this. A tear escaped her eye. She quickly wiped it away as she saw Detective Dobbs walking toward her.

"Mrs. Petrone." He extended his bony hand and put down the bag from Dunkin Donuts he carried. "I brought some coffee," he said as he sat next to her.

"Good," she said. Her nerves were frazzled from the caffeine she had consumed before she came, but she accepted the cup graciously.

He pulled a small bag from his pocket and handed it to her. "Pepper spray."

"Oh, thank you. How much do I owe you?"

He shook his head. "Just tell me why you need protection." His eyes bored into hers.

This was a man you didn't lie to. He would know. She took a deep breath and began with her buying the townhouse, Watkins's visit, Andrew Marcus and Cassandra Dolton and the genealogy class. She hesitated before taking a sip of coffee. It was strong and hot. She felt perspiration run down her armpits and between her breasts.

"What else?" he asked.

She nodded and continued with the lecture by Rupert and her two visits to the Society. She omitted nothing, including her attempt to locate Mrs. Morganson, the blue car following her, and her chase by the police. She ended with the flowers and the visit from Marcus. Net was physically and emotionally exhausted when she finished.

Dobbs slowly shook his head. "I sure didn't expect anything like this when you asked to see me. Have you talked to Vince about all this?"

"No!" she said vehemently. "I can't endanger my family. These people are ruthless. I don't want to put Vince and Melissa and the children in any kind of danger." She went on to tell him about Melissa's mother's bridge club and her warning to them. She put her head in her hands and moaned. "You can see why I can't tell all this to anyone, can't you?"

"Yeah. Now you say that this Watkins has alerted the Morgansons to the scam?"

"He said he would, but told me to stay out of it."

"Good advice," Dobbs agreed. "Let me see what I can find out about these people. In the meantime, do *nothing* but your usual routine. They probably do have someone watching you, but, if you don't seem to pose a threat, they'll eventually leave you alone. After all, two women coming to harm in the same townhouse in such a short time would raise a red flag. Tell me, can you trust this Marcus fellow?"

"I didn't think so at first, but, when he came to pick up the flowers, he told me he was a private investigator working undercover. Said the less I knew, the better."

"Hmm." Dobbs rubbed his chin. "He may have been hired by some wealthy family who was cheated out of their inheritance by this Society." He grabbed Net's hand and stared into her eyes. "Whatever you do, don't put the man in danger. They won't hesitate to kill him."

"That's just what he said," she whispered.

"Now, go home and act as normal as possible. I'll call you when I find out something. And, if you suspect that someone is following you, try and get the license plate number and the make of the car, okay?"

"I will." As she stood up she tottered so that Dobbs had to grab her. "Are you all right?"

"I think so," she said. "I feel like I'm living a movie—one that's nearing its climax." She shivered.

He walked her to her car and tried to reassure her that he would take care of everything, but Net had her doubts.

Chapter 37

Every time the phone rang, Net jumped. Now it seemed to jangle her nerves. She grabbed it almost viscously. "Hello."

"Hi, Doll. You okay?"

"Oh, Sam. Sure, I'm fine."

"You sounded a little uptight."

She feigned a laugh. "I've been getting so many calls for donations for causes that I didn't even know existed."

"You could just let your answering machine weed them out. Then call back only the people you want to talk to."

"Yeah, I suppose I could, but it rings seven times before the machine picks up and that would drive me crazy."

Now he laughed. "Me, too."

"Are we still set for Saturday?" she asked.

"Absolutely. I was just calling to say I'll pick you up a little earlier so we don't have to rush through dinner. Is that all right with you?"

"Of course. I'll be ready." Dear Sam, always so eager to please. They made small talk for a few minutes, Net telling him how the children were growing every time she saw them and he mentioning an old friend who had passed away.

When she put down the phone, Net indulged herself in a few moments of nostalgia recalling the old days and how simple their lives had been. But that was a time gone by that couldn't be recaptured.

* * *

Saturday turned out to be picture perfect, the weather mild, the sky clear. As Sam pulled into the driveway, Net saw Ruth watering a rose bush in front of her house. Her friend waved and said, "Have a good time."

We will," Sam called back. Net made sure to activate the alarm as she left, then, as Sam held the car door open, she got in and smiled at Ruth. Tonight she felt relaxed and knew she would enjoy the evening.

The restaurant in the old neighborhood was just as Net remembered. Neapolitan love songs played in the background; the fragrance of garlic and Italian spices filled the room. Red and white checkered table clothes covered the round tables, each sporting an empty Chianti bottle holding a candle with wax dripping down the side.

Net murmured a contented sigh as Sam held out her chair. "This is wonderful."

"Yeah, isn't it?"

The waiter greeted them as if they were family. "What kinda wine you like?" he asked in a heavy accent.

Sam looked at Net questioningly.

"You chose," she said. "Anything is fine with me."

He studied the wine list and chose a Valpolicello. "I think you'll like this," he said smiling at Net.

"I'm sure I will."

They chose an antipasto with calamari and artichoke hearts, followed by pasta with pesto sauce, one of Net's favorites.

"Sam, this is delicious," she said dipping a piece of crusty bread in oil and parmesan cheese. "Such a treat."

"You could have this kind of food every day, if you wanted, Doll," he said. The expression in his eyes almost melted Net's heart. She knew all too well what he meant.

"If I ate like this every day, I'd be as fat as Mama Gina." She laughed to break the tension she felt building up.

They skipped dessert, even though it was tempting, but time was short and they didn't want to miss the opening act of the play.

As Sam had said, the theater was remodeled and they had great seats. The play was about a typical Italian family and all the problems that ensued when the daughter got pregnant by her Jewish boyfriend. Each family was forced to accept the culture of the other and, in the end, everyone came together. It was well acted and Net and Sam both enjoyed it.

On the way home, Net felt a sadness. She had so enjoyed the evening that going back to reality was not to her liking. "Sam, I can't thank you enough for this lovely time." It sounded lame, even to her ears, but it was all she could say.

"It was great," he said squeezing her hand. Neither said anything else until they were at her door. She opened it and deactivated the alarm.

"Do you want to come in?" she asked

"No, it's late. I'd better get on home." He took her in his arms and kissed her, long and hard. She didn't resist. Then he turned abruptly and was gone.

She though about that kiss for a long time. It was nice, but it wasn't Joe. Fool, she told herself. It will never be Joe, but he's a good man. That night she laid awake, thinking and wondering.

Chapter 38

These days Net glared at the phone every time it rang. I must get my emotions under control, she told herself as she lifted the instrument off the charger.

"Hello." She tried to sound as calm as possible but even she could hear the quaver in her voice.

"Mrs. Petrone, George Watkins here."

"Oh," she sighed with relief. "How are you?"

"Tolerable. I want to tell you something encouraging," he said.

"I like that word."

"Can you meet me for lunch?"

"Of course. The same place we met before?" She visualized the quaint restaurant.

"No," he said a little too quickly, Net thought. "Let's meet at Centennial Park in Orland. Do you know where that is?"

Strange that he would chose the same place she had met Dobbs. "Sure, but why there?"

"Because it's a public place. I'll explain when I see you. There's a gazebo across from the water park. We'll meet there. I'll pick up sandwiches and something cool to drink. All right?"

"Fine. What time?"

"One this afternoon."

Before she could say another word, she heard the click. "I swear, all this intrigue is driving me to distraction. I'll never read another mystery as long as I live," she said aloud. Should she tell Ruth? Not now. She would wait until she heard what he had to say.

* * *

The hot muggy day brought hoards of mothers with children to the water park. Net found a parking spot a long way off and slowly walked toward the gazebo, but there appeared to be a group picnicking there. She noticed a man wearing shorts and a tee shirt with Centennial Park emblazoned across the chest and presumed he was a guard. He smiled and nodded to her. She smiled back.

It took her a while to find George Watkins in the crowd. He waved her over to a spot under a tree where he had a blanket spread on the grass.

"Sorry," he said. "It's the best I could do."

"This is fine," she replied as he helped her to sit down. Getting up will be another matter, she thought.

George handed her a ham sandwich with a pickle on the side and an iced latte. "I thought it was too hot for anything else," he said. "I hope this is to your liking."

She smiled. "I haven't been on a picnic in a long time. How I envy those kids their energy," she said watching a few playing kickball in the grass. "This is a good sandwich," she took a generous bite.

"Just keep watching the children and smile and nod your head from time to time as you listen to what I have to tell you," he said. "We can't be too careful."

Net thought the precautions a little over done but, with the strange things that had been happening lately, she went along.

"Mrs. Morganson is safe," he said.

"Oh, thank God."

As she turned her head, he held up his hand. "No matter what I say, keep smiling and watching the children.

She nodded.

"I contacted her sons, explained what had happened to my mother and they immediately took over. Had her examined by her physician who felt she was under duress when she signed that will. Then a trip to the lawyer's office and a new will revoking the previous one. Mrs. Morganson is safely tucked away at a Spa in Colorado for an indefinite period of time."

Net continued to watch the children but found Watkins's statement hard to believe. "So fast?"

"You can accomplish anything if you have enough money. It seems there have been a few complaints about this organization, but the authorities have not been able to find any concrete proof of fraud. I think Brother Rupert will be under closer scrutiny from now on." He looked at the children and pointed to one of them. "You were so concerned that I wanted to relieve your mind about that woman."

"Thank you. I appreciate it." She was debating whether to tell him about Melissa's mother's friends but decided not to, neither did she tell him about Detective Dobbs. He had enough to worry about.

"Now we'd better leave," he said. "I believe we're being watched."

Net frowned as she glanced around.

"Keep smiling and looking at the kids. There's a fellow over there who's pretending to be a guard but he's been watching us all the time. Give me your hand and I'll pull you up."

With some difficulty, and the man's help, Net managed to get off the ground. As he walked her to her car, they continued to laugh and converse about nothing in particular. From the corner of her eye Net saw the man who had greeted her when she arrived. He was talking on a cell phone. Suddenly she felt vulnerable.

"We won't meet again," Watkins said. "Take care of yourself."

She quickly got in the car, locked the doors and started the engine. How would this all end? Would she ever feel safe again?

* * *

From that day on, nothing was the same. Net went through her daily ritual: the pool, lunches with Ruth and some of the other residents, scheduled outings, but she always felt someone was watching her.

"I can't live this way," she said to Ruth one morning. "I'm so paranoid that I examine everyone I come in contact with. I've got to stop this."

Ruth screwed up her face. "Why don't you talk to someone?"

"Like who?"

"Well ..." Ruth hesitated. "Maybe a priest or a ..." She left the sentence unfinished.

"Or a psychiatrist, huh?" Net finished it for her. "I know that's what you're thinking."

"Couldn't hurt," her friend said.

Net bit down on her lower lip and fisted her hands. "I'll think about it."

She hadn't been inside a Catholic Church since Joe died. Hadn't been able to accept the fact that a benevolent Deity had taken him from her. God had nothing to do with it. From the injustices she had seen throughout her life, she had come to the conclusion that whatever God there might be, did not take away our loved ones on a whim. There had to be something else.

She had studied other religious beliefs of people throughout the world and through the ages. The theory of reincarnation and karma made the most sense, but she still hadn't been able to wrap her mind around it.

She put away some dishes that sat on the drain board, and dragged herself to bed. After reading a few pages of her book, her eyes began to close, the book fell from her hands, and she dozed. But her sleep was soon interrupted by a terrifying dream.

She walks into a huge cathedral with a high vaulted ceiling. The confessional beckons to her. Net slowly opens the door and kneels down. When the priest's window slides open, she lowers her eyes and whispers the long forgotten phrases, "Forgive me Father, for I have sinned. It is years since my last confession."

There is no response from the shadowy figure behind the mesh.

"Father, there is something I must talk to you about. I carry a great burden on my soul."

The man behind the mesh turns his full face to her. "You cannot escape me. Tell anyone and you, too, will die." It is Brother Rupert.

Net shrinks back as he utters a demonic laugh. She pushes herself off the kneeler and grabs the door. But the handle is gone. She pushes with all her might, but it won't budge. She tries to scream, but no sound comes from her throat. All she hears is the laughter growing louder as she sinks to the floor.

Net sat up with a start, perspiration dotting her forehead. She heaved a sigh of relief as she realized it was only a dream. She decided then and there that she could tell no one. She would have to live with the paranoia. But deep inside she knew it wouldn't stop, could feel that the situation would come to a conclusion; it had to; and, somehow, it included her.

Chapter 39

She glared at him through bloodshot eyes. "You promised to take me away. I can't stand my life anymore; have migraines almost every day; can't sleep. When I helped you convince my mother-in-law to sign away everything to the Society, you promised to give me enough money to care for that poor excuse of a son of mine." Her mousy brown hair fell across her eyes. As she brushed it away, she rubbed her forehead. Another migraine on the way. She paced, pursed her lips and stomped. "I'm tired of wiping his drool and cleaning his ass."

"Easy, Verena, I know it's hard right now, but your husband and brother-in-law have us tied up in court. It won't be long, I promise you, and I'll have enough money to take you away."

"You'd better," she said bitterly. "I can't even bear to go home. And I'm tired of following that Petrone woman. God, what a boring life she leads: goes to the health club, visits her son, outings with the other old folks. How long do I have to keep that up?" She stood in front of him, tapping her foot, and clenching and unclenching her fists.

"Not much longer," he said, trying to sooth her. "Why don't you go on home and take something for that migraine?"

Her voice softened. "You said it would be just the two of us." She walked seductively up to him, put her arms around his neck, and kissed him passionately, but he barely responded.

"That wasn't much of a kiss," she said, pouting.

He patted her on the backside. "Be patient, just a little longer. I've almost reached my goal. I have my eyes on one more client. Then, it's done."

She didn't like the way he spoke the last words. "You'd better not try and put one over on me, Rupert, or whatever your real name is. One word to my husband and you're finished."

He grabbed her wrists, his eyes narrowed to tiny slits. "Don't ... ever ... threaten ... me. Do you understand?"

"Ow, you're hurting me." She whined and squirmed. "I didn't mean it, you know that. I love you, just want to be with you, always."

Slowly he released her. "And you will, my dear, you will." He opened a drawer, took out a bundle of bills, and handed them to her. "To make things easier at home, just until ..."

After she left, Sandra Dolton came into the room. Rupert looked at her. "Did you hear all that?"

"I did. The woman is becoming a nuisance. Are we finished with her?" Sandra sidled up to him and began stroking his back.

He turned to her. "I believe so. I think we may have to arrange a little accident for poor Sister Verena."

Chapter 40

Net began to relax as one day followed the next and nothing untoward happened. She hadn't seen the blue car and didn't get the prickly feeling that someone was following her. She stood before the statue of St. Anthony on her dresser. "I'm sorry if I've been disrespectful. Please give me this one answer and I'll let it go. Is my Donna ... gone forever? Or can I still live with hope? Amen."

She made the sign of the cross three times and left the room to answer the ringing phone.

"Hello."

"Aunt Net, it's Lane."

Who else would call her aunt? Lena, or Lane, was the only niece she had. "How is the budding artist?"

"Fantastic! I painted another still life with that goblet and sold it in a month. I swear that thing is a good luck charm. Thanks so much for giving it to me, and for believing in me."

Net could hear the excitement in the girl's voice. She was so pleased. At least someone's life was going well. But, just maybe, her own worries would soon be over. "So what's next?" she asked.

"Well, I've decided to take a course in art restoration."

"Is there a future in that?" Net asked.

"Could be, if I'm good enough. And," she hesitated for just a moment, "and, I have a new boyfriend."

"I don't know if I can handle all this good news." Net laughed. "What does he do?" In the past Lane's choice of male companions had been less than encouraging.

"He has a degree in anthropology, but there aren't any jobs in that field. So he wants to take the police exam and work up to detective. Isn't that cool?"

"Very interesting," Net said, a policeman and an art restorer—not exactly high income jobs as far as she knew. "What does your mother say about all this?"

Lane let out a frustrated breath. "She thinks I'm 'grasping at straws', as she put it; says I can do better. But I don't think she cares much what I do. She's off on a Mediterranean cruise with the new man in her life."

Damn that Molly, Net cursed to herself. Why can't she take some interest in her only daughter? I would give anything to have mine back. "Well, I care and I have faith in your decisions. Keep me posted."

Later that day, as Net was preparing to make a batch of cookies, Detective Dobbs called.

"Mrs. Petrone, how are you?' he asked, concern in his voice.

"I'm fine. I don't think I'm being followed anymore and am beginning to relax."

"Good. I tried to get some information on that Society, but they're very secretive. They're not listed as a not-for-profit organization. In fact, I couldn't fine any listing for them at all."

"Hmm, that's strange," she said, "but I'm not surprised. They're up to no good and are not about to advertise that."

"They do appear to have a business selling rain forest grown coffee. It's called SFB coffee and is legitimate. Of course, that could be a cover to avoid suspicion of illegal activities. They also have a group of young people working with Save the Whales."

"That's it, huh?" she said.

"I'm afraid so. I'll contact Mr. Watkins and see how he's doing contesting the will. Again, I'm ordering you to stay out of the whole affair." His commanding tone of voice left no doubt in Net's mind.

"I will, definitely," she promised.

* * *

George Watkins's phone rang just as he was in the middle of working on an important report. He pushed the intercom button and said, in a frustrated voice, "Angela, I thought I told you to hold all my calls."

"Sorry Mr. Watkins, but it's your brother. He says it's important."

"All right. Put him through." George tapped his foot nervously on the floor. Now what?

"George, it's Bob."

"Yeah, what's up? Is Luke okay?"

He heard the almost hysterical note in his brother's voice. "Something is really wrong with Myra. I don't even know her anymore. She's been spending more time with that church group and last night she brought home a big wad of cash—practically threw it at me. Said she was finished taking care of Luke and that I should hire someone." He let out a deep breath that turned into a groan.

"How much money?"

"Five thousand dollars in hundred dollar bills."

"Whew! Where in God's name did she get that much money?"

"She wouldn't say." Bob sounded as if he were on the verge of tears. "I'm wondering if she's gambling or prostituting herself."

George visualized Myra's plain face and bulky body. Certainly not prostitution. "You've got to find out where she got that money, Bob. The pressures at home and the migraines may be doing funny things to her mind."

"Huh, when I mentioned seeing a doctor, she hit the roof. Said she needed some space and I should just leave her alone."

George thought for a moment. "Do you know anyone who can follow her and see where she goes?" An ugly thought was forming in his mind. "I don't want to scare you, but she may be putting herself in danger."

"Oh God, as if I don't have enough on my plate now. I'll talk to a guy I know and see what I can do. And thanks, George, for all your support."

When he disconnected the call, George Watkins sat for a long time staring out the window at a bank of clouds building up over the city. Was Myra doing something illegal? Whatever it was, all he could do was wait.

Chapter 40

A few days later, Net was on her way to Vince's house for a family dinner. He finally had a break at work and they decided to celebrate.

As she drove along, her eyes grew wide as she saw the blue car—again. She was sure it was the same car because she had noticed a dent in the front bumper the last time. It was directly behind her.

"Oh no. I thought I was free of you. Got to get the license number."

She squinted through the rear view mirror, trying to read the number, and failed to notice the stoplight turn red. The nose of her car was through the intersection when she realized what she had done. She slammed on the brake, but the blue car didn't stop. It rammed into her rear bumper catapulting her into the stream of traffic. A van going through the green light was unable to stop and hit the rear driver's side of her car.

She heard the crunch of metal against metal. "*Madonna mia,* what's happening?"

She felt as if she were an observer as a fence appeared to come toward her. She was frozen, unable to move. Her car careened through the fence and came to rest on a grassy area. Only then did she realize that she was in a cemetery.

"Oh *Dio,* am I dead?" She moved her arms and legs. No, she was very much alive and unhurt.

A man came up to her and asked if she was all right.

"I think so, but I'm not sure what just happened. What about the people in the other car?"

"They're okay," he said. "I saw that blue car hit you from behind then speed away."

"You did?" Now they would have to believe her.

"I wrote down the make of the car and the license number. I think it was a woman driving," he said.

"You're an angel. That car has been following me for weeks and I don't know why. Now I can find out who it is." She let out a sigh of relief. Now would this nightmare be over?

"Stay here," the man said. "The police will want to question you. Do you want me to stay with you?"

"I'm all right," she told him. But was she? Net sat still, her entire body trembling and her head beginning to pound. She tried to reconstruct the chain of events, but her mind was a blank.

The police arrived on the scene quickly and she gave her statement. She saw the officer talking to the witness, before he came back to her.

"Mrs. Petrone, I can see the damage to the rear of your car where you were hit and pushed, but you say you were preoccupied and didn't notice the light turn red."

"Officer, I really don't know what happened. That blue car was following me—tried to get the license number—felt the crash ...." She couldn't go on.

"All right, just try and relax. The car that hit you got away, but we have the license number. The paramedics will be here soon to check you out."

Net sat, stunned. "I had better call my son." Oh God, what will Vince say? That I shouldn't be driving? Shivering, she pulled a cell phone out of her purse and began fiddling with it. Finally tears cascaded down her cheeks.

"Here, let me help you with that." It was the kindly man who had witnessed the accident. "What number do you want to call?"

She gave him Vince's number and he punched it in. "Here, it's ringing," he said handing it to her.

"Hello," Vince answered.

"Oh *Dio*, I've been in an accident. Please come here."

"Ma, are you hurt? What happened?"

She began blubbering and crying until the man took the phone from her and gave Vince the location.

At that moment, the officer came up to her again. "Mrs. Petrone, do you know a Robert Watkins?"

"Who? Robert Watkins? No, I don't know anybody by that name."

"The car that hit you is registered to him. Is there any reason you can think of as to why a stranger would be following you?"

She shook her head as her energy began draining away.

"You'd better put your head back," the officer said. "You look a little pale."

At that moment the paramedics arrived and checked Net's blood pressure and pulse, then her neurological signs.

"I can't find anything wrong, but do you want to go to the hospital for a more thorough exam?" the young man asked.

"No. I want to go home." She laid her head back against the seat rest and tried to think, but her mind was a blur.

* * *

Net looked up to see her son's concerned face looking in the car window.

"Ma, are you okay? What the hell happened?" he opened the door and helped her out as the officer came up to speak with him. He explained the incident as Vince listened, keeping one eye on his mother. She held on to the car, seeming a bit unsteady.

Vince exchanged the insurance information with the driver of the other car involved in the accident and then turned to the officer. "Does she have to do anything else?"

"No, all the paperwork is done. You need to make sure the car is drivable."

Vince took Net by the arm and helped her from the car. She saw another man she didn't recognize. He took her other arm.

"This is Tom, my next door neighbor," Vince said. "He's a mechanic. He'll check out the car."

She nodded, but said nothing.

They watched Tom look under the hood, and then slowly drive the car out of the cemetery and onto the side road. "If seems okay," he said. "I think most of the damage is to the body."

Vince turned to his mother. "Tom will drive your car and you come with me. We'll go to my house, talk to the insurance company, and decide where to take it for repairs. I know a good body shop. I'll take care of everything. Right now, let's get you home so you can rest."

* * *

Later after Vince made all the necessary calls, and Net was properly fussed over, she felt drained.

The adrenaline rush had subsided and all she wanted to do was lie down.

"Grandma," Dominic said, walking solemnly toward her. "I got you a flower to make you feel better." He handed her a lovely pink dahlia he picked from the garden.

"Thank you, honey. It makes me feel much better." She hugged and kissed the boy and fought back the tears that welled up in her eyes.

Vince and Melissa wanted her to stay, but she insisted on going home, making excuses that the police and the insurance company might need to talk with her. She really wanted to be alone and try to sort it all out.

After saying goodbye, Vince drove her home. She insisted that she didn't need a rental car right now because Ruth would gladly take her anywhere she needed to go.

"Now you call me if there are any problems, you hear?" he told her. "If I'm in court, leave a message with my secretary and I'll call back." He went inside, made sure that Net was steady on her feet and didn't need anything, then gave her a hug and kiss and drove away.

Shall I call Ruth now? she wondered as she made her way to the bedroom. No, I'll lie down for a while, and then I'll call her. She glanced at St. Anthony's statue but didn't have the strength to talk to him. With a sigh, she lay down on the bed and soon fell asleep.

Chapter 42

"What? Are you out of your mind?" Rupert roared. "You actually hit that woman? Were there witnesses?"

He shook her shoulders with such force that her head snapped back.

Ow," she whined. "I don't know what I was thinking. Don't be mad at me, Rupert, baby."

He winced, pursed his lips and tensed his hands on her arms. Then, thinking of a solution, he relaxed his hold on her. "It will be all right, Sister Verena. I'll fix everything."

His eyes narrowed to slits, but she didn't notice as she nestled in his forced embrace.

"You're upset," he cajoled. "Sit down and drink some of this brandy, then Sandra will bring us some tea."

He sent a message to Sandra Dolton with his eyes. Words weren't necessary. She nodded and went to do his bidding.

He smiled as he settled the distraught woman in a chair. Everyone did his bidding. He had a special calling and would have all that he desired. He cajoled her into drinking a generous amount of the strong liqueur.

When the tea arrived, Sister Verena was visibly relaxed. He handed her a cup. She took a sip. "It tastes very sweet."

He smiled. "I've taken the liberty to add a mild sedative, my dear. After what you have been through, you need to rest. Stay here, with me, tonight." His hand caressed her cheek and brushed back her hair.

She finished the tea and soon her eyes began to close. "You're so good to me Rupert. What would I do without you?"

"You won't have to worry about that ever again."

She fell back against the cushions of the couch in a deep, drugged sleep.

Rupert took the cup out of her hand before she dropped it. He walked into the kitchen area and addressed Sandra. "Go outside and crush this cup. Bury it where no one will find it. Is there any other evidence that she was here ?"

"Only her purse, and we can put it next to her in the car."

"Good." His eyes narrowed. "We're a good team, you and I."

"I hope we remain that way."

He patted her cheek. "Hurry now, I want to get this over with before the drug wears off. Get her keys from her purse and drive her car into the garage. Be sure to wear gloves so there are no fingerprints except hers."

Sandra nodded, smiled, and did as she was told.

* * *

George Watkins picked up the ringing phone. These days it was either his lawyer calling with bad news or his brother. Today he didn't want to talk to either one.

"Hello," he said with little enthusiasm.

"George, it's Bob." His brother's voice sounded distraught. "I've just had a visit from the police saying that my car was in a hit and run accident."

"What? Were you driving it?" George knew his brother was a responsible driver and would never leave the scene of an accident.

"No, Myra had the car," he almost shouted.

"Where is she?"

"I have no idea. She isn't answering her cell phone. Said she had a few errands to run and hasn't come back. What'll I do?" Bob sounded on the verge of tears.

George let out a long sigh. "There's nothing you can do until she shows up. Then take her directly to the police station. The sooner she confesses, the better it will be for her."

"Okay."

His brother's reply was scarcely audible. What was happening to his family? First, his mother was scammed by that damned Society, and now Myra going off the deep end. Bob said she was

191

involved with some church group. Could it possibly be the same people? Would she be so stupid? He shook his head and went into the bathroom where he swallowed three aspirin tablets to ease his pounding headache.

* * *

Net tossed and turned, dreaming of portents of danger and evil. When she awoke, she was sweating and trembling. She turned to the statue sitting benignly on her dresser. "Oh St. Anthony, please help me to get out of this mess once and for all."

A knocking at the door brought her to her senses. She glanced at her reflection in the mirror, patted down her wayward hair and hurried to see who it was. Through the peep hole she saw Ruth's welcome face.

She opened the door and literally fell into her friend's arms. "Oh, Ruth, I'm so glad to see you."

"What's wrong? Did something happen?"

With a sigh Net led her to the sofa. "Sit and I'll tell you everything."

For the next half-hour Ruth sat, her hands clasped in front of her, and listened.

"I can't believe all these things are happening to you."

"Neither can I. Oh, how I wish I had never heard of that Society or any of those people." She put her elbows on the table, and rested her head in her hands. "The *Malocchio*," she whispered. "Oh *Dio*."

At that moment the doorbell rang. "I'll see who it is," Ruth said.

"I don't want to see anybody," Net said.

"All right."

A moment later, Ruth returned followed by Sam. "Net, Vince called me. I had to come." He stood there, an expression of such concern on his face that she couldn't send him away.

"Oh Sam, I'm so miserable." She began to sob.

He sat next to her and put his arm around her shoulder. "I'm here and I'll stay as long as you want me."

"I think I'll go home," Ruth said. "You're in good hands. And remember, I'm right next door if you need me."

"Thank you, my dear friend." Net started to get up from her chair, but Sam stopped her. Always the gentleman, he walked Ruth to the door, exchanged a few words, then went back to Net.

"Now you lie down and I'll be right here if you need anything," he instructed.

"What would I do without you?" she asked, stretching out on the sofa and wanting nothing more than to be taken care of.

"I'll always be here for you. You know that. Come on, let me help you. Are you comfortable?" he asked, placing a throw over her bare feet.

"Uh hum," she murmured.

Sam put on a CD of soft, soothing music and sat in a chair next to her. She felt comforted and safe and soon fell into a dreamless sleep.

* * *

By ten PM there was no sign of Myra, and the police had not found the car. George went over to his brother's house to lend moral support. He vacillated over sharing his suspicion with his brother. But Myra was Bob's wife, and he had a right to know the truth.

"Bob, pour me a generous glass of Scotch, neat, and one for yourself. I must tell you something."

With shaking hands, Bob poured the liquor, handed a glass to his brother, and waited.

George took a swallow, grimaced, and began. "I'm afraid that Myra may have gotten involved with that Society."

Bob gazed at him in disbelief. "The one that scammed Mom?"

George nodded.

"But ... but ... how do you know?"

"I have no proof, just a sinking feeling. Where is she? Why has her behavior changed? Isn't that what happened to Mom?"

Bob put down his glass and held his head in his hands and moaned. "Oh God."

"I may be wrong." George reached out his hand to his brother. "But all we can do now is wait."

Chapter 43

Marcus was becoming desperate. He knew Rupert was getting ready to shut down the operation. If Marcus could find the list of potential candidates with those circled in red who had signed over their assets and later died a, so called, "natural death", he might have something to trigger an investigation.

He had done a cursory search, but found nothing. He would give it one more try. In the middle of the night, he drove to the building where the Society met. He had a duplicate set of keys made. If he couldn't find it tonight, he would have to concentrate on something else—the Watkins will. He believed it existed and was convinced it was hidden somewhere in Net's townhouse.

As he drove slowly to the back of the building, he noticed Sandra Dolton's car parked close to the rear exit door. No one should be there at that hour. He turned off his driving lights and inched his car into a copse of trees behind the garage. Quietly he crept from the car, careful not to slam the door, and hid in the bushes.

Within minutes he saw Sandra come out the back door holding something in her hand. She went into the garage and came out carrying a spade. Finding a spot where the earth was soft, she dug a hole and put something into it. Then he saw her hit it with the edge of the spade and heard a crunching sound. She carefully shoveled the dirt back into the hole and covered it with a paving stone that was lying nearby.

When she appeared satisfied, she returned the spade to the garage. Then he watched as she backed a blue car inside and closed the overhead door.

Marcus frowned. Those two were up to something and he intended to find out just what it was.

* * *

"Sandra, are you ready?" Rupert asked.

"Yes, I backed her car into the garage and obscured the license plates with mud. My car is ready."

"Good work," he said. "I can always count on you."

A smile that never reached her eyes sent him a message. I'll have to be careful with that one, he thought. Perhaps I will take her with me after all.

Both wearing gloves, they carried Myra's inert body through the back and into the garage. She murmured as they lay her on the back seat of the car. Rupert shushed her as he sat in the driver's seat and inched the car out of the garage. Sandra closed the overhead door. Carefully they locked the center, making sure that no signs of Sister Verena remained.

* * *

Marcus didn't have to wait too long. He noticed that the front bumper on the car had been damaged and the license plates were covered with mud, but he was able to make out a few of the numbers. He jotted them down on a pad of paper.

Within minutes two cars drove away, Rupert behind the wheel of the blue car and Sandra following in hers.

He would never have a better time than this. As soon as they were out of sight, he let himself into the building and began a thorough search. After an hour he came up empty handed again. They must have destroyed all the lists. But when he searched the kitchen, be found something just as good as a list. Now he had to find the missing will.

But what had Sandra buried? Evidence perhaps? He quickly retrieved the spade from the garage, moved the paving stone and carefully began to dig. He found shards of a smashed cup. He ran back to his car for an evidence bag and carefully placed as much of the cup as he could find into the bag. He took some of the surrounding soil, too. Then he filled the hole, replaced the paving stone and put the spade back in the garage.

* * *

As Rupert drove slowly, he was grateful that it was a moonless night, making them less likely to be observed. Taking the back roads and streets that were likely to be deserted at that hour, they drove to an abandoned quarry half-filled with water.

Rupert gunned the engine and expertly skidded around a curve, leaving clear tire tracks. He stopped just at the edge of the quarry. He put the car in park but left the motor running, and placed the half empty bottle of brandy on the seat. Then he carefully climbed out and, with Sandra's help, managed to get Myra's body into the driver's seat. She made more sounds, but he ignored them. Soon she would be gone. He fastened the seat belt as her head fell forward onto the steering wheel.

He made sure the windows were cracked, then put the car in drive and shut the door. With a little nudging from the two of them, the vehicle began to move forward. It dipped over the side and crashed into the water. The front gradually sank down until only the rear end of the car was visible.

They put the two pairs of gloves in the trunk of Sandra's car. Rupert turned to her and smiled. "We do make a good team, my dear. Now I think we've earned a drink, and then, you may satisfy me." He licked his lips and caressed her arms as they climbed into her car and slowly drove away.

Chapter 44

Sam fussed over Net until all she wanted was to be left alone. He cooked a supper of linguine with oil and garlic, a dish they relished as kids. Along with a green salad and a glass of wine, she felt much better.

"You always make me feel good, Sam," she said over her second glass. She realized it might not have been the wisest thing to say. She didn't want to encourage him with false hopes.

"I like to do things for you. Makes me feel needed." He smiled and tipped his wine glass to her.

They cleared the table together, stacked the dishwasher, and put the food away. They decided to go outside and enjoy the mid-summer evening. Ruth came out and Net called her over. Her friend was hesitant, but Net insisted. The three spent an hour in pleasant conversation.

When the sun began to set, Sam gave a sigh and said, "I'll leave you in Ruth's capable hands. Is there anything you want before I go?"

"Nothing," she said.

"If you need a ride somewhere, just call me."

"Ruth is right here," she said. Seeing the look of disappointment on his face, added, "but if she's not available, I'll call you for sure."

"Okay. Sounds good." He gave her a hug and kiss on the cheek, said goodbye to Ruth, and left.

Net heaved a sigh. "I don't want to encourage him too much." A furrow formed between her eyes as she slowly shook her head.

"Unrequited love is a real heartache," Ruth said.

"I know, but I can't force myself to love him the way he wants."

"I understand. Will you be all right alone or do you want me to stay with you tonight?"

"Of course I'm all right. I'm not a child. Just because I've come to a bump in the road, doesn't mean I have to fall apart."

Ruth smiled. "Okay, call if you need me."

"I will." Net went into her house, double locked the doors and set the alarm.

* * *

The next few days went by in a blur. Net tried to go about her usual routine, but she did everything by rote. Ruth took her to her water aerobics class; they attended a lecture in the committee room of the center. When they left, she had no idea what it was all about. Her mind refused to absorb anything.

Will I ever feel normal again? she asked herself. Will this feeling of fear ever leave me? She constantly looked around her to make sure no strangers were about. She did receive a call from Vince.

"Ma, the body shop has ordered the parts for your car. It's probably going to be at least a week. I asked them to give it priority and they agreed. You can rent a car. It's covered by your insurance policy, you know. The rental company will bring it right to your house."

"Really?" Net wasn't aware of that. "Let me think about it."

"Okay. Now I gotta go back to court. Bye."

"That boy," she muttered. "Always in a hurry He's going to work himself to death." Suddenly she realized what she just said and made the sign of the cross three times.

She hesitated a moment until she was composed, and called Ruth to ask her opinion.

"I can drive you to the water aerobic classes and Sam would be delighted if you need him, so I see no need to rent a car."

"Sounds good," Net said. "We'll see how that works out."

Net had the TV on a news station just so she could hear another voice. Something caught her attention.

"We go live now to the quarry where the auto is being removed," the announcer was saying.

She hurried into the living room and watched wide-eyed as an equipment crew pulled a battered blue car out of the water. Could it possibly be the car that had been following her? "No," she said aloud. "How many blue cars are on the road? What are the possibilities that it could be the same one?"

The announcer's voice continued. "We do not know the identity of the occupant but it appears to be a woman behind the wheel. No other information is available at this time."

The screen switched to a commercial. Net had an uncomfortable feeling. She thought about the name of the owner of the car that had caused the accident, Robert Watkins. Should she call George and ask him? She paced. Indecision did not sit well with her. "I'm going to call," she said with determination. She looked at the number on the card he had given her then checked the time. Would he still be at the office? Why not try. She punched in the number and his secretary answered.

"May I speak with Mr. Watkins?" Net asked.

"I'm sorry, he was called away on a family emergency. Is there something I can help you with?"

"No, thank you. I'll call tomorrow." After replacing the phone on the charger, Net continued to pace. His cell phone was listed on the card but she hesitated to bother him. Perhaps something was wrong with the nephew.

"Why don't I mind my own business?"

To occupy her mind she decided to repot a plant that had outgrown its present home. Roots peeked out of the bottom of the pot. By the time she finished the task, Ruth was at her door to take her to a movie. She pushed all other thoughts into the recesses of her mind.

* * *

"Brother Andrew, may I speak with you for a moment?" Rupert called.

Andrew Marcus was always wary when Rupert wanted something from him. Feigning confidence, he walked into the office "What can I do for you?" he asked nodding to his superior.

Rupert's face wore an expression of disappointment. "You haven't brought in any prospects lately." He pushed out his bottom lip and furrowed his forehead. "I thought you were more committed to the cause than you appear to be."

Damn phony, Marcus thought. "I was looking for Sandra. Have a new genealogy class scheduled at a rather upscale retirement home on the North shore. There should be a few good prospects there."

Rupert smiled, but only with his thin lips. "Good. Our workers in the field need more money if they are going to make a difference. And this time, I want only prospects with no family ties. Too many complications."

"I understand," Marcus said. "Is Sandra here today?"

"I'm afraid not. I sent her on an errand. She'll be sorry she missed you."

Marcus knew he was lying as he had seen Sandra's car in the back of the building. "Too bad. Please ask her to call me at her earliest convenience. Now I have an appointment with the activity director of that home. I'll try and solidify the dates."

"You do that. And get back to me." Rupert pushed himself away from his desk and straightened his silk tie.

With those words Marcus knew he was dismissed. He couldn't wait to get out of there. Rupert was acting suspicious, wanted to know his every move. Marcus had noticed the absence of Sister Verena, but asked no questions. When he saw the news about the car found in the quarry, he knew what they had done.

Now he feared for Mrs. Petrone. Myra had been assigned to follow her. What happened? He would have to contact Net, and soon. Rupert was frustrated that he couldn't collect the Watkins money. He, too, wondered if there was a second will. From past experience, Marcus knew Rupert would go to any length to find and destroy it and anyone associated with it.

Chapter 45

The ringing of the phone practically made Net jump out of her chair. She was so antsy these days.

"Hello."

"Mrs. Petrone, Andrew Marcus here."

This was a surprise. She hadn't expected to hear from him again. But nothing was as she presumed it to be.

"How are you?" she asked. It seemed like a lame question but was all she could think of at the moment.

"I must speak with you," he said, a note of urgency in his voice.

"What about?" She hesitated. "Shall I meet you somewhere?"

"No, I'll come to you. I'll be on foot and dressed as one of the grounds keepers. Watch for me about noon and go out on your patio. I'll be working around the bushes."

"All right." She heard the disconnect. More cloak and dagger stuff. Why couldn't people just leave her alone?

She fussed and paced until the hands of the clock inched toward noon. Then she took a sandwich and a glass of milk, went out back, and sat at her small table on the miniscule patio. She didn't feel hungry but thought she should make some pretense of normalcy—whatever that was.

As was her habit, she brought a book along and opened it without reading a word. She didn't hear him come up, but soon a man was loosening the soil around the bushes.

"Don't look up," Marcus said. 'Ignore me and eat your lunch. But listen to what I have to say."

She nodded, turned the page of the book, and took a small bite of the sandwich.

"I'm sure you saw the news report of the car that was pulled out of the quarry the other day."

She gave a slight nod.

"The woman was Myra Watkins, the sister-in-law of George Watkins. The same man who's been looking for his mother's will."

Net almost choked. She coughed and took a swallow of milk, then looked at him.

"Keep your eyes down," he commanded. "Rupert and Sandra Dolton killed her. I'm not sure why, but they have a way of disposing of people who are no longer needed. She had become a follower of Rupert, probably anticipating some exciting escape from her dull life.

"I came to warn you. Rupert is preparing to shut down his operation. Too many people are making inquiries. The Morganson's lawyers are talking with Rupert's crooked lawyer and asking some very pointed questions." He hesitated for a moment, poking around in the soil.

"If he can collect on the Watkins estate, he will disappear. He has money stashed in off- shore accounts. No one knows where. But, he, too, believes there is another will. Apparently old Mrs. Watkins said something to Sandra about it. And Rupert's convinced it's hidden somewhere in your townhouse." He gave her a fleeting glance. "So, be extra careful."

Net sat, her mouth full of bread and cheese, unable to swallow, nor to move, for that matter.

Marcus stood, tipped his cap to her, and walked off toward the wooded area on the far side of the pond.

* * *

Net was in a state of shock. Time seemed to stand still. Were these people that diabolical? She finally shook her head clear and pulled herself off the chair. Where had she put the morning paper? After searching the kitchen and living room, she remembered she had tossed it into the recycling bin. She went into the garage and pulled it out.

Back in the kitchen, Net searched for the obituaries. There it was: Myra Watkins, age forty-five, loving wife of Robert Watkins, mother of Luke ... She read no more. Should she go to the wake as a sign of respect? Or just pretend she didn't know about it?

"*Mama mia,* what should I do? I'll ask Ruth. See what she says."

She saw her friend's car pull into her driveway. Net went outside and waved to her.

"What's wrong?" Ruth asked. "I can see by the expression on your face that something has happened."

Net took a deep breath. "Come inside. I have to talk to you."

They sat in the cheery kitchen, sunshine streaming in the widow. It seemed a world away from what Net had heard from Marcus.

"You want something to drink?" she asked.

"No. Just talk."

Hesitantly Net began with the call from Marcus, the secret visit, and checking the obituaries. "I feel like I'm in a horror movie."

Ruth sat back, her face wreathed in a frown. "I can't believe this."

"Do you think I should go to the wake, as a sign of respect?" Net asked.

"Absolutely not. I think we should examine every nook and cranny of this house for that will. If Rupert believes it's here, he'll send some thugs after it." Her face assumed an expression of concern. "Net, I think you should tell Vince about all this. You may be in danger."

"No," She stamped her foot. "I will not put my son and his family in danger, too. So far, I'm the only one they're watching. I want to leave it that way."

"Stubborn Italian," Ruth muttered. "But I suppose I'd feel the same way." She got up from her chair. "Let's get to work. Where shall we start?"

Net let out a breath. "We've been though all this before and found nothing. But, okay, we start in the kitchen and go through every room."

By evening they were both exhausted and had only searched half the house. "Let's call it a day," Net said. "We can pick up tomorrow. This is a waste of time and energy." She sat in a chair, too tired to move another step.

"No," Ruth said. "We have to be thorough. I'll be over right after breakfast and we'll finish."

"And, if we don't find anything?"

Ruth shrugged. "Then we have to assume that either the will was destroyed or there never was another one."

* * *

True to their promise, they tackled the search once again. Ruth had boundless energy. She moved chairs and prodded the bricks on the fireplace searching for loose ones. "This is where people in the movies always hide things, behind loose bricks."

"Those are fake, in case you hadn't noticed," Net said. "I'm ready to give this up. One place I really didn't bother with too much the first time was the guest bathroom. Not much in there, but I'll look just the same." She went into the bathroom while Ruth finished the living room.

Half-heartedly she looked in the toilet tank, under the lid, and behind it. This was where the crooks always hid the guns in the movies—nothing. Then she opened the medicine cabinet. The old shelving paper was coming loose and Net had promised herself to remove it. This was as good a time as any.

She only kept a few items in here so it took but a short time to empty the cabinet. The paper came off easily. Suddenly something dropped from under the piece she held in her hand. She picked it up—a scrap of torn paper. Something was written on it.

"Ruth," she called excitedly. "I found something."

Ruth came running in, her hair escaping from the bandana she had tied around it. "What?"

"Look at this. There's something written on it." She made a tsking sound. "I don't have my glasses. Can you read it?"

Ruth took the paper, squinted, and held it at arm's length. "The handwriting is really shaky. I think it says—umm—'Made a mistake ... Must make it right ... soon ...'"

"What else?" Net asked looking over her shoulder.

"That's all. There's no signature, either."

"Do you think old Mrs. Watkins wrote it?" Net pondered.

"Who knows," Ruth answered. "Her son could verify the handwriting, but this would never stand up in court. It says nothing about a will and isn't signed."

"I suppose not, but it does give more credence to another will, don't you think?"

Ruth shrugged.

"What shall I do, call George Watkins?"

"No." Ruth was adamant. "I have an idea. Let's make a copy and you can send that to Mr. Watkins and explain where you found it. I can keep the original in my strong box if you like."

"Where do we make a copy?"

I'll drive up to the center. There's a copy machine there." She grabbed the scrap of paper, put it in her pocket and hurried out the door.

Within a half-hour Net had the note written and, with the copy, put it in the mail box while Ruth took the original home with her.

Chapter 45

Net trudged back from the mailbox, her energy draining out with every step. She inadvertently glanced behind her expecting to see it lying on the sidewalk.

"Oh *Dio*, will I ever be free of this curse?" she muttered, unlocking her door. "There goes that damn phone. Can't people leave me alone?"

She grabbed it rather forcefully and said a gruff, "Hello."

"Well, you don't sound very welcoming," a familiar voice said.

"Molly? Are you all right?" She hadn't seen nor heard from her sister since Lane's art show. It seemed like another lifetime.

"Oh," Molly groaned theatrically. "It's my daughter."

"Lane? What happened? Is she hurt?"

"God no, worse than that. She's dating a policeman." Molly let out another groan.

"She told me about it and was very excited. I don't see anything wrong with that," Net said, confused by her sister's reaction.

"You don't?" Molly was adamant. "*My* daughter with a policeman, a public servant? She deserves, at least, a diplomat."

Net shook her head and let out a breath. "There's nothing wrong with public servants. Where would we be without them? Huh?"

"You're much too practical. I know we need them, but not with *my* daughter." Again she emphasized the word *my*.

"Don't get upset for nothing. Dating doesn't mean she's going to marry the guy. If he's a nice fellow, I'm happy for her. You always seem to have a man in your life, sister dear." Her words held a note of sarcasm. Right now she felt like throttling Molly.

A sound, half groan and half sigh, issued from the phone. "Gordon Masters left me, for a younger woman." There was actual panic in Molly's voice. Was she beginning to feel her age?

Suddenly Net realized where all this was coming from. She glanced at the wall calendar and noticed Molly's birthday in red, in just a few days. "Why don't we go out for lunch to celebrate your birthday," she suggested.

"Don't mention that day. I want to erase it from the calendar."

"Well, we'll celebrate your un-birthday. Isn't that what they did in *Alice in Wonderland?*"

"I would like to see you, Net." Molly's tone was almost pleading.

Would wonders never cease. Usually Molly wanted nothing to do with her older sister. "Settled," Net said. "When and where?"

"Are you free tomorrow?"

"Sure." She had picked up her car the previous day, earlier than anticipated, and she wouldn't have to worry about the blue car anymore. It was a good feeling. Then guilt set in. A woman had died, possibly been murdered. But she couldn't worry about that. It was out of her control. The sisters decided on a restaurant in Little Italy, one she knew well. Sam had taken her there many times and she remembered exactly where it was. With warm good-byes and the prospect of seeing each other the following day, Net sat back and analyzed the situation.

Molly would be sixty years old. To Net that sounded young, since she was considerably older. But it was all relative. Molly had been in the limelight for many years. Her youthful good looks served her well. She might be showing her age, Net thought. Well, tomorrow would tell. And why had she chosen the restaurant on Taylor Street? That was obvious. She didn't want to be seen by any of her hoity-toity friends without a man on her arm, and, God forbid, with an older woman.

* * *

The next day dawned bright and sunny. Net was actually looking forward to an afternoon with her sister. What to wear? Examining her wardrobe, she frowned at every article of clothing. I have to go on a shopping spree, she promised herself. As soon as all this intrigue is over.

She settled on a pair of navy blue slacks and a flowered tunic top embellished with summer jewelry. She was never one for ostentation. God only knows what Molly will be wearing, she told herself. What you see is what you get, had always been her motto. It was good enough for Joe Petrone. The thought of Joe brought tears to her eyes. "Stop it," she scolded. If Molly sees me with red eyes, she'll have a fit.

When Net arrived at the Taylor Street area, she was surprised at all the traffic. It was a weekday, but also summer. Lots of people came out for Italian ice and other goodies. She drove round and round until, finally, someone pulled out and she was able to park.

As she walked into the restaurant the smells of garlic and Italian spices filled her with nostalgia. A crooner sang softly in the background, the old songs they used to hear as children. It felt like coming home. Oh how she missed the old homestead in Melrose Park. Enough of this.

Looking around, she spotted Molly sitting at a table in the corner. At first glance she hardly recognized her. The svelte figure was gone. She had gained weight, rounding out her face. It gave her a softer look. She stood aside and examined her sister for a minute: no false eyelashes, no heavy makeup, only a little blush and orange colored lipstick to complement her flowered blue and orange dress. Net couldn't believe it.

As she walked up to Molly, her face wreathed in smiles, she whispered, "*Ciao, picolla sorella.*"

Molly's eyes opened wide. Then she, too, smiled. "You used to call me that when we were kids, 'little sister.'"

Net gave her a loud smack on the cheek. "You look wonderful."

"That's not true and you know it. I'm fat and look at all these wrinkles. I'm thinking of Botox."

Net grabbed her sister's hands. "Molly, a few pounds don't hurt. Your face actually looks younger, and I love your hair."

The long blonde locks were gone, replaced by a pixie cut dyed a soft brown. "You really think so?" Molly's eyes begged her sister for the truth.

"Yes, I do. Now stop obsessing about age. It's only a number. And we both inherited good Italian genes, okay?"

She hesitated for a moment, and then whispered, "Okay."

The waiter came up to them and asked if they would like something to drink. Net knew Molly liked white wine. "Chardonnay?" she asked.

Her sister nodded.

"Bring us a bottle, please."

"Yes Ma'am. Right away."

"If we get drunk we won't be able to drive home," Molly said. She had relaxed and seemed to be enjoying Net's company.

Net shrugged. "Then we'll find someplace to stay for the night." She grinned.

"All right," Molly said with a sigh. "In two days I'll be sixty years old." She squeezed her eyes shut. "And what do I have to show for it? A string of men who only associated with me to show me off. And now, they're choosing younger women." She looked down at her hands clutched on the table in front of her, the knuckles sporting arthritic nodules.

"You have a daughter," Net said. "A beautiful, ambitious young girl."

Molly frowned. "Every time I see her I remember how old I am."

Net sat forward. "I would give anything to have my Donna back, no matter how old I am."

Molly cringed. "I'm sorry. I almost forgot. It's been so long."

The waiter came up with their wine, opened the bottle and poured a little in Net's glass. She tasted it, nodded, and he proceeded to fill both glasses. "Would you like to order an appetizer?" he asked glancing at the untouched menus.

"How about we start with bruschetta and then, eggplant parmesan?" They both said the entree at the same time and laughed.

"Excellent choice, ladies," he said and left.

They lifted their wine glasses and Net said, "To new beginnings, for both of us."

"I'll drink to that," Molly said. "And what's going on in your life?"

For a moment Net considered telling her about Rupert and the Society but she had promised herself to put it entirely out of her mind, at least for one day. Instead she told Molly about the remains that were found, her contacting Detective Dobbs, and giving a DNA sample.

"That must have been a horrible experience for you," Molly said, a furrow appearing between her eyes. "I should have been with you." Her voice actually sounded contrite.

"Sam went with me," Net said. "I couldn't have gone through with it without him."

At that moment the appetizer arrived and they each sampled a piece of the crusty bread covered with succulent tomatoes and spices.

"Good old Sam," Molly said between bites. "Why don't you marry the guy?"

Net shook her head. "I love him like a brother. There will never be another Joe Petrone. He was the love of my life. It wouldn't be fair to Sam."

Molly sighed. "Some people marry for companionship. I've never felt passionate about any man, even Lane's father. I guess I don't have it in me." She reached for another chunk of the tasty bread. "This is delicious."

Their conversation turned to the mundane as they savored their meal. They laughed when the stringy cheese hung down from the eggplant and, sometimes, attached itself to their chins.

Net felt a new connection with her sister as they left the restaurant, one they had never had, even as children. "Let's walk for a while and then get some Italian ice," she suggested.

"Good idea," Molly agreed.

The traditional neighborhood buildings and the sounds of varied dialects gave both women a feeling of nostalgia.

"This is nice," Molly said, as she munched on a cone of lemon ice. "I've been so wrapped up in myself that I forgot how relaxing the old ways can be." She turned to her sister. "What about you? Do you miss all this?"

"I do, but life changes and we have to change with it. Molly, please take a good look at your daughter before the rift between you two becomes too wide to cross."

Molly sighed. "You're right. She has to live her own life whether I agree with it or not." She stopped walking and turned to Net. "Will you help me? I don't know how to start."

Net thought for a moment. "Neither you nor Lane has seen Vince's new baby. She's adorable. How about I call them and arrange a family picnic? That way you can reach out to her with other family members around and it won't be so difficult."

"That might work, but what if she doesn't want to see me?"

"Eh, don't be so negative. You two love each other, but you don't know how to show it. I'll have a talk with her and set it all up. How does that sound?"

"Sounds great." Then Molly did something she hadn't done in years. She gave her sister a big hug. "And she can even bring the policeman." They both laughed.

* * *

Later, as Net drove home, she reflected on the enjoyable time she spent with Molly. "Family must stay together," she said aloud.

When she pulled into the garage, she realized she hadn't thought about the Society for almost a whole day. But now it came back to her mind in full force. What would happen next?

* * *

Net gazed out her west window at the setting sun. Pinks and reds streaked across the sky. It was beautiful. Life is beautiful, she thought still reminiscing about her day and planning the picnic with Vince and his family. She took a deep breath and let it out slowly.

As she turned around, she noticed the blinking light on the answering machine. I'm not going to listen to it, she thought. But maybe it was important. She almost hoped it would be some charity soliciting a contribution. Then she could simply erase it.

Shaking her head, she hesitantly pressed the red blinking button.

"Mrs. Petrone, this is George Watkins," he said excitedly. "I received your letter. Call me on my cell phone as soon as you can. Thanks."

She frowned. Now where was his card with all the numbers on it? On the fridge, of course. She retrieved the card and, with a feeling of trepidation, punched in the numbers. He answered on the second ring.

"This is Net Petrone answering your call."

"Yes, thanks for calling. I was so encouraged by the note you found. It was in my mother's handwriting."

"But it wasn't signed and doesn't say anything specific," Net said.

"No, but it does lend some credence to our claim that Mother wasn't in her right mind when she signed that will."

It sounded like a long shot to Net but she didn't say it.

"We're still fighting with that Society," he said. Then his voice softened. "I don't know if you heard, but we've had a family tragedy."

Net knew all about it but feigned ignorance. "What happened?"

He explained about Myra's strange behavior and her accidental death.

"I'm so sorry," Net said. "Your nephew must be heartbroken."

"He is, but he's a strong boy." Watkins hesitated a moment then said, "Strange, but Myra had a double indemnity insurance policy for twenty thousand dollars. So my brother will have enough money for Luke's care for quite a while."

Net hesitated, then asked, "Are they sure it was an accident?"

"Why do you ask that?"

"No reason. I just wondered," she lied.

"Yes, there was no evidence of any foul play and they didn't think it was suicide. I want to thank you for your concern for my family and, if you should find the will ..."

"I know," Net said. "I'll keep looking."

Chapter 47

"This place appears to have a preponderance of wealthy women," Sandra Dolton said as she and Marcus examined the bejeweled matrons filing into the conference room.

Marcus was preoccupied and paid no attention to her observations.

"What's wrong?" Sandra asked. "Didn't you hear me?"

"Huh? Oh, I was thinking about something else." He turned to Sandra. "After this introductory class, we have to talk." His expression left a lot unsaid.

She nodded then turned as the activity director came prancing up to them. She, like everyone else in the room, exuded wealth. Her outfit was expertly tailored and her hair beautifully coifed. Ignoring Sandra, she held out her hand sporting a glittering bracelet and an emerald ring.

"I'm Shirley Pennington. We spoke on the phone and you are Professor Marcus."

He took her hand and gave a slight bow of his head. "Delighted. This is my partner, Sandra Dolton."

"Charmed," Shirley said, but kept gripping Marcus's hand. "I am so looking forward to your presentation. I've been interested in investigating my ancestors for quite some time. Who knows what one might uncover?" She laughed as Marcus extricated his hand.

"How many people have signed up?" Sandra asked.

"Let me see." She opened her folder. "It appears that we have fifteen residents and five guests." She addressed her answer to Sandra but continued to flirt with Marcus.

"Do you have enough handouts?" he asked Sandra.

"Plenty."

"If you'll excuse us, Miss Pennington, we need to go over a few items."

"Of course. You can sit at that table near the windows. I'll be here if you need anything."

"Thank you," Marcus said, eager to distance himself from the woman.

"She was ready to snatch you up," Sandra said, a sneer on her face.

Marcus ignored the remark as they sat at the table, spread out their material, and smiled at the eager participants.

When Miss Pennington closed the door, Marcus stood, walked out from behind the table, and greeted the audience. He began his talk, attempting to sound enthusiastic about the subject of genealogy, but his mind was mulling over something quite different.

When their allotted time was up and Sandra had dispensed the questionnaires and information on researching one's ancestors, Marcus turned toward the windows and gazed outside. He paid little attention to the manicured lawn and the well tended flowerbeds. All he could see was Rupert's diabolical face when he had confronted Marcus the previous day.

"Brother Marcus, I have the feeling that you are no longer committed to the cause. Am I right?" His eyes had bored into Marcus like two drills.

"I am as dedicated to the cause as I ever was, Brother Rupert. I've been occupied with a few personal issues of late."

Rupert's hands clenched into fists. "Personal problems do not matter. Only the cause—the environment—the devastation. We need to raise more and more funds to fight. And if human lives are sacrificed, it's a small price to pay." His face took on a dark red hue; his breath came in short gasps. Marcus's eyes narrowed as he studied the man. Something was obviously wrong with him. Lately he has been demonstrating disturbing behavior. At one moment he was calm and serene, and the next, almost unable to contain his fury when things didn't go his way. Was he mentally ill? Marcus knew he was a narcissist, but did it go beyond that? He would have to be extra cautious.

Within moments, Rupert regained his composure. "If you wish to leave the community, I will release you from any further duties." He had turned and walked away leaving Marcus to ponder his words.

Marcus knew all too well what the consequences would be.

"Oh Professor, I am so excited about searching my past ..."

Women surrounded Marcus and bombarded him with questions.

"Ladies I am so pleased with your enthusiasm. Please write down all your questions and we will address them at the next meeting. Now Miss Dolton and I have another class," he glanced at his watch, "and we're running late."

* * *

Marcus and Sandra sat in a back booth of a remote snack shop. Neither had spoken since they left the retirement center. He took a swallow of coffee and looked at her with such intensity that she frowned.

"Rupert thinks you are no longer committed to the cause," she said.

His expression didn't change. "And what do you think?"

She turned her head slightly and bit her bottom lip. "I'm not sure. I've been watching you and don't notice any change in your behavior. But," she hesitated for just a moment, "something about you is different. Call it intuition." She rested her arms on the table and smiled. Her eyes narrowed into slits, not unlike a cat stalking a mouse.

He took in a deep breath. "If you must know, I've had a serious personal issue that has occupied my time. And, I am working on the syllabus for my fall class at the University. I do have to earn a living, my dear."

"Those are logical responses," she said, still scrutinizing him. "I'll put them in my report to Rupert. But let me warn you, he's having you followed and watched very closely."

"Thanks for your concern, but I'm well aware of all that. I'm not a fool, Sandra, and I can be just as cagey as you and Rupert. Remember that."

She nodded, apparently satisfied with his answer. "Now to get down to business. What do you think of this group of wealthy widows you managed to charm today?"

"To be honest with you, I think they are much too healthy to fit into Rupert's grand plan. It's a waste of our time. I say we go through with the six weeks orientation class and look for greener pastures."

"I agree," she said. "They exude money but I saw no walkers, canes, nor wheelchairs. I did post the announcement of Rupert's presentation on the bulletin board. We'll see how many turn up. And, they may be generous in their contributions."

They finished their coffee and went their individual ways.

As Marcus drove to the university, he wondered how much time he had before Rupert would find him dispensable. The man was furious because he hadn't yet been able to collect on the Watkins will. Marcus feared for Mrs. Petrone's safety. He was certain Rupert would send a team to search her townhouse again, especially since she had found a paper hinting that something was amiss and Watkins's lawyer was taking full advantage of it. He felt compelled to protect her. She was an innocent woman embroiled in a diabolical plot. He must warn her, again, to have no further contact with George Watkins.

Chapter 48

Net wondered what might happen next. She was encouraged by her reunion with Molly and eager to return to a normal lifestyle. But, since she had found the scrap of paper in the bathroom, she felt certain that the will must be somewhere in the house.

As she walked around, a dust rag in her hand, she kept recapping everything that had happened since she moved here. She longed for the old simple life in Melrose Park; wished she and Joe and Sam were children again, living a carefree, fun-filled life.

As if he had received a subliminal message from her, Sam called. "Hi, Doll, how are you? We haven't talked in a while."

"Oh, I was just reminiscing about the old days. I'm okay," she said with little enthusiasm.

"You don't sound like it. Where's that lilt in your voice?"

She let out a humph. "I guess it's taking a day off. By the way, I had lunch with Molly the other day."

"No kidding? What prompted that?"

Net told him about the meeting and Molly's fear of growing old. "I think I did talk her into reconnecting with her daughter."

"That's a good thing," Sam said. "Family is everything."

There was a wistful tone in his voice. Net knew he regretted never having children of his own, but he had a slew of nieces and nephews that he doted on.

"I haven't heard anything from Detective Dobbs," Net said. "Have you?"

"It's too soon, only a couple weeks. He did say it might be over a month, remember?"

"Yes, I do." She glanced out at the golden sunshine. What was she doing in the house?

As if he read her thoughts, Sam said, "Suppose I come over and we go for a drive. No place special. When we get hungry, we'll stop someplace to eat. How does that sound?"

"It sounds great. You're like a tonic, Sam. One dose and I feel better all ready."

"That's me. A little bit of love is the best medicine."

* * *

The following day Ruth came over right after breakfast. "Is there anywhere we haven't searched?" she asked Net.

"I can't think of any place else. I suppose we could go out on the patio and see if there's any hiding place there."

"Let's give it a once over," Ruth said.

They opened the patio door and scrutinized the area but there was absolutely nowhere to hide anything. Besides, the weather would destroy any papers unless they were sealed in plastic. The search proved fruitless.

The women returned to the kitchen and replenished their energy with iced tea and cookies.

"The garage seems to be the most likely place," Net said, "but it was completely empty when I moved in except for that box that George Watkins retrieved.

"No clues in there, huh?" Ruth asked.

Net shook her head. "Only the items Lane used for her still life painting. But we could go around and see if there are any loose boards."

"Good idea," Ruth said. "Are you up for it?"

"I guess."

A thorough search of the garage turned up nothing but spiders and some mouse droppings.

"Damn," Net said, "I'll have to get something to get rid of those rodents. I certainly don't want them in the house."

"Absolutely," Ruth said. "I really don't think there's anything hidden in this house. If there ever was, it's gone now."

Net let out an exhausted breath. "I agree. I'm up for a nap. How about you?"

"Me, too. I'll see you later," Ruth said, opening the door.

"Thanks, my friend. I wouldn't have done such a thorough job without you."

"No problem. I always did like a mystery." She waved and headed back to her townhouse.

As she watched Ruth enter her house, Net glimpsed someone out of the corner of her eye. Was it one of the grounds keepers? When she turned around, he was gone. Now I'm seeing things, she thought. But a chill ran up her spine as she went inside and locked and bolted the doors. Then, just to be on the safe side, she set the alarm.

* * *

As darkness cloaked the area, Net felt more alone than she ever had in her life. She would have called Ruth but remembered her friend had gone to help at the animal shelter. Maybe Net should get involved, too. She did like animals. She would give it some thought. But for now, all she felt was self pity.

"Joe," she shouted. "Why did you leave me? I need you."

She had read in books that some bereaved people felt their loved ones around them, protecting and comforting them. But she knew Joe had gone wherever the dead go, and left her all alone. She threw herself on the couch and wept bitter tears, wailing and moaning as most Italian women did. When she had cried herself out, she scolded, "Stop it. This behavior is doing nothing but giving you swollen eyes."

She wiggled around trying to get comfortable then realized that Ruth had moved the couch next to the wall where the rug was bunched up. "Damn. I'm going to smooth that out right now."

She moved the piece of furniture away from the wall then retrieved the reacher she was given when she left the hospital. As she poked at the carpet, she realized that the corner wasn't nailed down.

"Hmm, that's strange," she muttered. Grabbing the corner with the reacher, she pulled. The rug folded back where someone had removed the nails. Since she couldn't get down on her hands and knees, Net poked and prodded with the tool, puiling the rug farther away from the wall. She spotted something white underneath. But when she tried to grab it, the rug sprang back.

I need something to hold that carpet down, she thought. My cane, that should do it. She took the cane out of the closet, pulled the carpet back and held it steady until she could plant her foot on it. Then, with the reacher, she pulled out a business-sized envelope. Her heart pounded and her breath came in small gasps. Could this be the will?

She glanced around, as if someone might be watching. Then she tucked the envelope in the pocket of her slacks.

She closed the blinds but realized that she hadn't had the one repaired yet covering the picture window. The louvers didn't close all the way. Must do that soon. She went into the dining room and, with shaking hands, carefully unsealed the envelope and pulled out a single sheet of paper. The hand writing was shaky but legible.

I, Ella Watkins, being of sound mind, hereby declare this to be my last will and testament. All previous wills are null and void.

I leave all my worldly goods to my sons, George and Robert Watkins, and to my grandson Luke Watkins for his care.

I withdraw any and all bequests to the Society for the Fifth Beneficence.

It was signed, dated, and witnessed by two of the residents. Net noted that one of them was the woman in the assisted living section who had insisted that she had witnessed the will.

"Oh *Dio!*" Net said as thunder rolled in the distance and the wind whistled outside the house. "What do I do now?"

First she pushed the rug back to its original position and shoved the couch over it. Where should she hide the will until she could turn it over to George Watkins? Where? Maybe in the bottom of the dresser drawer under all her clothes? No, not safe. As various places popped into her mind, she knew exactly where to put it—St Anthony. There was an opening in the bottom of the statue where people were supposed to put their prayer requests.

Carefully Net rolled the will and pushed it into the hole then breathed a sigh of relief. But now, she had to cover it with something. What? After pacing the floor trying to think of the proper substance she remembered a piece of felt she had left over from a project she did long ago.

She looked in all her drawers and finally found it. By now she was exhausted, the adrenaline rush beginning to wane. Had to finish this job. She cut the felt so that it fit nicely over the bottom of the statue, then glued it on. There, now it looked like it had always been there to protect the furniture.

"St. Anthony, please guard this paper. It's a matter of life and death." She held her *corno* with her left hand and made the sign of the cross three times with her right. Where shall I put the statue, she wondered. I'll leave it right here on the dresser, where it belongs.

A loud clap of thunder made her jump. Taking short deep breaths, she sat in her lounge chair to wait out the longest night of her life.

Chapter 49

Rupert paced, his face a mask of fury. "So, that's all you found out?" he shouted at Sandra. "Personal problems?" He turned to her, fists clenched, his color an unhealthy reddish purple. "I give you an important assignment and you bring me nothing."

She sat, one knee crossed over the other appearing relaxed, but every muscle in her body was ready to spring into action. "What did you expect me to do, torture him? I truly believe that he knows nothing." She slipped her hand inside the shoulder bag that hung at her side and caressed the small pistol that lay there. She would use it if necessary.

"But that Petrone woman knows, I'm certain of that," he insisted. "Bring that will and a nice fat reward is waiting for you." He smiled, but it was diabolical. He took a thick envelope from his desk drawer and spilled the contents out with a flourish. Hundred dollar bills cascaded from the envelope onto the desk top. Again he grinned, as he methodically picked them up and replaced everything in the drawer. His eyes narrowed and his mouth set in a horizontal slash. Then he sat back and relaxed. "I have a brilliant plan to test his loyalty."

Her expression remained unreadable but in her mind she was certain he was ready to erupt.

"Call him, now," Rupert demanded. "Tell him the two of you are going to the Petrone woman's house. Use whatever means necessary. Force her to give up that will."

"Have you lost your mind? Don't you think that if she had found it, she would have given it to Watkins by now?" Sandra backed away from him, not trusting his reactions.

"It has to be there!" he shouted. "If she won't tell you, get rid of her, anyway necessary.

Burn the place down," he yelled. "But get rid of that will. I want that money." His eyes blazed with madness.

Sandra decided then and there that this would be her last assignment. She had enough money squirreled away to live comfortably in some remote country. He never found out that she had been sneaking small amounts of the contributions on a regular basis. Rupert never guessed that she could outsmart him.

He began pacing again and muttering incomprehensible words. "Take incendiary devices ... a tear gas bomb ..." Then his ranting turned toward everyone who cared nothing for the environment: the oil companies, factories spewing pollutants into the atmosphere, corrupt politicians ... His voice rose with each word. His entire body shook.

Sandra realized that, in his present frame of mind, he was a dangerous man. But Rupert always kept his hands clean, left the dirty work to his minions. Myra Watkins was the only one he had personally eliminated. She remembered the look in his eyes as he watched her car splash into the quarry. He had actually enjoyed it.

What happened to the dedicated environmentalist she knew for so many years? This man was a stranger, one she didn't trust.

"Well, what are you waiting for? Didn't you hear what I said?"

She nodded, turned, and left the room.

* * *

Marcus looked at the clock: ten-thirty. A storm raged outside more severe than the recent ones to hit the area. This type of weather made him nervous. He examined the paper in front of him—his completed report to the client who had hired him. He was satisfied that he now had proof—a lowly tea bag would prove Rupert a murderer.

By a stroke of luck he had found a cupboard unlocked. It stored tea bags of every variety the Society used, including the lethal ones that precipitated the heart attacks in susceptible people. He had taken only two, fearing the number was closely watched, and then crept away, unseen.

He included the tea bag, carefully sealed in plastic, in the manila envelope with instructions to have it analyzed by a lab. With a sigh of relief, he put the envelope aside. In the morning he would take it to the Post Office and send it by overnight mail. Then his job was done. But terminating his relationship with the Society was another matter.

He smiled. It would be satisfying to watch the police investigate Rupert and his bogus operation; obtain his secret files and offshore accounts. Then lock him up along with Sandra Dolton.

He knew he wouldn't sleep much that night so he sat in a lounge chair and attempted to read. As his eyes began to close, he was jolted awake by the ringing of the phone. Who would be calling at this hour? The hands of the clock pointed to eleven. He decided not to answer. It was probably a wrong number. But as the answering machine kicked in, he heard Sandra Dolton's voice. A chill ran up his spine.

"Marcus, I know you're there. Pick up the phone. We have an important mission."

He wanted to tell her to go to hell, but he wasn't ready yet. Grabbing the phone, he grumbled, "This had better be good. Do you know what time it is? And, in case you haven't noticed, there's a storm out there."

"Rupert is losing it," she said. "We have one more assignment—the Watkins will. I'm to pick you up and go to the Petrone townhouse. Rupert is convinced she has the will and we're to get it."

Marcus clutched the phone so hard his hand turned white. "She doesn't know anything about it," he said.

"She was snooping around," Sandra said, "Rupert had someone watching her and that's enough to make him suspicious."

Marcus let out a frustrated breath. "She's just a nosy old woman with nothing better to do."

"Doesn't matter," Sandra continued as if she hadn't heard him. "When Rupert says jump, well, you know the consequences if it's not high enough."

Marcus knew only too well. There were enough thugs on his payroll to make anyone's life a hell. I have to warn Net, to protect her, Marcus thought. He hesitated for a moment. "That's a gated community in case you didn't know. The bars to the entrance are locked at this time of night."

"Well how do the residents get in if they're out late?" she asked.

"I believe there's a key pad that raises the gates." Marcus tried to come up with a plan that would stall Sandra.

"There has to be another way to get in there," Sandra said. "What do they do in emergencies?"

"They probably have the code on file with the police and ambulance services. I don't know. Why don't I scout around and see if there's another access road? Then I'll call you and we can meet. We're not going to get far in this storm anyway." He tried to sound convincing but knew she didn't believe him.

"Oh no. I don't trust you–partner," she said with scorn.

"My dear Sandra, trust has to be earned and neither one of us has done that. I'll meet you at the entrance in a half-hour."

"Why can't I pick you up?" she asked.

"For the simple reason that I want to take my own car. It's a four wheel drive and more reliable than yours. If that doesn't satisfy you, go alone."

He could hear her taking deep breaths. "All right, and, by the way, which townhouse is hers? They all look alike."

He gave her the address but not the directions. "It's near the pond," he said, knowing full well there were three ponds on the property.

"You'd better not be screwing around with me, Marcus."

"Or you'll do what? Kill me? I'm not a fool. I have a document that I sent to my lawyer telling him all about your precious Society. He has instructions to open it if anything happens to me." Would she realize he was bluffing? He had to take the chance. He knew by her silence that she was weighing the possibility.

"All right, you bastard, a half-hour."

Chapter 50

Marcus took a .45 caliber pistol out of his safe and placed it in the glove compartment of the car. He had to be prepared for every contingency.

The rain came down in sheets with such force that the wipers couldn't keep up. He took the short cut that he had devised the last time he saw Net, but the going was slow. He could barely see the road, even with the high beams on. On some streets the water came halfway up his tires. Few cars were out on a night like this, only the foolish and the desperate.

When he found the access road, it was a river of mud. He got stuck twice and finally stopped the car next to the fence. "God, I hope they haven't repaired that hole," he muttered.

He put the pistol in his pocket, slipped on his black slicker and boots, and began to search along the fence.

* * *

Sandra drove faster than the weather allowed and soon realized she would be in a ditch if she didn't slow down. She felt like turning back and telling Rupert they couldn't make it because of the storm. But she knew what his response would be—no excuses. Besides, she thought of the large sum of money he had promised her when this task was completed. Then she would make her move.

Finally, after an hour, she reached the entrance. "Now where the hell is Marcus?" she asked between gritted teeth. He could be in a ditch somewhere, but he would have called on her cell phone. She punched in his number but got the only the message.

"You have reached Professor Marcus. I am unavailable at this time. Please leave a message."

"Damn him." She threw the phone down on the seat.

She saw the empty guardhouse. Wooden arms extended across the road on either side blocking the access. She knew it wouldn't take much to ram through, but it would surely set off an alarm. She couldn't take the chance. Fortunately the storm was passing; the rain now a steady drizzle.

Searching the area she almost missed a spot off to the side that was under construction. I'm in luck, she thought. Better check it out. She alighted from the car and, sloshing through the puddles, examined the spot where a tree had been removed. A large hole remained, filled with water and debris. Someone had covered it with a piece of sturdy wood. Was it strong enough for her to drive over it? She stooped down and checked. It appeared to be. If she maneuvered her small car just right, she could squeeze through. On the other hand, her tires might sink into the mud leaving her stranded.

She scoured the area, found some brush and branches knocked down by the storm, and covered the mud the best she could. Getting back into the car, she cursed both Rupert and Marcus. She backed up, put the engine in third gear, and, as carefully as she could, inched the vehicle over the wood and brush. The wheels began to spin. Okay, she told herself, back up a little and try again. She did, and the third time managed to get through the narrow opening.

Perspiration mingled with the rain running down her face from her soaked hair. Finally she was on the road. As if on cue, the rain stopped; the clouds scudded by revealing a brilliant moon. It bathed the entire area in an eerie light.

"Great, that's all I need. If I could shoot out that moonlight, I would," she muttered as she drove slowly and without headlights down the road. At least she would be able to read the signs.

* * *

After searching for what seemed like an hour, Marcus finally found the broken area of the fence. He crawled through mud and rainwater, soaking his clothes. Finally he was able to stand. Gripping the fence, he stretched his back and gritted his teeth. He had to get to Net in time.

At that moment the rain stopped, the clouds separated, and the moon lit up the night sky. "Damn! There goes my cover." He ran toward the pond because it was the fastest way but, if Sandra had somehow been able to get through the gate, she would most likely spot him. He listened carefully for the sound of a car—nothing.

When he did reach the cover of the townhouses, he saw Sandra's car going slowly down the street, lights out, as if the driver were checking the signs. He ducked behind a garage. Had she seen him? He couldn't be sure. By now she must realize that he had betrayed her and would be out for blood. She wouldn't hesitate to kill him.

Cautiously Marcus emerged from hiding just as Sandra's car crept down the street. He ran behind the row of houses until he spotted Net's. He barreled across the street knowing that Sandra would have to drive down to the end of the street before she could reach him.

By now his breath was coming in rasping gasps. When he reached Net's house, he rang the doorbell and pounded on the door to alert her. Then he went around to the back knocking at the windows as hard as he could. "Mrs. Petrone," he called, "It's Andrew Marcus. Let me in. We're both in danger." He went from window to window and to the back door. In the distance he heard the car as it came closer and closer.

* * *

Net was in a half sleep in the lounge chair. Did she hear something? Was someone outside? Her eyes popped open. She cautiously went to the window and saw a car, with its lights out, moving slowly down the street. Net was certain someone was outside. She was just about to call security when the doorbell rang and someone pounded on the door. What was happening? That was Marcus's voice at the back door calling. The word 'danger' was the only one that registered in her mind. Peeking through the kitchen window she saw him bedraggled and soaked. Should she call the police? She moved back and shook her head.

"Mrs. Petrone, you're in danger. Please let me in."

The tone of his voice convinced her to open the door. She deactivated the alarm and let him in. "What in the world is wrong?" she asked.

"Hurry. No time to lose. Activate the alarm and call 911."

She pushed the alarm code and ran into the living room to grab the portable phone. She was standing directly in front of the picture window, the louvers of the blinds half open.

"No!" he yelled. He tackled her as two shots slammed through the glass shattering it. The alarm let out a loud wail.

Net fell to the floor, hitting her head on the edge of the coffee table. For a moment she was disoriented, and then she heard Sandra Dolton's voice through the door.

"I know you're in there Marcus. Come out or I'll kill you both."

What? Why? Is this really happening? In a fog Net felt herself being dragged toward the back of the house. Something warm and sticky soaked through her blouse.

The window smashed, again, with the impact of a missile. Immediately tear gas filled the room. Net began to cough, her eyes stinging.

"Bathroom," Marcus whispered.

By now her mind was beginning to clear. She crawled into the bathroom, Marcus behind her. He slammed the door shut. "Towels," he whispered.

The moonlight coming through the small window was enough for her to see that he was covered in blood. Quickly she opened the window to let in fresh air, and threw him a towel. He shoved it along the bottom of the door.

She realized she still had the phone clutched in her hand. With shaking fingers she punched in 911 and called for help. Then she pressed the call button on the wall that alerted security.

Only then could she turn her attention to the injured man lying on the floor. "Don't die, Marcus, please," she begged. He moaned as she pressed a wet towel against the wound in his shoulder but blood soon saturated the cloth.

"Stay with me," she said. That's what they always said on television, but this was real life. "Help is coming." Then she began to pray in Italian, her heart and head pounding in rhythm.

As the sirens in the distance grew louder, the pounding on the door ceased. She collapsed beside Marcus and pressed on the oozing wound as her lips uttered a prayer.

Chapter 51

It seemed like hours before help arrived but in reality it was only moments. Everything happened as if in a fog. The house filled with people—paramedics working on Marcus, firemen opening windows and doors, police searching every room.

"Come with me, Ma'am," a man said helping Net to a gurney. Before she knew what was happening, she was being loaded into an ambulance.

"Net!" Ruth screamed, running up to her friend. "You're covered with blood."

Ruth was crying. Net had never seen her cry before.

"We're taking her to Palos Hospital," the paramedic said. "You can meet us there."

Net had never been in an ambulance. She still wasn't sure of what actually happened. Her head ached, and she wasn't thinking clearly. As the vehicle sped down the road, a female paramedic removed Net's blouse and examined her chest, wiping away the blood and putting sticky patches on her. Someone else put an IV in her arm.

"My friend—how is he?" she asked, almost afraid to hear the answer.

"He's in another ambulance on the way to a trauma center. Don't worry, they'll take good care of him."

Isn't that what they always said? Even if folks were at death's door. She lay there praying fervently for Marcus. He had saved her life. "*Oh Dio,*" she moaned.

When they reached the emergency room, the medical staff rolled Net into an examining room. A white-coated young doctor looking much too young to have so much responsibility, smiled down at her.

"My head hurts," she whispered.

"You have a gash on your forehead," he said. "We'll patch that up with some glue. Take only a few minutes." He shone a flashlight into her eyes. He told her to follow his finger had her look from side to side, up and down. "I think you're fine, but we'll do an MRI just to be certain. At most you have a mild concussion."

"My friend, Andrew Marcus, what happened to him?" she asked anxiously.

"Not to worry. I spoke with the doctor at Loyola. They have him stabilized and will be taking him to surgery shortly. If you're up to it, a police officer would like to speak with you."

She nodded as he led a young officer into the cubicle.

"Please tell me exactly what happened, Mrs. Petrone. Start from the beginning."

"By now her head was fairly clear. "You must find Sandra Dolton. She's dangerous." In halting tones, she told him about Sandra and Rupert and gave him the address of the building where the meetings were held.

"We'll send someone out there immediately. We will have to question you further at a later date."

The doctor returned and gave the officer a look of dismissal. "If you're finished, I need to tend to this gash." The policeman left and the doctor expertly patched up Net's cut, put a dressing over it, and went to order the MRI.

At that moment she heard Vince's raised voice in the hallway. "I insist on seeing my mother ..." She didn't hear the rest. Then Ruth's voice begged to see her. In a moment they were both ushered into the cubicle.

"Ma ...." Vince sounded like a little boy. "What happened?" He sat next to her stroking her cheek as tears streamed down his face.

"I'm all right. Some crazy person shot through the window." Her eyes met Ruth's telling her not to say any more.

He gave her a questioning look. "I don't understand how some lunatic got into a gated community and just happened to shoot through your window. There's something you're not telling me."

Just then an orderly came in and told them Net was going for the MRI. He directed Vince and Ruth to the waiting room.

* * *

Sandra Dolton drove at top speed keeping only her parking lights on for visibility. As the sirens came closer, she floored the gas pedal and rammed through the wooden arm barring the exit. Police cars, ambulances, and a fire engine sped through the entryway.

Had they seen her? At this point she hoped they were unaware of what happened. All she could do was hope and pray. Pray? That was a laugh. She was a criminal and, if caught, she knew the consequences.

Fortunately, she reached the center without encountering anyone. The rain had slowed to a drizzle making driving less hazardous. Sandra took that as a good sign. When she unlocked the door, she heard nothing.

"Rupert," she called. No answer. Where the hell was he? Searching the rooms she noticed a light under the door to his private office. "Rupert." She barged in and was met with a startled look. He was hurriedly emptying the money from the safe into a duffle bag.

"What the hell are you doing?" she screamed.

"Preparing for us to get out of here," he answered continuing his task.

She didn't believe the "us" for one minute.

He turned to her. "What happened?"

"Marcus betrayed us," she answered. "Everything went wrong. I didn't get the will and ended up shooting somebody, not sure if it was Marcus or the woman." By now she was breathing hard.

His eyes blazed as he got up, advanced toward her, and slapped her across the face. "You stupid bitch! Now you've ruined everything. Why didn't you kill them both? If one of them is alive, the police will be here at any moment."

Sandra seethed with anger, her eyes narrowed, fists clenched. "How dare you," she growled. "I've done your bidding since you started this grand scheme of yours and this is the thanks I get?" She pulled the gun out of her purse, her hand steady as she aimed it at him.

He lifted his hands in supplication. "You know I didn't mean that. Come on, let's both get out of here. We have our fake passports and …"

232

Before he could utter another word, she pulled the trigger. Rupert fell backwards from the impact, his hands grasping his belly as blood flowed freely from the wound.

"You lying bastard. I should put one through your head, but maybe you'll bleed to death before anyone finds you." She went to the safe and shoved more money into the duffel bag.

"Sandra," he pleaded. "Don't leave me like this, please. You ... know ... I ... love ... you ..." His voice trailed off.

"Huh, all you love is power and money. Now you can go back to the environment and your miserable body can fertilize the earth." She lifted the bag over her shoulder and was about to hurry out of the room, when she heard pounding on the doors.

"Police! Open up!"

"Shit." she ran to the back, slid the bolt on the rear door, and was met by a burly policeman with a gun in his hand.

"Put the gun down, slowly, sister," he commanded. "And drop the bag—now!"

She did as she was told as packets of money spilled out onto the floor and the gun slid across the room.

"Hands on your head, lady. Do it!"

Uttering a few expletives, Sandra complied.

"There's a man bleeding in here," another officer shouted as he called for an ambulance.

The first officer cuffed Sandra and read her rights. Then he led his prisoner to a waiting police car, her head hanging, all the bravado gone.

Chapter 52

By the time Net returned from the MRI, Ruth had told Vince the entire nightmarish story. He walked into the cubicle where his mother lay, a look of disbelief on his face.

As soon as Net saw him, she knew. He sat next to her, took her hand in his, and held it tight. "Ma, why didn't you tell me about all this?" The expression on his face was one of confusion and, a touch of guilt. "How could you get involved in something so dangerous without consulting me?"

"Eh, I didn't know it would turn out this way. I just wanted to help Mr. Watkins find the will." She shrugged. "Then, one thing led to another and suddenly I was mixed up in this mess."

"But why didn't you tell me?" he persisted.

"You were so busy. Melissa said you came home late every night and left early in the morning. I didn't want to burden you with something that seemed futile, at least at first." She turned her head away and wiped a tear that sneaked from her eye. She felt his hand caress her cheek and turned toward him.

"Then, when I realized these people were diabolical, I didn't want to put the family in any danger. You do understand, don't you?" She ran her hand through his tight curly hair and, for the first time, noticed a touch of gray at the sides.

"I should have been there for you," he said, shaking his head.

"Well, let's just say I had an unplanned adventure, and I'm sure it's over now."

At that moment a man in a business suit came into the cubicle and introduced himself as Detective Adams. "Mrs. Petrone, I thought you would like to know that, thanks to your accurate information, we have apprehended both of the perps. The center is being examined by the crime squad as we speak. Are you up to giving me a complete statement?" He glanced from her to Vince.

"Can my son stay?" she asked. "He's my lawyer."

He nodded.

"All right. Hand me that glass of water, Vince, and I'll start from the beginning." An hour later Net was exhausted after reliving all that had happened.

"That's quite a story," the detective said. "You put yourself in a precarious situation, my dear lady. May I ask why?"

Net held her hands up. "I guess I read too many mysteries. No more adventures for me. I promise." She grabbed her *corno* and gazed directly at her son who was still holding her hand.

Detective Adams got up to leave but Net stopped him. "Before you go, can you please check on the condition of Andrew Marcus? I think I heard somebody say Loyola. The man saved my life."

"I'll make a call. Be right back." True to his word the detective returned in a few minutes with an encouraging report. "They've just finished surgery and his condition is stable. The doctor expects him to make a full recovery."

Net let out a deep sigh. "That *is* good news. He's a dedicated man."

Shortly after, the doctor came in and told Net she was free to leave. The MRI was negative and all the tests were within normal limits.

"You're coming home with me," Vince said in a no nonsense tone.

"Yes, but first I must talk with Ruth. Vince, go and check me out. Here are my Medicare card and my supplement, in case they don't have them. And send Ruth in, please. " She handed her wallet to her son as Ruth entered the cubicle.

"I'll need some clothes," she said. "I'm sure the police will let you into my bedroom for that. After all, no one was in the house except me and Marcus."

"Okay." Ruth nodded. "I'll fill up a suitcase with underwear, pajamas, slacks and tops. Will that be enough?"

"Get some toiletries, too." Then Net whispered, "and the statue of St. Anthony on my dresser."

Ruth frowned in confusion. "Why do you need that?"

"I found the will and it's inside the statue." Net kept her voice down and glanced around as if someone might be listening.

"Where was it?"

"I'll explain everything when you get to Vince's house with my things."

"What if they won't let me take it?" Ruth asked.

"Tell them I'm a very superstitious woman and attribute my salvation to the saint. They

can dust it for prints, if they want to. They'll only find mine." She hesitated for a moment. "I have faith in you, Ruth. I know you'll talk them into it."

"Well, I hope you're right. I'll leave now and meet you at Vince's house."

* * *

Later Net was comfortably settled in Vince's spare room with Dominic fussing over her.

"Grandma, how did you get hurt? You got a bandage on your head."

"Oh honey, you know how sometimes people trip and fall down. That's what happened, but I hit my head on the table." She certainly wasn't about to tell the child what really happened.

"Be a good boy and get Grandma a glass of juice."

"Sure. What kind?"

She smiled. "Surprise me."

A short time later, Vince peeked into the room. "Ma, Ruth is here with your things."

"Oh good. Send her in and, Vince, please stay. You need to see something."

He let out a breath. "I swear, Ma, you're full of secrets."

Ruth bustled into the room with two suitcases and a bag.

"Did you get it?" Net asked.

"Yes. They did dust it for prints and then let me take it. I must say I did some fast talking," she said, preening.

"Fine work. Vince, take that statue of St. Anthony and remove the felt from the bottom, carefully."

He did as instructed then examined the hole in the bottom of the statue. "There's something in here."

"Exactly," Net said. "It's the Watkins will."

He cautiously removed it using tweezers so as not to damage the document. Then he read it twice, rubbing his hand over his chin. "This is legal all right, dated, signed, and witnessed by two people. It negates any previous documents. I'll call Mr. Watkins and have him pick it up and take it to his lawyer."

"Where did you find it?" Ruth asked. "We went over that place with a fine toothed comb."

Net gave them a smug expression. "Remember the corner of the rug that didn't lay quite right? I lifted it and there it was."

"Oh for heaven's sakes. The one place we never thought to look."

Net turned to her son. "As long as the living room needs to be cleaned and repainted, do I have enough money to have the carpet removed and hardwood floors put in?"

"You got plenty, Ma. I'll see that it's done. Now I'm going to call Mr. Watkins.

* * *

Later Detective Adams paid Net a visit and reported that Rupert and Sandra, as well as some of their minions, were locked up. Rupert was in the hospital with a gunshot wound to the abdomen, but was expected to recover. He again thanked her for her quick thinking and assistance in uncovering the illegal Society for the Fifth Beneficence.

Chapter 53

A few months later Net heard the whole story from Marcus who had fully recovered. They sat in the back booth of a coffee shop.

"From my sources," Marcus said, "Sandra has agreed to testify against Rupert. She'll probably get a reduced sentence."

"Those people." Net blew out a breath. "So unscrupulous. What will happen to Rupert?"

"If the justice system works as it should, he'll be convicted of murdering Myra Watkins, and be sentenced to prison for life without parole."

"What about all the money they scammed from those women?"

"I believe Sandra may have access to the offshore accounts and some of the money may be returned. But I can't be sure."

"Well, I guess that's it," Net said, reaching for his hand. "Thank you for saving my life."

He smiled as he gave her hand a squeeze. "I think you reciprocated and saved mine also. Stay safe, dear lady, and out of trouble."

"Oh, I will, you can be sure of that."

Epilogue

When Net moved back into her newly renovated townhouse, Sam came over with a bottle of champagne to celebrate. He had been hovering over her, showering her with flowers and candy.

"This is great," he said admiring the light bamboo floors. "It gives it a whole different look."

"That's what I wanted. Now I just need to settle down and live a quiet life with no surprises."

Sam took her hand, his eyes filled with love. "If anything had happened to you … " He didn't finish the sentence but wiped a tear from his eye.

Net kissed his cheek and gave him a hug which he returned with tenderness.

She glanced out the window and noticed the mail truck.

"Sam, would you get the mail? I just saw the truck drive by."

"Sure." He walked out the door and came back with a bundle of catalogues and an official looking letter.

"Uh, here's one you been waiting for. It's from the crime lab."

Net felt a chill run through her body. "Oh God, do I really want to know?"

"You want me to open it?" he asked.

"Please."

He carefully slit the envelope with his pocket knife and pulled out a single sheet of paper. A furrow appeared between his eyebrows as he read it.

"Well?" Net's voice quavered.

"No match," he said. "It's not Donna."

Net began to shake as Sam held her close. Then a flood of tears unleashed all over his shirt. He grabbed some tissues and handed them to her.

" I'm so glad you're here with me. I know she's alive. I feel it in my heart."

He nodded. "Ya gotta have hope. Sometimes that's all that makes life worth living. How about we open the champagne now? We have two things to celebrate."

He popped the cork and filled two flutes with the bubbly. "To the new townhouse and to hope."

Net knew what he hoped for and she wouldn't take that away from him. Someday her Donna would come home and, who knows, her feelings toward him might just change.

Made in the USA
Monee, IL
20 July 2022

10033334R00143